FALSE CHARITY

FALSE CHARITY

Veronica Heley

This first world edition published in Great Britain 2007 by
SEVERN HOUSE PUBLISHERS LTD of
9–15 High Street, Sutton, Surrey SM1 1DF.
This first world edition published in the USA 2007 by
SEVERN HOUSE PUBLISHERS INC of
595 Madison Avenue, New York, N.Y. 10022.

British Library Cataloguing in Publication Data

Heley, Veronica
  False charity
  1. Widows - England - London - Fiction 2. Detective and
  mystery stories
  I. Title
  823.9'14[F]

ISBN-13: 978-0-7278-6527-4   (cased)
ISBN-13: 978-1-84751-022-8   (trade paper)

All Severn House titles are printed on acid-free paper.

Typeset by Palimpsest Book Production Ltd.,
Grangemouth, Stirlingshire, Scotland.
Printed and bound in Great Britain by
MPG Books Ltd., Bodmin, Cornwall.

One

S he was desperate to get home without breaking down.
She'd been running on too little sleep and too much coffee for days. There was no one to meet her at the airport. Instead, there was a message from her son to say he'd been unavoidably detained. She couldn't manage the two heavy suitcases on the Underground by herself, so hailed a taxi and gave her address in Kensington. In the taxi she tried to sit upright and not sag even though she ached with tiredness.

If Hamilton had been with her, he'd have helped her to relax. He'd probably have used the 'lost' time in traffic jams to remember friends who were in trouble, in sickness and in health. She couldn't do that. Not yet.

It was over six months since Bea and her husband had left London on their long-planned trip around the world. He'd made it as far as New Zealand, but she was returning alone. She would not weep. Not in public, anyway.

Tuesday, late afternoon
He let the bloodied paperweight drop from his hands. It bounded away from the body and rolled under the coffee table.

Large tears appeared on his cheeks as his mother came into the room. 'It wasn't my fault, Mummy!' From childhood he'd relied on his mother to get him out of trouble, and he was sure he could rely on her for this, too. 'I told him what you said and he laughed! He turned his back on me, as if I didn't count. I only hit him to teach him a lesson. It was all your fault, anyway. You should have come straight up with me. Richie should have parked the car by himself.'

He was a spoilt child in a nineteen-year-old body, holding out bloodied hands in supplication.

She pushed his hands aside, diamond earrings swinging as she knelt beside the body to feel for a pulse.

'What . . .!' A smallish man with a rounded stomach followed the woman in. He blinked rapidly. 'He can't be dead! We decided, you arranged, we agreed to pay him off.'

She screamed, lunging at the youth. 'Can't I trust you even to keep him talking for two minutes? Useless creature!' She slapped his face open-handed, first one cheek and then the other. The slaps sounded like gunshots in that stuffy room.

Instead of giving ground the lad grovelled, clutching at her, burying his face in the floating fabric of her dress. 'It wasn't my fault, Mummy!'

The woman battled to control her temper. She was a handsome woman in her early forties; most of the time she looked ten years younger. Her son was the only weakness she allowed herself, but it was a weakness which was beginning to incise lines between her nose and chin.

The older man kept well away from the rug on which the corpse lay. To his eye, the man on the floor had been hit not once but many times. Once to knock him down, perhaps, but many times more to pound his skull to pieces. 'He's gone too far this time. I know he's your son, but—' The woman made a sharp movement, and he bit off the rest of what he was saying. After a moment he muttered, 'We'd better pack, hadn't we? We can be at Heathrow in an hour.'

'Let . . . me . . . think!' Eventually she relaxed. 'We've invested too much time and effort to run. We've made a pretty penny with the other two functions, but it's nothing to what we're due to make this weekend. After that, yes; we'll disappear.' Hers was the deciding voice.

She surveyed the room. 'Look on the bright side. We don't have to cut him a share now, which means there's more in the kitty for us. No one but us three knows he was to visit us tonight. There's not much blood, except on the rug. We'll dump that in a wheelie bin somewhere. Clothes can be drycleaned.'

'But the body?'

'Mummy, Mummy,' said the boy, still on his knees. 'You forgive me, Mummy?'

She stroked his forehead under the fringe of dark hair. 'There, there,' she said. 'There, there.'

*   *   *

Tuesday, late afternoon to evening

Bea Abbot leaned forward in the taxi as they reached her home territory. Nothing much seemed to have changed while she'd been away. The taxi turned off the busy High Street and made its way up the hill to a quiet side road. The ornate ironwork of the Victorian balconies and railings glistened black against the white of the house fronts. The tall windows gleamed a welcome.

She longed for a shower and bed, but as she paid off the taxi and heaved her cases up the steps, the front door of the house was flung open to shouts of 'Surprise!' and 'Welcome home, darling!'

She tried to look delighted. Someone took the cases from her and stowed them under the stairs while she smoothed down the jacket of her cream trouser suit and shook her head to settle her ash-blonde hair. As hands reached out to greet her, she stretched her mouth into a smile and accepted kisses and good wishes all round.

'Dear Bea, you're looking well. How many hours is the flight from New Zealand? You must be exhausted.'

Did she look that tired? A sideways glance at the mirror in the hall assured her that she didn't look bad for sixty.

'Dear Hamilton, how we'll miss him!'

It appeared that a number of their friends had assembled to celebrate her return. Her tall son Max surged forward to give her a hug and hold her close. She could feel his love for her, and it almost melted her into tears. But no, she must be strong. No more tears. Not yet, anyway.

Then it was the turn of her friends. 'Darling, you look fabulous. Did Hamilton ask you not to go into mourning for him?' A scratchy comment from an old acquaintance who'd worn nothing but black for years.

Bea almost lost her smile. 'Seeing me in black depressed him.'

'Darling, so sad!'

'Dear heart, we've missed you both so much.'

Drinks circulated, nibbles ditto. The tall doors between the first-floor drawing and dining rooms had been thrown open so that guests could spread themselves out. Sympathy cards were double-stacked on the mantelpiece. Max had been dealing with most of the formalities that follow a death, thank goodness.

The rooms had been decked with flowers, the antique furniture shone with polish . . . not that you could see much of it for people.

Max raised his glass and tapped on it with a knife to obtain silence. He also cleared his throat, which was a little trick he'd developed since his election to the House of Commons.

Dear Max, thought Bea, *I do hope he's not going to make a speech* . . . She'd been through a lot in recent months, no, years; it was almost three years since her dear husband had started on the downward slope and she'd retired from the agency to look after him. She was feeling dizzy with tiredness. She touched her lips to the glass of champagne someone had kindly put into her hand and set it aside. Champagne didn't help when you were as tired as she was. She wondered if she could get a cup of good coffee to perk her up. She parked her hip on the back of her settee and held on to her smile.

'Mother, ladies and gentlemen, and those of you who are also our friends!' Subdued laughter. Most people were relaxed enough to listen without looking at their watches. The phone rang in the agency rooms downstairs. Bea looked round for someone to answer it. Then relaxed. The Abbot Agency was being wound up. Someone else would deal with it. She didn't recognize the sound as the Voice of Doom.

Instead, she thought what a pity it was that Max hadn't inherited his father's – her first husband's – charm; though to give him his due, Max was a lot better looking than Piers had ever been. Tall, dark and handsome sounded good, until you added a little too much weight around the chin and midriff. It was hard work, attention to detail, marriage to an ambitious woman and a dogged belief in his political party that had got Max into Parliament at the third attempt, even though he hadn't an original thought in his head.

Bea killed that thought as being unfair and possibly untrue. Max was a good boy, and would be a faithful representative of his constituency.

Max conducted his speech with his free hand. 'It's wonderful to see so many of you here to welcome my dear mother back from her travels. We've all missed her enormously, haven't we? Welcome back, Mother!'

Glasses were lifted in a toast, to which Bea bowed and smiled. That part of Bea's mind which was feeling waspish remarked that it had suited Max and his wife very well to live rent-free in this prestigious London address while Bea and Hamilton had been away. Max's constituency and his chief residence were in the Midlands and it would have cost him the earth to buy a similar London house for the long months when Parliament was sitting.

The other part of her mind said, But he's a good lad at bottom, and he really worries about me. I'm not so sure about that anorexic wife of his, but . . . no, I won't think about that now.

'. . . today's gathering is both a sad and a happy occasion. Happy, because a wonderful lady has been restored to us. Sad, too, because my wonderful Super Dad – who was always better than a real father to me – has, after a long, brave fight, left his earthly remains on some . . .'

I do hope, thought Bea, that he's not going to say, 'on some foreign shore'.

'. . . foreign shore,' said Max. 'We shall all miss him tremendously.'

'True. True. Here's to Hamilton.'

Max gestured to the mantelpiece on which stood a silver-framed photograph of a dark-haired, round-faced man, smiling benignly down on the gathering. Max brightened up. 'No one can doubt that he had a good time while he was with us, that he wore out, instead of rusting out.'

'Hear, hear.'

'He fought a good fight,' said Max. 'Cancer takes no prisoners, they say, and if he had any regrets at the end, it must have been that he wasn't given enough time to retire to the seaside and work on his golf handicap after going around the world. He will be remembered not only as a brilliant party-giver – I fancy he may be looking down on us now, and wondering if the champagne will go round—'

Subdued laughter.

'He will also long be remembered for running the highly successful Abbot Agency, with its watchword of "discretion". Over the years the agency has solved countless problems for people in distress. My dear mother only bowed out of it when Hamilton fell ill, and he only handed on the baton to me when he grew too frail to direct operations himself. I hope, I think, I didn't let him down when I took over from him, but now I've got a new career it's time to wind up the agency, too. Here's to an honourable retirement for the Abbot Agency.'

'Hear, hear. The Abbot Agency.'

Bea sighed. It was the end of an era.

Again a phone bell trilled.

The phone continued to trill, and she realized to her horror that it was her own mobile which was ringing. Fishing it out of her jacket, she flicked it off, noticing as she did so that the call was from Piers, her first husband. They were good enough friends, nowadays. He'd phoned her in New Zealand after the papers had reported Hamilton's death. Nice of him. But she didn't want to speak to him now.

Max was winding down. 'After her long years of service to the agency, followed by more years of loving care to Hamilton, we welcome my dear mother back home to a well-earned rest. Looking a million dollars as she does, I'm sure she'll soon be enjoying a good time on the golf course at the seaside, and in the club house afterwards. To Mother.'

'Bea!' came the well-drilled chorus. Most of the women wore sympathetic smiles for a woman of sixty who might look younger than her years, but was not and never had been a bimbo.

Oh, well, thought Bea. I hope Max finds himself a better speech writer soon.

With many glances at watches, people began to pay their respects to Bea and drift away.

'So sad, dear, but you've always been so strong.'

'I just wish you weren't leaving the neighbourhood.'

'Dear Bea, you must come round to see us sometime before you go.'

Arms went round her shoulders. A lot of air-kissing went on, and promises were made to keep in touch. Some of them were meant.

Max was looking at the clock on the mantelpiece. Busy, busy. The very picture of a man on whose shoulders the fate of the world, or his constituency, rested. Bea knew she was being unfair to him because he really was fond of her, but she was too tired to guard her thoughts.

Max put his arm around her shoulders and gave her a hug. She allowed herself to rest against him for a moment of much needed comfort.

'Mother, I'm afraid I'm going to be late if I don't . . .

committee meeting . . . but you can cope, can't you? Maggie will fill you in. That's the girl who's been helping me close up the agency. I've let her use a room on the top floor, but she knows she has to be out by the end of the week. Must dash. I'll come round tomorrow and we can have a good chat, tidy up the loose ends.'

Was Maggie the person manning the phones at the agency downstairs?

Following Max came his over-thin – not to say haggard – wife, Nicole, clutching her tiny Yorkshire terrier, which was wearing a tartan bow in its topknot. 'Dear Bea, so good to see you coping so well, considering.'

Bea had a moment's disorientation. Fatigue, of course. The room faded out and she clutched at something, anything, to avoid falling. Then she was all right again, and could hear and see as before. She discovered she'd grasped Nicole's arm in her moment of weakness, and apologized. 'Sorry, I'm more tired than I thought. What was it you were saying?'

Nicole gave her a look full of doubt, meaning, Was the old dear still compos mentis? Had grief turned her mind to jelly? Nicole said, 'I was saying that I don't think there's much to discuss, but I'll pop in tomorrow morning to go over a couple of things with you. Dear Hamilton, I shall miss him so much. You must come down to us some weekend; not this weekend, though. Some constituency function, you know.'

On her way out Nicole brushed past an occasional table, causing it to totter and the glasses on it to fall. Nicole didn't notice in her haste to catch up with Max. Bea righted the table, thankful that the glasses that had stood on it were almost empty. The carpet might need shampooing, though.

She braced herself. The room was in disarray, with bottles, glasses, ashtrays – yes, some people had been smoking – and nibbles strewn on every surface. Also on the carpet. Max and Nicole had been living here for quite a while and various pieces of furniture had been moved to different positions. Ornaments had been switched round. Bea shrugged, thinking it wouldn't take her long to clear up . . . if only the room didn't keep swaying around her.

Then it settled. The silence was welcome. The bell at the agency door downstairs rang sharply but Bea refused to react. Enough was enough.

The sun had come out, and dust motes danced in the beams that shot through the half-open French windows at the back of the house. Bea thrust open the doors and went out on to the iron-work balcony to get a breath of fresh air. It was going to be a warm evening.

Curling iron-work stairs led down into the garden, which was not large but was protected on three sides by tall brick walls topped with spiky railings.

Bea saw that the sycamore tree in the corner had not been lopped that summer, so that it threw a canopy of green over the bottom part of the garden. Everything had been well looked after; the paved area around the modern fountain in the centre was weed-free, and the rambling roses trained to climb the walls had been dead-headed. Huge pots filled with busy Lizzies and ivy-leaved geraniums had been watered recently.

Garden chairs and a table had been placed beneath the tree, and Bea imagined Max and Nicole hosting a barbecue down there. Important people would attend; up-and-coming politicians, journalists, perhaps? People with money, definitely. Her mind went further back down the years . . . she remembered the boy Max riding his bike round and round, pretending it was a motorbike going vroom-vroom while Hamilton cooked the evening meal on the barbecue that he'd built himself. Later on, the four of them had been accustomed to eat alfresco meals at a trestle table Hamilton had found in a junk shop somewhere. She wondered where that table had gone.

Just to look at the garden lifted her spirits.

Neither Max nor Nicole were particularly light-hearted. Both were deeply serious about Max's career. Nicole showed no signs of producing children and this had been a source of sorrow to Hamilton and Bea. Ah well, thought Bea. There's still time. Hopefully.

Bea's dear husband Hamilton had been light-hearted on the surface, but he'd had a deep sympathy for the underdog and the wronged in society, particularly if they couldn't afford to hire expensive lawyers or go to the police.

Bea mourned his loss, greatly. They'd been together for many years; years of hard work in which they'd earned a good living while having the satisfaction of knowing they'd righted a lot of wrongs. Hamilton had been a good stepfather to Max. She didn't like to think how her son might have turned out if

Hamilton hadn't been around to lend some stability to their lives. Max wasn't perfect – too much under the thumb of his wife – but then, who was?

She thought she'd done most of her mourning for Hamilton during the years he'd taken to die, though now and then something came back to catch at her throat and make her shake with the pain of her loss. They hadn't been lovers for a long time, but they'd always been good friends. What did the future hold for her? She couldn't think, daren't think. Was too tired to think.

She took out her mobile phone and listened to the message Piers had left on it. 'Welcome back, and when can I drop round?' She shook her head. Piers was best kept at a distance. She deleted the message.

The agency doorbell rang again. Wasn't it after office hours? Usually the strident doorbell was muted by the last person to leave the office at the end of the working day, which was when the telephone was switched to Hamilton and Bea's living quarters. Presumably the Maggie person was still working.

It needn't concern her any more. Hamilton's will had been a simple affair; everything to her, with keepsakes to the children and one or two old friends.

Hamilton had advised her to close the business, sell the house and leave the area to make a fresh start, but now the time had come to put his plan into action, she realized that the last thing she wanted to do was retire to the seaside and play golf. That had been Hamilton's dream, not hers. So what should she do?

She'd think of something. Tomorrow.

Now she must find an apron and start clearing up from the party. Trust Max to give a party in someone else's house and leave them to do the washing-up.

Someone had swept into the room behind her. A stick-thin girl with hair dyed pink, wearing too short a skirt over thin legs that didn't warrant such exposure. Bea stifled a 'Tut!' and brought out a social smile. 'You must be Maggie? Have you come to help me clear up? That's kind of you.'

'Welcome home, Mrs Abbot. You can safely leave everything to me, you know. Max said you might be glad of a hand after your journey.' The girl couldn't be more than twenty, but had the bossy manner of a good nanny. She bustled around, making a little too much noise for Bea's tired brain. Bea thought that anyone watching might imagine Maggie was the hostess, and Bea the guest.

Bea said 'Thank you,' and tried not to wince as the girl clashed glasses together. Bea was so tired that her head was buzzing but she told herself that the girl meant no harm, and with jet lag it was better to keep going till bedtime if she could, allowing her body to recover its natural clock the quickest way.

The doorbell rang again downstairs, and the girl said, 'Tsk! Can't they read? Didn't they see the notice I put on the door?'

'I'll get a tray,' said Bea. She went through to the kitchen at the back of the house to fetch a tray and an apron. The kitchen, she noticed with resignation, was in a mess. Now that *would* need cleaning up before she went to bed. She could never sleep easily if her kitchen were in a mess.

Maggie came through with a double handful of dirty glasses, which she plonked down on the sink. 'It's probably that awful woman again. Nothing for you to worry about. I'll pop down and tell her to get lost.'

Someone was already coming up the stairs, someone who didn't mean to be fobbed off by Maggie or anyone. 'She's back, isn't she? Out of my way, girl.'

'Now wait a minute . . .!' said Maggie.

A head of curly blonde hair hove into view, and Bea smiled. 'Well, well. A voice from the past. How are you, Coral? Long time no see.'

Coral Payne was no more than five foot tall, with a big bust and the organizational ability of a sergeant major. She was also an excellent caterer who'd been on the agency books for years.

'Bea Abbot, you're a sight for sore eyes. I'm really, really sorry to hear about poor Hamilton but now you're back, you can put everything right again.'

Which was when alarm bells began to ring for Bea.

Tuesday, early evening
Lena seated herself on the settee, removing her earrings. 'He was gay, wasn't he?'

The body still lay where it had fallen. A fly droned around the room.

Richie shook his head. 'I wouldn't have said so, no.'

The boy picked up the hint she'd given them. 'I'm sure he

was. Gay men often go cruising and meet with trouble, don't they? Of course he played the field. I overheard him saying so, the day I was at the hotel—'

'Mixing business with pleasure,' said Richie. 'If you hadn't given the receptionist your phone number, he'd never have known how to contact us.'

'How was I to know he'd recognized me? It was just bad luck that he'd worked at a place we'd done before. He shouldn't have tried to blackmail us. It's his own fault that this happened.'

Richie persisted. 'You should have walked out as soon as he recognized you. We could have cancelled the function, got clean away.'

'That's enough,' said Lena.

Noel turned a sunny smile on his mother. 'So what do we do with the body, then?'

'We'll wrap him in a shower curtain and in a couple of hours' time when everything's quiet we'll carry him down to the garage. We'll pretend he's drunk if anyone sees. Put him in the boot of the car, and dump him on Hampstead Heath. Being gay, it'll cause no surprise if he's found up there, beaten to death.'

A dark stubble was beginning to show on the older man's chin. 'Hang about, Lena. He'll have taken some precautions, maybe told someone about us?'

'Why would he have done that? He wanted to join us, not destroy us. He won't have told anyone.'

Richie pointed his finger at her. 'He might have told the receptionist.'

Noel brushed that aside. 'He told her he needed my number to check up on something for Saturday. She's too dumb to work it out. I'll take her out again, make sure she forgets.'

Lena was frowning. 'That reminds me. We need to get rid of his mobile phone, if it's got Noel's number on it.'

'What a fool he was,' said the boy, grinning. He put on a camp accent. '"I know what you're up to. I can help you, if you cut me in."' The boy rocked with laughter. 'He said, "Cut me in!" and we cut him up!'

Richie grimaced. 'If you hadn't lost your temper, we could have paid him off and no one any the wiser.'

The woman shook her head. 'I never liked the idea of cutting him in. This way is better.' She needed to convince herself of that.

Two

Tuesday, evening

Coral surveyed the mess left by the party. 'Left you to clear up, have they? Not surprised. Give me an apron and I'll help you get things straight while we talk, right?'

'Oh, come on, now.' Maggie put both hands on her non-existent hips, preparing to do battle. 'Mrs Payne, you know Max said he couldn't help you.'

'What young Max said is neither here nor there,' declared Coral, seizing an apron, and tying herself into it with little jerks. 'Mrs Abbot is here now, and we don't have to take any more notice of Mr Hufflepuff.'

Bea repressed a grin. That description of Max was all too accurate, though of course she'd never hurt him by using it to his face. 'Coral, dear, I'm delighted to see you, but I've only just flown in from the other side of the world and I'm shattered.'

Coral cleared a space on the kitchen table, though how she'd done it, Bea couldn't imagine, for it had looked impossible a moment before. 'I told Max, why don't you get me and my team to cater for your mother's homecoming? But no, he wouldn't hear of it. That one always was penny wise and pound foolish. Maggie, make yourself useful; take a tray and start collecting glasses from the other room. Bea, you could do with a cuppa and a bite to eat, if I know anything about it.'

Maggie squawked, 'You can't just come in here and—'

Coral began to rinse glasses and stack them in the dishwasher. 'Mrs Abbot and I have worked together more times than you've had hot lunches, girl. She knows I wouldn't be invading her privacy like this unless it was important, and it seems to me it's just as well that I did. Can't you see she needs something hot inside her and a quiet sit down and chat before she sleeps off that terrible journey, because she didn't eat anything on the plane, I'll be bound? First she must eat; then we'll talk.'

Coral pulled out a kitchen stool, removed a couple of dirty plates, wiped the stool down, and gave Bea a gentle push in its direction.

Bea reached for a kitchen tissue, and blew her nose. 'Thank you, Coral. Maggie, it's all right. Coral and I are old friends.'

'Yes, but Max said that I wasn't to let Mrs Payne bother you now the agency is closing down.' The girl's chin stuck way out. Really, she was a very plain-looking creature.

Coral slapped the door of the dishwasher shut. 'Tip the rest of those nasty little bought canapés into the bin, and let's see what we can find in the way of proper food in the cupboards, shall we? I remember how it was when my husband died. I kept myself so busy I forgot to eat properly, and then one day I tripped over the cat and sat down and howled for hours and hours. Then I made myself a big cottage pie, ate the lot, and felt much better.'

'I'm just fine,' said Bea.

'You're far too thin,' said Coral. 'I always say that when a woman's head looks too big for her body, she's been neglecting herself. Or dieting too hard. Which is it this time?' The kettle boiled and she made Bea tea in a giant mug, sugaring it liberally.

Bea began to laugh, with a trace of hysteria. 'After Hamilton died, I flew on to the South Island of New Zealand because we'd booked the flights and he'd been looking forward to it. It seemed logical at the time to carry on with our schedule, though now I think it was ridiculous. The scenery was spectacular but I couldn't eat anything. I'm so glad he managed to see so much of the world before he died. He enjoyed everything right up to the end.' She blew her nose again.

Coral nodded, emphatically. 'That was Hamilton, all right.'

'Coral, do you remember when you were doing that big wedding in the middle of the holiday season and we couldn't get enough help for love or money, and Hamilton filled in as master of ceremonies, and Max and I helped out? And Max emptied a tray of champagne flutes into the bin, and Hamilton took the blame?'

Coral was laughing. 'Max wouldn't like his pals at the House of Commons to hear that he'd once earned money as a waiter, would he?'

'Oh, I don't know. They might think it proved he understood the working man. Let's see what's for supper.' She checked
the fridge and freezer. Nicole had stocked up for her with some
frozen meals; a pleasant surprise. The child Maggie was looking
thunderous, so Bea tried to defuse the situation.

'Don't look so shocked, Maggie. In those days we turned
our hands to anything. Silver service, escorting children around
London, clearing houses when old people died, and worse!'

There was a tinge of mischief in her tone. Maggie looked
stunned, but Coral giggled. 'I remember when . . .'

'Not in front of the child,' said Bea, mock serious. 'It was
hard work, Maggie, but it was fun, too. Or is distance lending
enchantment? Will you join us in a scratch supper, Coral?'

Between them Coral and Maggie cleared up the mess left
by the party, while Bea put some frozen meals into the
microwave. She wondered if Nicole ever did any cooking; probably not.

Maggie declined to join them for supper, but insisted on
dealing with the stains on the carpet next door while Coral and
Bea ate at the kitchen table. Bea wondered if the child was a
snob but reckoned she'd probably been trained by Max not to
associate with 'the help'.

Bea ate as much as she could. It wasn't as much as she
should, perhaps, but better than she had been doing lately.

Afterwards she and Coral had some coffee in the sitting
room, so that they could sit by the open French windows and
look out over the garden in the quiet of the early evening.
Planes droned on overhead on their way to Heathrow Airport,
but they were never more than a background reminder of the
world outside. Bea pushed back fatigue, eased off her shoes
and sighed with relief.

'I must try to keep awake for another hour, if I can. So,
what's the matter, Coral?'

For the first time Coral looked unsure of herself. Her tiny
feet hardly touched the ground, seated as she was in a Victorian
button-backed armchair. 'Maybe I should apologize, breaking
in on you the day you got back. Truth to tell, I got my dander
up good and proper and forgot you might be too tired to listen.'

'It must be important or you wouldn't have come.'

'It's important, yes. Max won't help, saying it isn't his responsibility, and maybe he's right in law. I know the difference

between right and wrong, and I say he's wrong. Of course, now he's an important person with a salary in Parliament, he doesn't want to be tidying up loose ends from the agency, and maybe I shouldn't have come bothering you but I didn't know what else to do. I've tried ringing him, loads of times, and coming round to speak to him. All he says is that I can take it to the small claims court if I wish. But I can't do that, can I? No more than I can go to the police.'

'Ah. No proof – of what?'

Coral shrugged. 'It was always a bother to me, keeping the wages straight, so I got my son-in-law to look after that side of things.'

Bea jerked herself awake. 'You let that no good son-in-law of yours keep your books? After the hash he made of costings for the open evening at the art gallery? I thought you said years ago, that you'd never let him loose on your books again.'

'He's gone and done a business degree since then, and my daughter's pregnant and begged me to give him another chance. And it was for a big do, wasn't it? Charity organization. Proper letterhead and a cabaret and little pin things to give away. There was to be an auction and the guest list was to die for.

'Max passed the job to me, said it would do me a lot of good, get my name known with a better circle of people, people who count. I'd just lost one of my oldest accounts when they moved out of London so I was looking for something to fill the gap. The function was to be held in the Garden Room at a big roadside pub down the Great West Road.

'Silver service, of course. I had to call in a few extra to help, and my sister helped out with preparing the food and though I say it myself, it was a sight for sore eyes and not much left over, I can tell you. The place was packed. Loads of people complimented me on the food and I thought I was on the up and up. Till the charity's cheque bounced.'

Bea drew in her breath. She knew how much these events could cost. 'How much were you out of pocket?' She'd noticed that two of her pictures were crooked on the wall, so she got up to straighten them.

'Thousands. Far more than I could afford to lose. That wasn't the worst of it. I rang Max and told him what had happened and he said he was sure there'd been some mistake, that he'd contact the people who ran the charity about it for me. Sure enough, they rang me the next day to apologize. A woman it was. Nice as pie. She said it must be some glitch or other and the cheque had probably been taken from the wrong account. Their accountant was on holiday but they'd send me a replacement cheque as soon as he got back.'

'And did they?' She plumped up some cushions.

'Wait for it! She said they wanted to make it up to me. She could charm for Britain, that one. She said they'd another function coming up, even bigger. Would I be interested in doing that for them? Meanwhile she'd see that I got my money as soon as possible. Like a fool, I believed her.

'The next function was at the Priory Country Club, much the same as the first one, only bigger. All bare shoulders and bling for the women and silk shirts for the men, if you know what I mean. It's true I got a cheque from the charity the day before the second event but of course there wasn't time for me to get it cleared by the bank beforehand. That bounced, too. As did their cheque for the second event.'

Bea felt dizzy. She climbed on to a low stool to straighten the mirror over the mantelpiece and had to hold on to it, to prevent herself from tumbling off. 'So you didn't get a penny for either? Why didn't you go to the police? No, don't tell me. Your son-in-law wasn't up to date with his book-keeping?'

'Something like that,' said Coral, in carefully neutral tones.

Bea surmised that he'd probably been paying the staff cash in hand without covering insurance or tax or keeping proper records. If that was the case, Coral couldn't go to the police without getting him and herself into trouble. Bea straightened the mirror, noting to her horror that there were gashes in the wall behind it. Was this where Max and Nicole had hung their plasma television? Well, the mirror would disguise the problem for the time being.

Coral attempted a smile. 'I'd forgotten you could never sit still for five minutes.'

Bea got off the stool, and sat. 'I'm listening. What did you do then?'

'I didn't let it rest, of course. I came straight back to Max but by that time he'd got into Parliament and lost interest in the agency, and was hardly ever here. That holy terror of a woman that used to keep the books here, she'd retired, and that girl Maggie is good at polishing furniture but hopeless in the office. When I finally got to see Max he said he was sorry, he didn't know what had gone wrong, but the agency wasn't liable for anything other than introducing us to the client.

'So I went round to the address on the charity's letterhead and, guess what . . . not a sign of them there! And their telephone number was out of service.'

'Ouch,' said Bea. 'A proper con job, and you can't go to the police.'

'Then I heard you were coming back after poor Mr Hamilton, ah well, we all have to meet our Maker some time, don't we, and I was glad you gave yourself a bit of a holiday afterwards even if it was by yourself.

'But the thing is, I've lost so much money that I don't know which way to turn. I help my daughter and son-in-law out with their mortgage, you see, and I haven't been able to pay it for four months. She, my daughter, is eight months pregnant and in a nervous state, and all my son-in-law will do is blame me for taking the job on. That's why, the moment I heard you were on your way back, I said to myself that you'd help me even if Max has washed his hands of it. I want you to find those dodgy dealers and make them pay up.'

Tired as she was, Bea shot up out of her chair. 'Coral, no! I couldn't.'

Coral folded her arms. 'Why not? If anyone can do it, you can.'

'What? We're not a detective agency. We don't hunt down criminals or follow erring wives or husbands. Besides, the agency is being closed down.'

'I'll believe that when the moon turns blue.'

'What?' Bea put her hands to her head. 'Which bit don't you understand?'

'You've never in your life turned your back on a job half done. How long have we known one another? Twenty years, maybe more. You and Mr Hamilton, God rest him, you've never let a client down.'

'Oh, come off it. There's been times when we've had to say we couldn't take a case, and when things haven't worked out quite as we'd have wanted them to.'

'And were there times when Mr Hamilton asked me to do a job without vetting the client properly?'

Well, no. Hamilton had never done that. Check, check and

check again; that was his motto. Bea knew, because she'd mostly been the one to do the checking when she'd worked for the agency. If what Coral had said was true, Max had not only failed to check the credentials of the 'charity' but then declined all responsibility in the matter. Which pressed the 'Ouch' button for Bea.

She pulled a face. 'Listen, Coral. I'm really, really sorry, but you must know that I haven't worked in the agency for years, and now it's being wound up I couldn't interfere, even if I wanted to.'

'Of course you could. You know right from wrong, same as I do, and you know this is wrong. As for young Max saying the agency's dead, well what's that to you? Who founded it, you or him?'

'Well, actually it was Hamilton who—'

'Inherited it from his aunt, who'd run it with a gaggle of distressed gentlewomen. Yes, I know. He told me some wild tales about how his aunts used to carry on in those days, and didn't we just laugh! Then you came to join him with that miserable little kid in tow, and it was you working all hours and finding good people to work for you, that's what turned the agency into something special. So don't tell me you couldn't interfere now.'

Bea pushed her mop of hair back from her face. Did it need cutting again? She'd had it cut in New Zealand, but hadn't been altogether pleased with the result. Now she was back, she must get her own hairdresser on the job.

She said, 'I'm tired, Coral. Bone weary and worn out. I feel like an old woman.'

Coral edged herself off her chair, and patted Bea's arm. 'I know, I know. I've been there, done that, bought the serial rights and sold them to the BBC. I said to myself, "Bea's maybe had the guts knocked out of her over this, and if she has, then she won't be able to help and I won't say anything to upset her." But I took one look at you, and I thought, You've still got a backbone, somewhere inside the jelly. You get a good night's sleep and I'll be round in the morning to hear what you have to say, right?'

Bea let Coral out of the front door. The road beyond was quiet, lined with cars displaying parking permits, since this was a residential parking area. Where had Max put her car? And Hamilton's? Wait a minute, hadn't Max said he'd take

Hamilton's car off her hands? She rubbed her forehead. She couldn't remember, couldn't think straight. She'd ask him about it in the morning.

Dusk was closing in. The white stucco of the houses looked ghostly in that light. It wasn't a very long street, but many of the tiny front gardens sported small flowering trees and there were window boxes everywhere. In this or any other light, the street looked charming. A moon showed itself over the roof opposite.

A light glowed in the basement below. Presumably Maggie had her quarters there? Hadn't Max said something about giving the girl a room, but that she had to be out at the end of the week? Maggie might look a figure of fun, but she knew how to clean a room. Even Coral had said that. So tomorrow, if Bea could stand Maggie's bossy ways, the girl could help her get the furniture back the way she liked it.

Tomorrow she'd think about what Coral had said. Not tonight. Anyway, what Coral wanted was quite out of the question. It was a nuisance not having the house to herself, but in a few days' time the girl would be gone and Bea could relax.

She went into the big reception room, and looked around her. It didn't look like her room at the moment, with this and that missing, and all the sympathy cards on the mantelpiece. She must look through them sometime.

She and Hamilton had spent most of their evenings in this room. Latterly Hamilton hadn't enjoyed big social events because of his slight but increasing deafness, so they'd mostly stayed in, she watching television or reading, and he playing patience. He'd played on a baize-covered table – now missing – in the window with real cards, not on a computer. He'd said there was something soothing about laying the cards out one on top of another, occupying the top of his mind while underneath his subconscious dealt with any problems that happened to be around. Oh, she was going to miss him so much.

She stood looking out over the darkening garden for a while. A moving light in the sky was not a falling star, but yet another plane making its way to land at Heathrow Airport. A breeze ruffled the leaves on the tree and above it rose the graceful spire of St Mary Abbot's church, a pale finger pointing upwards into the night sky.

She shut and locked first the windows and then the burglar-proof grille inside, turned off the lights in the kitchen and sitting room and set the burglar alarm. Now to get her luggage up to her bedroom. She dragged the cases out from under the stairs and stopped. They were too heavy for her to haul up to the first floor. The flight back from New Zealand was taking its toll. She consulted her watch to see what time it was, but couldn't focus on it.

She would leave the cases where they were, take a shower and fall into bed. If she couldn't find a nightdress then she'd do without.

She reached her bedroom at last and with thankfulness saw that Nicole had put clean linen on the king-size bed. Don't think about Hamilton dying in a hospital bed far away. Don't think about the lonely cemetery in which he now lay, on the other side of the world.

The en suite bathroom had been cleaned, and fresh towels laid out. Thank you, Nicole. She wondered whether Max and Nicole had enjoyed sleeping in this big bedroom. She hoped they had. There was a trace of a powdery scent in the air; Nicole's. Bea hefted up one of the sash windows as far as the burglar lock would allow. The scent would soon go. Nicole had even thought of putting a small posy of flowers in a vase on the dressing table.

Bea decided to rescue her own toiletries from her luggage in the morning. At that moment she became aware of music filtering down from the floor above. Not jazz, not pop. A string quartet? Suddenly it was muted.

She stiffened. Was that Maggie up there? But, wasn't Maggie still working downstairs in the basement?

Perhaps the girl had crept up the stairs after her? If so, Bea could ask her to help by bringing up at least one of her suitcases.

Bea had already shucked off her shoes, so she went up the stairs to the top floor without making a noise. It wasn't that she'd meant to startle Maggie; it was just how it happened.

On the top floor there were three doors. Here Max had once held sway. The room at the front of the house had been his bedroom, and the room behind had been set aside for games, with model railways on the floor at first, computers and a drum kit later. The third door led to the second bathroom.

Bea opened the door to the front bedroom and a strange man leaped to his feet in alarm.

'Who . . .? What . . .?'

He gaped. He was young enough to be her son. No, her grandson. A student, perhaps? Overly thin and undersized. Brown eyes wide with anxiety. Dark hair that grew in a whorl at the back of his head and probably never stayed down. Not old enough to shave? Scrupulously clean, sweatshirt and jeans a trifle too large for him, bare feet.

She blinked. 'Are you a burglar?' Which sounded absurd, even to herself.

He made an inarticulate noise. He looked terrified.

This was the larger of the two rooms on the top floor, with windows overlooking the street. The room was furnished much as Max had left it except that a computer now rested on the desk next to a television set, and there was a microwave oven and kettle on a stand nearby. Plus the room was far tidier than it had ever been when Max had been living in it.

Footsteps came up the stairs and Maggie entered, bearing a foil-covered frozen meal. She took in the situation and gave an unconvincing laugh, which was far too loud and grated on the ear. 'I can explain.'

Bea said, 'Does he live here, too?'

'Sort of. He's been helping me out with the agency work, and he doesn't have anywhere else to go.'

'Max didn't mention him. Does Max know he's here?'

'I told Max he was my boyfriend, which he's not, of course. Just a waif and stray.'

'You can't be both a waif and a stray,' said Bea, over-tired. 'One or the other. Does he have a name?'

The boy gibbered, so Maggie helped him out. 'Oliver Ingram. He's an idiot. Mostly.' She spoke in the dispassionate tones of an elder sister referring to a subnormal younger brother.

Bea couldn't think of anything to say.

'I'll explain in the morning,' said Maggie, talking to Bea now in much the same tone as she'd referred to the boy. 'Now don't you worry about a thing, Mrs Abbot. You get yourself to bed and I'll bring you up a nice cup of tea in the morning.'

Bea stifled an impulse to tear Maggie off a strip for speaking to her as if she were a small child, and then another one to laugh. 'Is Oliver strong enough to bring up my suitcases? They're too heavy for me.'

'We'll do it between us,' said Maggie. She turned to the boy and said, 'And don't you play that loud music of yours any more. Use your ear-phones, like I told you.' She caught Bea's eye and said, 'Teenagers!' with another of her unconvincing, braying laughs.

Oliver gave an impression of a nodding puppet, but managed to haul one of Bea's suitcases up the stairs and deposit it in her room without banging into the banisters or dropping them on his bare feet. Maggie carted the other case up with the minimum of effort. Obviously there were some muscles in that sinewy frame of hers.

Bea disinterred her toilet things and a nightdress, had a hasty shower and tumbled into bed. Before she turned out the light, she picked up a book Hamilton had left behind by mistake. It had a soft leather cover with his initials on it in gold, and he'd used it so much that some of the leaves were loose. He'd missed it on their first night away but she'd bought him another. He'd grumbled that the print in the new one was too small, but he'd used it right to the end. It had been buried with him.

It comforted her a little to hold his book in her hands, a book he'd read every day of his life. It seemed to bring him closer. She didn't bother to open it. Besides, she'd left her reading glasses somewhere. Where was her second pair, the ones she used for reading in bed?

What was the prayer her mother had always said over her, as she tucked her up in bed at night? 'Now I lay me down to sleep, guardian angels round me keep . . .' Bea couldn't remember the rest of it. At one time, when she was maybe seven or eight, she'd had bad dreams about a grey monster. Her mother had taught her another prayer which had worked well at the time. 'Matthew, Mark, Luke and John, guard the bed that I lie on.'

Very comforting thoughts, those. But not much help now. Bea wasn't sure she believed in guardian angels nowadays, or indeed believed in anything much. Hamilton had held strong beliefs. She wished, how she wished, that she could share his certainty about a God who loved her and was prepared to die for her.

She lay there, longing for sleep and fearing that it would elude her, as it had eluded her every night since Hamilton died. Hours passed, and still she could not sleep, but stared into the darkness.

*   *   *

Wednesday, morning
It was past two in the morning, but they were used to being
up into the small hours and showed no signs of strain. All three
had changed into T-shirts and jeans. The night was warm. They
wouldn't need jackets.

Wearing gloves, Richie searched the body, relieving it of all
identity, including mobile phone, keys, wallet and watch. Also
the silver bracelet on the left wrist.

The two men bundled the body into the shower curtain, and
checked the time.

There were only ten flats in the block, with parking below.
The street outside saw very little traffic at night. It was one of
the main reasons they'd chosen the place.

'Ready?' said Lena. The two men nodded and bent to pick
up the body. Lena followed them out of the flat, carrying the
rug in a bin bag. They would make it look like a robbery.
Everyone would think the man had gone looking for talent on
Hampstead Heath, fallen in with the wrong crowd, got mugged
and left for dead. End of story.

Three

Wednesday, morning

Bea woke to find it was broad daylight. She was surprised to find that she had actually fallen asleep for a while. She still felt draggingly tired, but told herself to stop whingeing and get on with the day.

Someone was bustling around the room. A mug of tea had been placed on her bedside table. The tea was in a china mug in a saucer with a lid on it to keep the contents hot. Now that was a good start to the morning.

'Don't you bother about anything, Mrs Abbot,' said Maggie, bossy as ever. The girl was now clad in a short lime green tunic which assaulted the eye. Where did she get her clothes from? 'I've unpacked as best I can, but I'm afraid there isn't any space in the dressing room so I couldn't hang anything up except behind the door. I expect you'll want most of your things washed or dry-cleaned. It's always the same after a holiday, isn't it?' And she gave another of her grating laughs.

Bea propped herself up in bed and sipped tea, trying to focus. 'That's kind of you, Maggie. Are you looking for a job as a housekeeper?'

'Oh, no. That's not what I want out of life at all. Max did say that he might be able to find me another job in an office if I made myself useful to you, but I wouldn't want to work as a housekeeper; no way.'

Bea thrust her hands back through her hair and shook her head to settle it. 'You could have fooled me. It was you who put clean sheets on the bed and cleaned the bathroom, wasn't it? Not Nicole.'

The girl made a dismissive movement with her hands. 'Well, Mrs Abbot was busy moving out. She said she didn't have the time to do it herself, so I said to her that you shouldn't have to come back after such a journey and find the place in a mess, and she said I could do it, couldn't I? So I did. I like everything neat and tidy around me.'

Bea edged herself off the bed and opened the door to her dressing room, which had been fitted out with cupboards and wardrobe space to hold all her and her husband's clothes. She couldn't get in because racks of Nicole's clothes, suitcases, and cardboard boxes had been packed shoulder-high into the space. Bea's disbelieving eye identified a plasma screen television, stereo, and other necessities for everyday life in the moneyed classes. 'What on earth . . .?'

Arms akimbo, Maggie nodded. 'I told Mrs Abbot you wouldn't be pleased, but she said there was no point taking her stuff away for such a short time.'

Did Nicole imagine that she was going to take over the house? But . . . too many conflicting thoughts collided in Bea's head. Her chief emotion was fury. How dare Nicole think she could casually take over Bea's home, when nothing, absolutely nothing, had been decided as to its future! Yes, Max had mentioned in one of his phone calls that perhaps she might sell the house to him when she moved, but she hadn't said yea or nay. She'd promised to think about it and had then put the whole thing out of her mind. It was too soon to make decisions about her future.

With an effort she told herself it would not be a good idea to criticize her daughter-in-law to Maggie. Bea modulated her voice from a screech of rage down to a pleasant tone. 'Thank you, Maggie. I'll be down in fifteen minutes. If you could put some coffee on for me?'

'Wouldn't you like some porridge? I always say, you should start the day as you mean to go on, with a full stomach. Or perhaps a couple of poached eggs? No, perhaps not eggs. Too many eggs are bad for you, they say.'

'Just coffee, please,' said Bea, feeling rather faint at the thought of a cooked breakfast.

'Very well. Will do. Now, when you come down, bring your dirty clothes, and I'll put them in the washing machine for you. Oh, and don't forget anything that needs dry-cleaning; I'll pop it into the shop later this morning.'

Bea bit back a sharp rejoinder, deciding it wasn't worth having a set-to about it. The girl meant well and after all, she'd be gone in a couple of days' time.

Bea dressed in the least creased of items from her luggage; a pale green silk top which looked like a T-shirt but wasn't, over cream silk-and-wool trousers. Peering into the mirror, she thought she looked hung-over but not too bad for her age. She darkened her eyelashes and eyebrows, added a spot of blusher to highlight her cheekbones, a dusting of power on her nose, and used a soft peachy lipstick. Her tan was good. Her eyes – Hamilton had always called them her 'eagle' eyes, because they were long-tailed and saw further than most – looked shadowed. They'd watched over a death-bed and it showed.

Which reminded her to slip the chain of her specs around her neck. Small print defeated her nowadays. She inspected herself at the full-length mirror, turning around to make sure she was properly turned out. Putting on my armour, she thought. Let battle commence. And don't let's forget that attack is the best form of defence.

Nicole arrived as Bea poured herself a third cup of black coffee. Nicole declined coffee and went straight into the sitting room, making it clear that neither she nor her pedigree dog normally spent time in a kitchen.

A clunking sound in the garden led Bea to unlock and open the grille and then the French windows on to the balcony, from which she saw Maggie dipping watering cans into the rain-water butts, to keep the flowers going. Was a hosepipe ban in operation? She was out of touch with much that had been happening in London while she'd been away.

Nicole had brought a laptop which she proceeded to set up, hardly thanking Bea for the present she'd brought back from New Zealand. Bea suppressed annoyance, for the gift had been expensive enough, in all truth.

'Now, Bea.' Nicole's own mother was older than Bea, but Nicole called her mother by her Christian name, too. Nicole had seated herself in Hamilton's favourite chair, the high-backed Victorian one. Bea told herself she wasn't going to get weepy at that time of morning.

'Thank you for the party yesterday, Nicole. It was a lovely thought.'

'Yes, well, there's lots of people who cared about Hamilton, and it's good PR for Max to keep in touch with everyone.'

'Indeed. You've looked after my little home beautifully, and the garden, too. Hamilton always used to say that houses are like people; they deteriorate if they're not looked after properly.'

'It's about the house that I—'

Bea went on the offensive. 'Now don't you worry. There's no way I'm going to charge you rent for the time you've been living here, even though I suppose I ought to have done so. I'm just glad it fitted in with your plans to move in for a while. You must give me your new address. Are you thinking of renting somewhere? The price of a flat near Westminster must be horrendous.'

'But Bea, I thought—'

'No need to worry about me. I can look after myself. Take my time, look about me, make no decisions about the future for a while. That's what Hamilton told me, and that's what I'm going to do.'

'But you're going to live on the South Coast and—'

'No, dear. That was Hamilton's idea, not mine. I really don't know what I'm going to do and where I'll end up, but I doubt very much it will be in a bungalow staring out to sea. I've always been a Londoner, you see.'

Nicole's colour rose. 'But I understood that—'

'Max did suggest buying this house from me if I did eventually decide to leave London, but I can't think about that yet. It's far too soon. I'm just glad I made it back home in one piece.'

Nicole hadn't been expecting this. 'But I got hold of a designer to draw up plans to remodel the house, bring it up to date. I've got quotes from the builders, and they can start on Monday. Look!' She turned the laptop to face Bea, who blinked. Her cream and gold sitting room was currently furnished with antiques handed down through Hamilton's family, while the designer's plan for this room screeched colour in vermilion and green, with minimalist furniture in plastic and glass.

Over her dead body! For the second time that morning, Bea felt her temper rise, but she subdued it and even managed a smile. 'I'm sure you can find something nearer to Westminster than this.'

'We can't possibly afford it. We're staying with friends until this house is ready.'

'Ah, that accounts for your having left so much stuff upstairs. Do get it shifted soon, won't you?'

'Yes. I mean, no. Listen; it wasn't my idea to buy the house off you, but when Max said you'd be leaving London, it seemed as if it were meant. Of course we get allowances for having to live in London while Max is at the House, but I want a decent place where we can entertain. My people have helped us buy a flat in the constituency, but we can't expect—'

'You must go to Marsh and Parsons, who'll find you somewhere to rent. They're the best estate agents around. Been here for ever. What did they say this house was worth, by the way?'

'Well, we didn't exactly ask. We thought you wouldn't want to charge the full market value, so as to keep it in the family.'

Bea counted to five and told herself that there was no point in antagonizing her loving son's wife. 'You thought I wouldn't need the full market price?'

'Yes. I mean, no. I mean . . . you won't need the full price to buy something down on the South Coast, and we didn't want to get into debt.'

Bea pointed to the laptop, and somehow hung on to a tone of sweet reason. 'Remodelling this house would cost you an arm and a leg, so I've saved you that much, and you're quite right about not wanting to get into debt. I'm sure you'll find a delightful place to rent. Somewhere on the river?'

'We've already spent so much money on architects. Look, this is the new wet room, and this the extension out into the garden.' Nicole showed Bea various designs which made her feel giddy. The architect would remove all the period features which made the house so charming.

Bea put a snap into her voice. 'Enough, Nicole. Please. Give it a rest.'

Nicole's face was white with rage, which made the blusher on her cheek-bones stand out. She snapped the laptop shut, considering her next argument. 'I don't think you've thought this through. Keeping this house going costs money, and I suppose there may be some inheritance tax to pay.'

'Don't you worry your head about that, dear. The house has been in my name for ever, and Hamilton left me well provided for. I am so proud of you and Max. And so was Hamilton. To think that a son of ours is now a Member of Parliament!'

What Hamilton had actually said was, 'He's a good lad and means well, though I'm not sure he's got what it takes to succeed in his new career. If he keeps his seat and makes his way up the ladder Nicole may stick with him, but if he stays a back-bencher I give that marriage five years at most.'

The front doorbell downstairs gave a sharp ring. Was that Coral arriving?

Bea picked up Nicole's little dog, which had been trying to sit on her foot. She stood, indicating that the meeting was over. 'It seems my next job is going to be finalizing the affairs of the agency. I gather we've a dissatisfied customer on our hands.'

Nicole was distracted, answered at random, probably worrying how she was going to break the bad news to Max. 'I suppose that girl Maggie can handle it although Max did say she was pretty useless in the office.'

'Do you know anything about Coral Payne, the caterer who got stung?'

'Oh, one of the troublemakers. Honestly, Bea. What a fuss about nothing.'

One of the troublemakers? How many dissatisfied customers were there?

Bea said, 'Have you any idea how Max came to meet the people who ripped her off?'

'We meet so many, I can't be expected to remember which one she means. I think it was some preview at the Royal

Academy. No, I remember now, it was at a charity function, Red Cross, or Mental Health or something like that. Perfectly charming woman, American, I think. Desperate to help the victims of whatever it was, somewhere in Asia. Knew about the agency, asked if Max could put her in touch with a reliable caterer. So he did. It was up to Mrs Payne to check them out.'

Was that true? Bea wasn't sure that it was, though she could see how Nicole might think so. Bea began to walk Nicole to the door. 'Was Max paid an introduction fee by Coral?'

Nicole shrugged. 'How should I know?'

Bea made a mental note to check. 'I'm sorry for Coral. Don't we have some insurance to cover bad debts?'

'I don't suppose it would cover Mrs Payne's bad debts. If she didn't have any insurance, then that's her fault, not ours.'

Bea opened the front door, and manoeuvred Nicole down the steps. Only then did she realize that she was still holding Nicole's little dog. Nicole came back for him with a bad grace – the dog objected to being removed from Bea's arms – and disappeared with him, looking at her watch, in the direction of the Tube station. Or to collect her car?

Only then did Bea remember that she hadn't asked Nicole about her own car. And Hamilton's. Bother. Well, she didn't need a car today, did she? There was a convenience store nearby and for anything else, there was Marks & Spencer's Food Hall in the High Street nearby.

She closed the front door behind her, and went down the outside steps to the basement, thinking about what she would say to Coral. It was out of the question for her to get involved, obviously. Although, wouldn't it make her as bad as Max, if she refused to accept the blame for the shortcomings of the agency?

The basement steps had been swept and a healthy-looking bay tree in a pot had been placed in the area below. Everything looked spotless. Full marks to Maggie. The girl might be one of the most irritating creatures alive, but she did know how to look after the house.

Bea tried the door into the basement, but it wouldn't open. She rang the bell and Maggie's voice requested identification before letting her in. A good safety precaution. The tiny vestibule and loo beyond was also clean and neat though perhaps could do with a lick of paint. But if the agency were closing, what did it matter? The basement could now be turned into a self-contained flat and let out for extra income. Or sold.

The reception room beyond seemed a trifle dim and perhaps a trifle dingy. Stick-thin Maggie was sitting at a desk in front of some filing cabinets. Coral was sitting on an upright chair with a fat file on her knee. The settee beside her was occupied by her podgy daughter – heavily pregnant – and fidgeting son-in-law.

Bea registered the fact that Maggie was looking annoyed before Coral sprang to her feet. 'You remember my daughter June, don't you?'

June was a blonde of sorts, with straggling hair tied back in a ponytail. On seeing Bea, she struggled to her feet, assisted by her husband. She was breathing hard and looked as if she'd go into labour any minute. 'I got it out of Mum last night, what's been going on.'

'She insisted on coming,' said Coral, looking worried.

'Threw a wobbly,' said June's husband. He was a weaselly type, more flash than faithful if Bea knew anything about human nature, but he did seem concerned for his wife.

June wobbled on her feet, but stayed upright. 'Mrs Abbot, you've got to get that money back for us or we won't be able to pay the mortgage, and it's four months owing now. It was all your fault, anyway, not Jake's.'

That's right, Bea remembered now that her husband's name was Jake.

'He shouldn't be blamed for it. He did everything that was proper, everything that he should have done and if anyone says otherwise, they'll have me to answer to.' Her colour was alarmingly high, and she had put on so much weight in pregnancy that she could have made two of her skinny husband, and been more than a match for Bea herself.

'Do calm down, dear,' said Coral, not sounding too sure that June would listen.

'That's more than enough,' said Bea, trying for authority.

At which June opened her mouth and screamed. In that small room, the effect was ear-splitting.

'What's happening?' shouted Jake.

'Give her room to breathe,' said Coral, ditching the file and clutching at June's wrist.

June took a deep breath and then, eyes goggling, screamed again.

Bea made another attempt to control the situation. 'June, shut up and listen to me!'

June screamed again.

Maggie shot across the room. 'Dial 999? Ambulance?'

June continued to scream.

'Yes, do that, Maggie.' Bea tried to attract Coral's attention. 'When's she due?'

'Not for another month, but you know how they are about dates!'

Jake was shaking June's arm, and she wasn't taking the slightest bit of notice. 'Shut up, girl! Shut up!' he was saying.

'Hysteria?' Bea shouted at Coral over June's continued screams.

Coral shrugged. 'It's her first. She's frightened. I don't know!'

Jake grabbed Bea's arm. 'Do something! Make her stop!'

'I would if I could, but—'

'Where's that ambulance? We've got to get her to hospital.'

Jake shouted in Bea's ear. 'Where's your car?'

She shouted back, 'Missing!'

Coral was vainly trying to get June to sit down again. June's face was bright red, her hair had come down and was hanging around her face. She continued to scream.

Coral dithered. 'I could take her in the van, I suppose.'

Maggie came off the phone and inserted herself into the group. 'There's a big pile-up on the High Street, and there may be a delay getting an ambulance through. Shall I call a taxi?'

Coral fished out her keys. 'I'll take her. *June!*' She shouted at her daughter. '*We're going to the hospital, now!*'

June gave a couple more screams, but didn't object as her husband and mother propelled her towards the door. By the time she'd got to the steps and was being pushed up them by the combined efforts of her family, she was weeping and gulping, but no longer screaming.

Maggie cancelled the call for an ambulance.

Bea sank into the nearest chair and covered her eyes with her hands. June's screams still seemed to echo through the room.

'Well, what a palaver.' Maggie screeched out a laugh, making Bea shudder. It seemed the girl had enjoyed the ruckus. 'So

what can I do for you now, Mrs Abbot? Some more coffee?
Take your clothes to the cleaners?'

'I'm all right for the moment, thanks.' Bea made an effort.
She picked up the file Coral had dropped on the floor, but
didn't attempt to open it. She felt shattered. She thought that
June had probably brought on that alarming attack quite delib-
erately, in order to bring pressure to bear on the agency. But
the consequences! If she lost the baby . . . it didn't bear thinking
about.

Bea inched herself to her feet, sent a bright smile in Maggie's
direction and took the door into the hall. In front of her, stairs
climbed to the first floor, but from the interview room on her
right – the office that had once been hers – she could hear the
clatter of computer keys. Would that be the boy Oliver?

She hesitated about going in to speak to Oliver but eventually
decided he could wait and, passing the tiny kitchen, went into
the inner sanctum from which Hamilton had once directed the
affairs of the agency. Because of the way the ground sloped, the
reception room on the street was semi-basement, but Hamilton's
large room at the back was at ground floor level, with another
grille protecting more French windows on to the garden.

This was where Hamilton or Bea had once welcomed clients
for a discreet, private chat. It was furnished as a sitting room
with comfortable chairs, and just one desk by the window for
Hamilton. The desk was no longer by the window, but had been
moved into the middle of the room, dominating it. Presumably
Max had preferred it that way, but it made a nonsense of
the friendly ambiance which had once been the trademark of the
agency. There was a stack of mail on the desk, awaiting Bea's
attention. More sympathy cards, letters, official-looking docu-
ments. Max had dealt with most of the forms that were needed
after a death but there were some things only Bea could deal
with.

With an effort she inched the desk back to the window again.
Hamilton had always liked to look out on the garden and the
trees beyond and it was indeed a pleasant scene. He could gaze
up at the sky, now blue as could be, with the spire of the church
just visible through the summer leafage. He'd done most of
his thinking in that big comfortable chair behind the desk,
swinging round now to look out of the window and now to
access his computer.

His computer wasn't there any more. Oh.

Max knew how to use a computer, didn't he? Yes, surely he did. Perhaps he'd stored Hamilton's computer somewhere else, thinking Bea would have no further need of it? Or was Oliver now using it in his room upstairs?

Well, it didn't really matter what had happened to the computer, did it? What mattered was that June shouldn't lose her baby, even if she had been responsible for bringing her labour on early. What mattered was that their mortgage should be paid, even if it was Jake's fault that Coral couldn't go to the police.

It was not a simple question of right and wrong, though right and wrong came into it. Coral and her son-in-law had probably been greedy, had not bothered to check the client out, had been lax in their book-keeping. Yes. But they hadn't deserved to lose all that money.

Bea opened the file, put on her reading glasses and discovered the total of how much they'd lost. Ouch. The agency could wash its hands of the affair. Naturally. They were not at fault in any way. Were they? No.

We-e-ll. Not in law, maybe. But yes, they were morally responsible, weren't they? Hamilton would certainly have said so. He used to quote some lines about being ready to right wrongs, or being a knight or something. She couldn't remember exactly what.

But there – Bea pushed the paperwork aside – this was no longer anything to do with her. She'd retired from the agency ages ago, and couldn't possibly be held responsible. A mistake had been made but mistakes do happen even in the best regulated families and it was not her problem. Was it?

She leaned back in her chair and closed her eyes.

Wednesday, morning
The team had slept late but now there was work to be done. They'd dumped the bin bag containing the stained rug in a wheelie bin in Camden Town. The washing machine was working on the shower curtain, and Richie had dropped off their clothes to be dry-cleaned.

Lena, dressed in a black leotard and sequined slippers, put on some rubber gloves to check out the victim's mobile phone. It was brand new, performing everything except the polka.

Noel was easing stylish boots over designer jeans. 'If I've got to get rid of my mobile, why can't I have his?'

'Don't be silly,' said his mother, accessing the address list. 'Ouch, he's got a couple – no, three – girls' telephone numbers in his memory.' She tapped her teeth. 'He said he was playing the field. Suppose he wasn't gay but—'

Noel pouted. 'He was gay.' He snatched the phone out of her hands. 'Swap you mine for this, right?' He fiddled with the phone. 'Who shall I send a photo to?'

Richie slid into the room, another phone to his ear. 'The hotel confirms the special offer on the wine. All right?'

'Sure,' said Lena, watching her son with a mixture of irritation and pleasure. 'Noel, you know you can't keep it.'

He whooped. 'Will you look at this!' He showed her an image of herself on the mobile.

She said, 'Look!' and pointed. Grabbed at the phone and missed.

Laughing, he opened his fingers and let the phone smash down on to the floor. And stamped on it. She drew the back of her hand across her forehead. 'Oh, Noel!'

'Was there anything on it?' asked Richie, through his teeth.

'You should have let me keep it,' said Noel, spreading his hands wide. 'Now look what you've made me do!'

Four

Wednesday, midday

Bea started up out of her nap. After a moment's disorientation, she adjusted her glasses and picked up Coral's file. Even though she was not responsible for the mess Coral had got into, she might be able to come up with a constructive suggestion.

The paperwork was not in chronological order. She spread the bits and pieces out on Hamilton's desk, trying to get a picture of what had been going on.

Maggie blundered into the room, all arms and legs. 'What can I do for you, you poor thing? How are you feeling? Jet lag's terrible, isn't it? Would some coffee help? I can make it in a trice.'

Bea told herself the girl was only trying to help. 'You can tell Oliver to come in. He's the computer buff around here, isn't he? I assume he's got Hamilton's computer and if so, tell him to return it, pronto.'

Silence. Maggie twisted her lips together, displaying reluctance to do as Bea had asked. Where did she buy her clothes and what colour had her hair been originally? She wouldn't be bad looking if she held herself better and paid a visit to a decent hairdresser. Was she anorexic, perhaps?

'Promise you'll be gentle with him,' said Maggie. 'He cries if people shout at him.'

Bea slammed her hands down on the desk. 'Heavens above!'

Maggie winced, but stood her ground.

'Oh, very well.' Bea moderated her voice. 'I promise to handle him as if he were made of glass. Just get him in here, fast.'

Oliver sidled into the room, looking about twelve years old. He was wearing a pair of moccasins in addition to the same casual gear as before. Bea gestured him to take a chair, which he only did after sending a pleading glance to Maggie. He was a finely cut lad, fine-boned – almost sparrow-boned. Too thin. If he put on a bit of weight, he might be handsome. There was a dusky tint to his skin. A mixed race ancestry, somewhere along the line?

'You too, Maggie. Sit.'

Maggie sprawled on the settee but Oliver sat on the edge of a chair, looking terrified. Bea repressed an impulse to blast him into outer space. He really was victim material.

'Now, I'd like an update, please. I want my husband's computer back. Also I need to know how many outstanding jobs we have on our books, what we owe, what is owing to us, and what sort of timescale to shut down we're talking about.'

Oliver gaped at her, wordless. Maggie shrugged, gazing out of the window, distancing herself from what was happening. Bea remembered that Maggie wasn't supposed to be much good at office work. All right. But what about Oliver?

Bea sat on her impatience. All right, an outright order to

Oliver didn't work. She'd try another way. She put on her Little Woman act, almost batting her eyelids in an effort to convince them that she was the original nitwit and he was the White Knight of the keyboard who could ride to her rescue. In a soft voice she said, 'You see how helpless I am, Oliver. Anyone could take me for a ride at the moment. I really need your help, to try to understand what's been going on.'

Oliver's narrow chest expanded as he got the point. Maggie gave a sharp nod, expressing approval of the way Bea was handling the boy.

Oliver said, in the tones of one who can hardly believe their ears, 'You want me to show you what I've been doing?'

Give the boy a cherry. 'Please.' She tried to sound humble.

Having reduced her request to words that he understood, Oliver was happy enough to bring in various spreadsheets and analyses of computer programmes that he'd been running. He laid them out on the desk, and began to explain them to her.

It was soon clear that while Maggie had been acting as receptionist and housekeeper for Max and Nicole, Oliver had been running what was left of the business.

'There's a bit of a gap at the beginning of the month,' said Oliver, as he began to wind down. 'Someone was keeping the books straight before me but she left and I'm sorry but I haven't been able to track every transaction down.'

'You've done a remarkable job,' said Bea, truthfully. 'I couldn't have done half as well.'

He managed to stop fidgeting at that, and even produced half a smile.

Bea put her elbows on her table, and rested her chin on her hands. 'Does my son know how much you've been doing?'

A shrug. 'He knew and he didn't know, if you know what I mean.' He shot a look at Maggie, asking for help. Shuffled his feet. 'He said he couldn't afford to pay me, but as I was Maggie's boyfriend—'

'Which he's not,' said Maggie, pugnacious in defence. 'I was sorry for him. Like a puppy left out in a storm, he was. And the room upstairs wasn't doing anything. To be frank, I'm not much good on the computer. I can produce the odd letter and make phone calls and that, but not this complicated stuff. So what I can't do, he does for me and I feed him and keep the house clean. And that's it, really.'

'My son mentioned that there might be some cases outstanding, possibly people who've had cause for complaint?'

Oliver and Maggie exchanged glances. Maggie said, 'One or two. But honest, nothing for us to worry about. Max had them checked out by his solicitor and we're in the clear.'

'Including Coral's case? Are we in the clear on that?'

'Yes,' said Oliver, but he looked unhappy about it.

'Yes,' said Maggie. 'Strictly to the letter of the law. Max explained it to me; there's always bad debts, and she should have been more careful.'

'Did she pay us an introduction fee?'

Oliver said, 'Yes, she did.'

Bea swung the big chair round and looked out over the garden. It was green and restful out there, and the temperature was rising. It would be another hot day. She unlocked and opened the grille and the French windows. Now she could hear the buzz of bees on the brightly coloured annuals in the big tubs outside. There were butterflies on the buddleia tree, and above the sycamore tree at the end of the garden rose the spire of the church.

She wasn't much of a churchgoer, though Hamilton had gone once a month and sometimes more often. Hamilton had been a Christian, not just on Sundays, but every day of the week as well.

As clearly as if he'd been at her elbow, she heard his voice. *Are we here just to make money, or to help people who can't help themselves?*

I can't! I'm too tired, too old. I've been out of it too long.

You can do it, girl!

Could she? Dare she? Suppose she tried to think like Hamilton; what would he have done in this case?

She sighed. She knew exactly what he'd have said. Help them, of course. She couldn't do it on her own; she'd been out of the business too long. What's more, she seemed to remember their computers had been updated some while back. Would she even know how to turn one on nowadays? So, she needed Oliver to help her.

If Oliver stayed for a while, presumably Maggie would have to stay, too. Bea quailed at the thought. The girl was bossy, loud and had a laugh that could drill through steel. Bea shuddered. Could she face living with that laugh? Even if it were only for a week? She sighed. She supposed she must. Indeed, she had very little choice if she wanted to go on living with a quiet mind.

She returned to her desk. 'I'd like to do something for Coral if I can. I understand you two are on notice to leave at the end of this week. Suppose I extend that deadline until the end of next week, which will give you more time to find somewhere else to go. If Oliver does any work for me, he gets paid for it, understood? I'd like to see what can be done to track down the con men who pretended to be a registered charity and took Coral for a ride. How does that strike you?'

Oliver and Maggie consulted one another without words. Oliver nodded.

Maggie said, 'What would we have to do?'

Bea shuffled papers, trying desperately to think what Hamilton would have said, if he'd still been here. He'd say, *First you check. Then you think. Only after that, you act.* So what would you check first? She handed some paperwork from the charity to Oliver.

'These people called themselves the International Relief Foundation, and the appeal fund was for helping the victims of the last tsunami. Find out everything you can about them.'

Oliver looked as if he wanted to drop the papers. 'How do we do that?'

Bea suppressed impatience. 'There's a charity number given at the bottom of the letterhead. Is it genuine? Check on the board members. Ring them up. See if you can find someone who'll talk to you about the charity they represent. Find out who is responsible for the day-to-day running. Is it one of the board members, or the secretary, or who? We need to find out how much of the information on the letterhead is genuine. If any.'

Oliver nodded. He still looked terrified, but maybe he'd do it. 'Off you go, then,' said Bea, and he scampered off, all eager beaver.

'Now, Maggie. At the bottom of this letter there's a signature which looks like Graham or Gordon Briggs, secretary. Coral says she spoke to an American woman, though. Can you find out who she is?'

Maggie pouted. 'How do I do that?'

Bea wanted to grind her teeth, but told herself it would be

too hard on her fillings. 'Well, for a start, it wouldn't be any good ringing the same people as Oliver. Coral told us about two places which have held events for these people. I want you to ring them and speak to whoever handles the bookings. Find out what they know about these people; for instance, who did they deal with at the charity? Can they give you a name? Does the charity have another address or telephone number, so that we can contact them? If you can, also find out if they've been paid for the functions the charity held there.'

At that moment her phone rang. She picked it up, saying smoothly, 'Abbot Agency, how may I help you?'

A man's voice, full of charm. With a laugh in it. 'At long last! I was beginning to think you'd given us up for good and were staying in the Southern Hemisphere.'

Piers, her first husband. 'What do you want, Piers?'

'There's a fine welcome. Can't I just want to see you for old times' sake?'

'I doubt it.'

'I'll drop round later, all right?' He put the phone down before she could tell him not to. Maggie was trying to look as if she were not dying of curiosity.

Bea said, 'My ex-husband. From the time before I married Hamilton.'

Maggie was trying to work it out. 'Max's father?'

'Yes. Not that he's been much of a father to . . . well, never mind. We've got work to do.'

She watched Maggie leave, guessing she'd probably go straight to Oliver with the news that Mrs Abbot's first husband had surfaced the day she got back from burying Hamilton. What next? Bea tried to open a drawer to find Hamilton's address and telephone book because there were one or two people she knew who might have come across the fake charity. She broke a fingernail. Bother. Now she had to find a nail file.

And 'bother' Piers, too. They'd married young; and it had been a disaster. After suffering four years of his tomcatting around, she'd thrown him out. He'd taken it as lightly as he took everything except his work, moving in with first one of his women and then another. Never staying long with anyone. Being a freelance portrait painter and wickedly attractive with it, he'd been able to do that.

For five long years he'd avoided her, during which time she'd worked all hours at all sorts of jobs to keep herself and Max. Maintenance cheques had arrived now and then. Never enough and never often enough, but she supposed Piers had been doing his best. The divorce went through unopposed.

Then one day he'd turned up on the doorstep asking for a bed for the night as if he'd never been away. Not that she'd let him in. Oh, no. Though it had taken all her willpower to resist his charm. Sometimes she wondered what would have happened if she had let him in . . . but no. Tomcats don't change their spots. Whatever.

Max had been nine when Piers returned. It was too late for him to play at fatherhood. Bea had been on the point of marrying Hamilton, and her son adored the large, laughing man who was always there for them.

After Hamilton adopted Max, the boy had declared he didn't want to see Piers any more. That should have been that, but for some reason – guilt, perhaps? – Piers had kept in touch with Bea. Every so often he'd give her a ring and ask her out for a meal; sometimes he'd ask after his son, though he didn't seem really interested in what she had to say. His career had taken off, the agency had thrived, they met without embarrassment.

She hadn't seen him for nearly a year. Tea at Fortnum and Mason's. They'd just been told that Hamilton's cancer had returned, and he'd refused further treatment in favour of going around the world, seeing everything he'd always wanted to see, doing everything he'd not had time for. Piers had been a good friend that day, said the right things, said she could always rely on him . . . though he hadn't said for what, the bastard.

Bea had to go and borrow a nail file from Maggie in the end. Then she got side-tracked as the front doorbell rang upstairs, and didn't stop. Bea guessed it was Piers. Bother!

'Shall I . . .?' asked Maggie, waving her arms in semaphore fashion.

'I'll go,' said Bea. Anything to stop him leaning on the bell. She opened the door. An orchid in a pot and a bottle of wine were thrust in her face. 'Welcome home,' said Piers, stepping inside the hall. 'By the way, have you got a bed for the night? I seem to be temporarily homeless.'

Wednesday, midday
The team was listening to the news on the television.

'. . . *taking his dog for a walk on the Heath stumbled across the body of a man early this morning. If anyone has any information, they should contact . . .'*

Lena used the remote to turn the television off. 'Home and dry. No identification. No problem. The keys went down a drain, the jewellery I wiped clean and dropped into a charity shop. We've been lucky. But Noel, don't you ever . . .!'

The lad pouted, and she bit back the rest of what she'd been about to say. She turned to Richie, who was folding menus with neat movements. 'What's the latest on the DJ? Can we get him again?'

'Cash up front. I've not been able to beat him down at all. Do we play?'

She tucked a strand of blonded hair behind one ear. 'Sometimes we have to spend, in order to rake it in. And the cabaret?'

'I've found a lad who's been on one of those talent shows on TV but never made it any further. He wants cash on the night.'

Lena nodded. 'Give him half in cash on the night, and a cheque for the rest.'

Noel yawned, grabbing the remote to turn the TV back on. Neither Lena nor Richie remonstrated, though Richie looked as if he'd like to do so.

Noel said, 'Is the Appealing Orphan coming out to play again?'

'She's upped her price,' said Lena. 'A minicab to pick her up and a fifty-pound note. I've told her not to embroider her story. Last time she said she'd lost five brothers and sisters, and six uncles and aunts. Two of each would be better.'

Richie nodded. 'One child lost, is a tragedy. Two thousand dead is news.'

'I think I'd better tell everyone about the tsunami, and let her add her voice at the end. That way, she can't exaggerate. She's so photogenic, we must use her.' Lena raised her voice. 'Do you hear me, Noel? You make sure Ana gets round to all the tables on Saturday night.'

Noel grunted, and switched channels.

Lena booted up her laptop. 'There's a thousand and one things still to do.'

Richie folded the last menu and pushed the pile aside. 'I'll go and collect the cosmetic samples we've been promised for giveaways, but it's going to take me a while because the warehouse is out in the sticks. Someone ought to check at the shop, see if there's any more requests for tickets. I suppose I could do that on my way back.'

Lena was frowning. 'I promised I'd drop a replacement cheque into the hotel. We have to let them have some money today or they'll cancel. I've still got to check on the caterers, get the balloons up, fetch my dress from the cleaners.'

'I'll collect the mail from the shop,' said Noel, losing interest in the television programme. 'Then on the way back I could drop the cheque in at the hotel, chat up the little receptionist, find out if our friend's been missed yet.'

Lena was uneasy. 'I'm not happy with your going anywhere near that girl. It was bad enough your taking her out for the evening, but to give her your phone number was asking for it.'

'It was only my mobile number, and she didn't know why the barman wanted it.'

Lena tried to convince herself he was right. 'I suppose she'd have tried to blackmail us, too, if she'd caught on.'

Noel shrugged and looked up at the ceiling. Richie glowered at Noel, but knew better than to say anything.

One of Lena's phones rang, she checked the label on it and answered. 'International Relief and Development Fund . . . oh, how are you? It was a good night, wasn't it! . . . What's that? Our cheque bounced? No! It's not possible. There must be some mistake. Give me the details and I'll get on to the bank straight away to sort it out.'

Five

Wednesday, lunchtime

Piers pulled a suitcase on wheels into the hall, closed the front door with his foot, and enveloped Bea in a hug.

She struggled free. 'How dare you!'

She would have hit him, only her hands were full. He laughed, slapped her behind and walked into the drawing room. She followed him, telling herself that the poet was right to warn people about guests bringing gifts, because you never knew what they were really after. The bottle of wine looked a good one. He'd spent money on that, and on the orchid, too.

Piers' gaze fell on Maggie. He gave her a slow inspection from her pink topknot to the awkward-looking feet, and identified her place in the household. 'Hello. I'm Piers. Could you come up with some coffee, do you think?'

Maggie simpered and scampered off, saying she'd see what she could do.

Like Max, Piers was tall and strongly built. Unlike Max, Piers hadn't an ounce of fat on him. He had a mop of dark hair becomingly streaked with grey. His skin was bronzed, his eyes hazel, and his chin looked as if someone had pushed it over to one side. He wore a checked wool shirt over well-cut jeans and the clothes looked right on him, despite the fact that he was now in his early sixties. Time had been kind to him in many ways, perhaps because he'd never burdened himself with family responsibilities.

'Piers,' said Bea, dumping the orchid on the mantelpiece out of the sun. 'Out!'

'Now, now. Don't be so hasty. So this is your home.' He looked all round. 'Nice place. Suits you. Are you going to keep it?'

'Yes,' said Bea. 'Piers, I can't give you a bed, so—'

'I got back from Scotland this morning. My tenant's not due to move out till Monday, so I thought I'd look you up.'

Maggie banged her way back into the room carrying a tray with a cafetière of fresh coffee and two mugs on it. She brought it to Piers as a puppy brings a toy to its master.

Piers thanked her with a smile, helped himself, and sank into a chair. 'Seriously, Bea, if there's anything I can do you've only to say.'

'Thank you, Piers,' said Bea, who didn't for a moment believe he meant it. 'Everything's under control.'

'Except for some old friend of hers who's in trouble,' said Maggie, interfering as usual. 'Max said she wasn't to worry about it, as it really is a lost cause.'

'Maggie,' warned Bea. 'Zip it!' And as Maggie opened her mouth to argue, Bea decided she'd had enough. 'Haven't you some work to do downstairs? Manning the phones, if you can't cope with the computer? And if you can't do that, can you find out if my old cleaner will come back to work for me?'

Maggie turned puce. 'I know my mother asked Max to give me a job, but surely you can find something better for me to do than scrubbing floors!'

Bea tried to be patient. 'Maggie, I didn't ask you to scrub floors, though I realize you probably have been doing so, but you really must not—'

'I'm leaving, right? Today. This afternoon!' Clumsy footsteps ran away down the hall.

Silence, while Bea wondered whether to go after the girl, or be thankful that she'd seen the last of her.

Piers said, 'Shall we change the subject? Or shall we talk about whatever mess you've got yourself into?'

'I haven't got myself into a mess. Coral has. Oh, never mind all that. Why are you here, Piers? Surely you're not trying to pick up where we left off all those years ago? We can't pretend you never left us.'

'No, I've regretted it many a time, but –' a shrug '– then I get down to work again and forget about everything else. I'd like to make amends, promise that I'd never leave you in the lurch again, but that would be a lie. Because I might.' Piers shook himself. 'I could do with a drink. Bea?'

'First tell me why you're here.'

Piers sat down, and took a deep breath. 'I'm no angel, I know, and you might have thought I walked away and forgot you, never felt any guilt. But I did. Feel guilty, I mean. Well, most of the time I didn't, but then it would come up and hit me, and I'd curse myself for losing you. So when Hamilton asked me to look after you—'

'What? When was this? You and Hamilton? But how did you know one another?'

'We met by chance at the National Portrait Gallery. I had something hanging there and he'd wandered in by chance. If it had been anyone else, I suppose he'd have looked right through me, but Hamilton, he wasn't like that, was he? We ended up having lunch together. After all, he'd gained what I'd lost. He was magnanimous. I rather think I apologized to him for having

walked out on you, but he seemed to understand how it is to
be driven by work. And what it is to run away from commitment. He was good about commitment, wasn't he?'

Bea nodded. Yes, if Hamilton had committed to anything,
he saw it through.

Piers said, 'You never cared to watch cricket, did you? He
liked it, and so did I. After that first meeting we used to run
into one another at Lords every now and then, perhaps twice
a year. He was restful to be with. I felt absolved from what
I'd done, deserting you and Max. Three years ago Hamilton
told me about the cancer. It was only at the start, and he hoped,
various treatments were being offered, well, you know about
that. It took years, didn't it? We kept in touch. He never
mentioned the cancer unless I asked him, right up to the last
time we met. It was then he said you might need some help
when he died. I said you wouldn't want help from me, no way.
He just smiled. So that's why I'm here. One unreliable old
man, offering whatever help you need.'

Bea blinked. This was all rather a lot to take in at once, and
it wasn't very good for the ego to feel that Piers had only come
looking for her because Hamilton had asked him to.

There was a noise at the door, and Maggie edged her way
in. She was red in the face, which clashed horribly with her
dyed hair. 'Sorry I flew off the handle. You were quite right,
I really am not much good at office work. So I'll fish your
washing out of the drier, take your dry-cleaning in, and be off.'

Part of Bea said 'Hurray!' but the other part said she couldn't
let the girl go like this. She extended her free hand to Maggie,
who came slowly across the room, angrily swiping the back
of her hand across her face. Bea looked around. 'I saw a box
of paper tissues somewhere.'

Piers made a long arm, rescued a box and handed it to
Maggie, who snorted and sniffed into one tissue after the other.

'What about the boy?' asked Bea. 'Is he leaving, too?'

Maggie wiped reddened eyes. 'He got thrown out by his
father. He's got nowhere to go. I'd better find him a hostel or
something. I don't think my mother would let him stay with
us.'

'What did he do?'

Maggie said, 'What you've got to understand is that it wasn't
his fault. He's the youngest in a family that's mad keen on

sport, and he's no good at it. He's brainy, mind. He's taken eight A levels and he thinks he got them all. The thing is, he's a computer buff.'

She took a deep breath. 'He accessed something on his father's computer, something he'd no right to be looking at. His father found out and beat him up. Then he threw him out. I found him in the park when I was taking Nicole's dog for a walk. Down by the water. I startled him and he almost jumped in. I was afraid that if I left him there, he really would jump.'

'Good heavens,' said Bea, feeling faint.

'So I brought him home – here – and found him some clothes. Got them at the charity shop, actually,' said Maggie, gaining confidence as her story progressed. 'I let him use the computer and he's done all the work I was supposed to be doing while I looked after the house. He's only a boy, you see.'

'How old is he?' asked Piers. 'Couldn't Social Services look after him?'

'He's just turned eighteen. They don't want to know if you're turned eighteen.'

'And you are – how old?'

'Twenty.' The girl sniffed hard, tossed her head, well into Don't Care mode. 'Divorced already. Can't cope with computers. Got fed up at home, waiting on Mummy hand and foot. She doesn't really want me around, anyway, showing her up before her friends, because she looks so young, still. No wonder she asked Max to find something for me, just to get me out of the house!' More angry sniffling.

Bea pulled the girl down on to the settee and put her arm around her. 'There, there. What on earth am I to do with you all, eh?'

'Throw us all out. Make a clean start,' said Piers. 'I'll be all right, you know. It's true I'd rented out my place for a couple of months while I was busy with some commissions out of town, but I can easily go to a hotel till Monday when my tenant leaves. I'm not short of a penny.'

Maggie was mopping up. 'I keep telling Oliver that he's got a marketable skill and could walk into a job anywhere, but he says that without his A level certificates, no one will employ him.'

'He should ask the school for them.'

'He can't. His father's the headmaster.'

Bea didn't know whether to laugh or scream. She chose laughter. It didn't sound merry, but it was better than tears. Looking up, she caught Hamilton's eye as he looked down from his photograph, and that sobered her up. Hamilton looked – of course it was a trick of the light – anxious.

'Well,' she said. 'First things first. Something to eat.'

Maggie cheered up at once. 'Leave that to me. What would you like? Pasta? Scrambled eggs? A fry-up? No, you'd better not have fried stuff. Bad for you. I'll do some pasta, right?' The girl could switch from Orphan Annie to Boadicea in three seconds flat.

Bea said, 'After we've eaten we'll have a Council of War. Piers, can you spare the time to eat with us?'

'I keep trying to tell you I'm at your disposal. I've got nothing on for ten days, when I'm due to paint another of the great but not so good. A politician, needless to say. At least there's something in their faces to paint. Which reminds me, Bea; you're getting very paintable. Care to sit for me some time?'

'In your dreams,' said Bea. 'I know what an old hag I look now.'

'You're just tired,' said Maggie, with accuracy but without compassion.

Piers looked at Bea with eyes that took in every line on her face, and the sag under her chin. 'You look like someone I'd like beside me in a fight. I think I could do you justice, now.'

Bea was flattered, but that didn't stop her worrying about more pressing matters. 'I must go and find Oliver. We don't want him doing anything stupid, do we? Oh, and Maggie, did I dream it, or did you come up to tell me that you'd found something which might help Coral?'

'Oh yes, that's it. Oliver thinks he knows how they worked the false address.'

Piers lifted both his hands in a gesture of surrender. 'I think it's about time I put my foot down with a firm hand. What exactly is all this about?'

Bea couldn't make out if he were serious or not but launched into the tale of Coral's woes, with Maggie chipping in every now and then.

'Good grief,' said Piers, when they'd finished. 'Can't the police—?'

'No,' said Bea, not bothering to elaborate. There was an awkward silence, and Maggie said, 'I'd better see about lunch,' and darted off.

Piers said, 'Am I right in thinking Coral would be in trouble with the taxman if she went to the police?'

'Something like that, yes. She trusted a member of her family to deal with – er – certain aspects of the book-keeping, and he let her down. She's putting it right.'

'I've been in trouble with the taxman myself till I wised up and got a good accountant. That's the trouble with freelance work. Feast or famine.'

'You're doing all right now?'

'Bless you, yes. Got a penthouse flat in the Barbican, and a shack in the South of France that I can retreat to when everything gets a bit much here. You don't need to worry about me.'

Bea sighed. 'I do, though. How come a busy man like you just happens to be able to drop everything and come to my rescue at a moment's notice?'

Was that a blush? 'I knew roughly when you'd be back after Hamilton died. I knew who I was due to paint around this time, so I built in a bit of leeway. I'm totally at your disposal for ten days, right?'

'Because Hamilton asked you to? I don't think I can accept your offer, Piers. Besides which, tracking down con men isn't exactly your scene, is it?'

He sat upright. 'I'm not going to track down con men. What I thought was, that there might be a family squabble going on that I could help you sort out. That I could come the heavy father act.' He laughed, shortly. 'Some father I've turned out to be. But now I'm here, well, yes. I'd like to help. It would take my mind off the dreary business of painting the sly, heavy faces of today's power merchants, which is all I seem to do nowadays.'

Bea didn't know whether to believe him or not. In the past he'd been so driven by his art that he'd never had time for anything else but bedding the nearest available woman and ingesting a certain amount of food. And that only when reminded to eat. He hadn't been selfish so much as absorbed by his art.

She said, 'I can't have you sleeping here.'

'No, of course not. I'll book into a hotel locally. Do you know one?'

'Maggie can do it for you.'

'Don't laugh, but I rather think I'd like to paint her, as well. All that gauche bravado. Why is she pretending to be Barbie doll?'

Bea shrugged. 'I only met her last night. There's a capable girl somewhere under all that camouflage, but her manner is unfortunate, to say the least. She talks to me as if I were a toddler, and her laugh drives me insane. I'll be glad to see the back of her.'

Maggie popped her head around the door, to say, 'Five minutes.'

Bea cringed. Had the girl overheard?

Maggie was frowning. 'Have you seen Oliver? I can't find him anywhere.'

At once Bea felt alarm. Knowing something of the boy's history, might the prospect of being thrown out of his home and separated from Maggie have driven him to despair once more? 'Piers, look downstairs. No, you won't know the way. Go down the steps outside the French windows. Look in the little shed at the bottom of the garden. Maggie, see if Oliver's taking anything from his room at the top of the house.'

Bea ran down the stairs to the basement, while Maggie thundered her way up the stairs. What was the child wearing on her feet?

The basement was eerily silent. Flickering light came from old-fashioned neon tubes overhead. Tiny spots of light showed where the computers were on standby. There was no Oliver in Hamilton's room, in the interview room, kitchen, reception room, or toilet.

Bea went back up the stairs, taking it at a more leisured pace. Thinking.

Maggie came skittering down from the top floor. 'Everything's just as he left it this morning when I went in to make his bed.' She reddened. 'Well, he's a boy and he's never had to make his own bed.'

'Then you should teach him,' said Bea. She swung into the sitting room and looked out of the French windows at the peaceful garden below.

Piers called up to her from where he stood at the end of the garden. 'Nothing. He's not in the shed and I don't think he's gone over the wall.'

He climbed the outside stairs to rejoin them in the sitting room. 'What do we do? Call the police?' He was only half joking.

Maggie caught her breath in dismay, but Bea said, 'Do you think he'd go without a word to you, Maggie?' Maggie shook her head.

'Then,' said Bea, 'I think we need to look in the place he'd find it easiest to leave messages. That would be on his computer, wouldn't it?'

'But,' said Maggie, 'he knows I'm not much good at computers. What would I look for?'

'Have you got an email address? Yes? Let's try that. Now, how many computers have we got? Where's the one Hamilton used to use? Is that the one Oliver's got in his bedroom up top, or the one he's been using in the interview room?'

'I don't know which one he'd use,' cried Maggie. 'The one in his bedroom, I suppose.'

'Where was he when you saw him last?'

'I don't know. I wasn't looking.'

Piers said, 'He went down the stairs, I think.'

Bea led the way. 'Piers, are you any good with computers?'

'I've got a laptop. Had to learn how to use some of the latest technology. My bet is that he'll use the one in his bedroom. On the top floor, is it?' He disappeared up the stairs.

Bea accessed the computer in the reception room, the one Maggie was supposed to use. She called up Windows Explorer to see what entries had been made most recently. There was nothing personal. She tried the email on the off-chance, but though Maggie had sent a couple recently, there hadn't been anything coming back in.

'Got it!' Piers shouted down the staircase. He came down, waving a piece of paper. 'In a file titled Home. Addressed to Maggie.'

Maggie rushed up to him, and read it out. '"See you later. Don't look for me. Thanks for everything. Oliver."'

'The idiot,' said Piers. 'What does he think he's playing at? Hide and seek? He'll end up as a rent boy if he's not careful, or living in a cardboard box. Or both.'

'Hide and seek,' mused Bea. '"Don't look for me." The idiot's hiding somewhere close. That's what he means by telling

Maggie not to look for him. We've got to search the house. Look in every space that might hold a skinny lad.'

'Not the river?' gasped Maggie.

'No, child. Not the river. Oliver's playing games with us. Now, shall we each take a floor?'

'My pasta!' shrieked Maggie and took the stairs up to the kitchen, two at a time.

'Are you sure, Bea?' said Piers. 'He could easily have slipped out behind our backs.'

'If there's anything I'm sure about, it's that that young limb depends on Maggie for everything. For crying out loud, she feeds him, clothes him and even makes his bed. He doesn't strike me as the bold sort who'd see running away as a big adventure. Let's open every cupboard, look in every small space before we give up and scream for the police.'

They searched the basement. Looked in all the nooks and crannies. Piers swore when he caught his hand on the metal edge of a filing cabinet, but otherwise went along with Bea's plan while making it clear he didn't really believe it would produce results.

They moved to the first floor where Maggie joined them. She said the pasta might be all right if they could eat straight away. Otherwise, she'd cook some fresh. They looked in every cupboard, even the kitchen ones. They looked under the sink in the cloakroom. They looked under the stairs, in the broom cupboard. They looked in the sideboard, even. Nothing.

'Let's start at the top and work down,' said Bea. They climbed to the top floor. More cupboards. Wardrobes. They even looked under the sink in the bathroom and inside the airing cupboard. They looked under beds, even, in case he was lying flat somewhere. Nothing. Piers was getting bored. He'd left Oliver's computer switched on, and sat down to play with it. What he found seemed to amused him.

'My, he's been a busy little boy, hasn't he?'

'Porn?' said Bea, getting progressively crosser.

'No, not porn. He doesn't strike me as being hooked on women yet.'

'Unlike you, you mean.'

They descended to Bea's bedroom floor, Maggie leading the way. Piers threw open the door to the spare bedroom, and arched his eyebrows as he saw it unused. So now he knew that Bea could give him a bed for the night if she wished.

So what! thought Bea.

The doorbell rang two storeys below. 'I'll go,' said Maggie.

Bea turned towards her own bedroom. 'That'll be Coral, I expect.' Noting his bewilderment Bea quickly brought him up to date. 'I'd better go down in a minute and see her. Find out if June's been kept in hospital.'

'Shall I give your bedroom the once-over?' suggested Piers, grinning.

'Certainly not,' said Bea. 'He wouldn't hide in here, anyway. Or would he?' But just in case, she tried it. Nothing under the bed, nothing in the en suite. She pulled open the door to the dressing room, packed with Nicole's bits and pieces. A large cardboard box confronted her, two inches from her nose. That hadn't been there last night.

She tugged at it. It wouldn't budge. 'Help me shift this, Piers.'

Maggie could be heard pounding up the stairs. 'Mrs Abbot, Mrs Abbot! You're needed!'

'One thing at a time,' said Bea. 'Pull, Piers. Put some welly into it!'

He tugged hard, trying to shift it right and left. 'It's heavy!'

'Heavy enough to contain Oliver?'

Maggie burst into the bedroom. 'Mrs Abbot, are you there?'

The box suddenly gave way, showering Piers with an avalanche of videos.

Piers staggered back, yelling, his arms up to defend himself from attack

Bea sighed. 'Come on out now, Oliver. There's a good boy.'

Wednesday, lunchtime
Lena had her laptop beside her, checking off lists, stuffing addressed envelopes with tickets.

Richie walked around the room, talking on a mobile. He cut it off, shrugging. 'Another dissatisfied customer. Lena, are you sure we ought to hang around for this next one?'

'It's not like you to lose your nerve, Richie. Haven't we done this time and time again?'

'You and I alone in the provinces, yes. It's been good, but—'

'There's no way they can trace us except through the mobile phones. Which one were you using?'

He consulted the label on it. 'Priory Gardens. That was the wine merchant.'

'Get rid of that phone. Find us a couple of new ones.'

Richie nodded, hardly listening. 'Noel's been gone a long time. Lena, you and I never put a foot wrong, but bringing in your son—'

She cut him off with a flick of an eyebrow. 'Forget it, Richie. He's part of the team now. With his looks and charm – and contacts – he can get to people we couldn't even hope to reach. We've doubled our take since he joined us, haven't we? True, he's young and he's made one or two small mistakes, but—'

'Killing a man isn't a small mistake.' Richie rubbed his hand over the back of his neck. 'I've never been involved in murder before.'

'Not murder.' She frowned. 'It was an accident.'

'You two make a good pair. You've got the brains and the nerve for this game, and he's got the polish from university. But he makes me nervous, Lena. Maybe after this next event, I should fade out.'

'I don't want to lose you, Richie.' Yet they both knew that if she had to choose between her son and her old partner, Noel would win.

Six

Wednesday, lunch to suppertime

With some difficulty Oliver let himself down on to the floor. Bea hoped he hadn't put his foot through anything valuable while making himself a nest in the hidey-hole, but didn't really care if he had. Nicole ought not to have left her stuff there. Besides – and here Bea grinned to herself – Nicole ought to have insured her things, oughtn't she?

Maggie was flushed with indignation. 'Oh, Oliver! How could you give me such a fright!'

Piers nursed his right wrist, cursing beneath his breath. Oliver looked as hangdog as a puppy who'd been caught making a mess on the best carpet, and about as young. He needed a wash and a brush up.

Coral Payne appeared behind Maggie. Coral had been crying.

Bea put her hands on her hips. 'For two pins I'd shove the lot of you out of the front door and go to bed for a fortnight. Coral, I'm sorry, my dear, but we've got a bit of a crisis on here. I hope June's all right?'

Coral tried to smile. 'It's not the end of the world, but they're keeping her in hospital on bed rest. Jake's staying with her.' She sat down on Bea's bed. 'Oh, dear, oh dear! I've come over all silly.'

Bea understood that June had gone into labour, but the hospital was trying to stop it, to prevent the baby being born prematurely. She sat beside Coral and gave her a hug. 'Come on, it's up to us to keep the show on the road. We women can never afford to give way, can we?'

Coral sniffed and shook her head.

Bea said, 'Tell yourself that June's in the best possible place for her at the moment. Is Jake going to ring you if there's any change? Yes? Good. So let's deal with the next item on the agenda. Piers, does that wrist of yours need a doctor?'

Piers waggled it a bit. 'It's not broken. Oliver, I think you and I should have a little chat.'

'Oh, no!' cried Maggie, arms akimbo. 'You can't beat him up just because he was scared.'

Oliver peeked up at Piers through his hair which had fallen over his eyes. He looked about eight years old. He'd ripped his jeans, too.

Piers took hold of Oliver's ear and led him out of the room. 'This isn't about my wrist. Let me deal with this, Bea. Up the stairs you go, my lad. You and I are going to have a nice quiet talk about your extramural activities.'

'Stop him, Mrs Abbot!' said Maggie, hopping from one foot to the other. 'He shouldn't, I mean, he can't just take him off like that. It's against the law.'

Piers' voice floated back down the stairs. 'What the lad's been up to is also against the law.'

Oliver emitted a squeak, but made no other protest. The door of his bedroom shut with a bang.

All of a sudden Bea felt extremely tired. This time yesterday she'd been on a plane flying back from the other side of the world. She'd been weary when she got on the plane, and too tired to think straight when she got off. Then there'd been the surprise party, and the unpleasant revelations about the agency. She hadn't slept well, and today had brought its own set of shocks.

She helped Coral to her feet, put her free arm round Maggie and urged them to the door. 'I think we'll all feel better when we've eaten, don't you?'

Coral's voice quavered but she managed, 'That's what I always say, too.'

Maggie dithered. It was clear she didn't know whether to charge to Oliver's rescue, or dish up lunch. 'Mrs Abbot, I hate to say it, but there's someone else turned up this morning, wanting to see Max. She's not on our books as a cleaner, but she says she's done a job for someone who is. Which is nonsense, isn't it? At least, I haven't heard of anyone passing a job on to anyone else. You'd better warn him, because when I said he wasn't here any more, she said she'd have to pay him a visit at the House of Commons. They won't let her in, though, will they?'

Bea couldn't take this in. 'No, my dear. I shouldn't think they would. You say you've got some food on the go?'

Maggie gave one last look up the stairs and then went into the kitchen to dish up. She served large soup bowls of pasta with mushrooms and tomatoes in a cheesy sauce. Bea put her head down and ate. She'd had enough of the world and its problems.

When they were clearing their plates, Piers came in, pushing Oliver before him. 'Now, boy. Make a clean breast of it.'

Oliver shifted his feet about, darted a glance at Maggie. Another at Bea. He said, 'It was all my father's fault.'

'No, it wasn't,' said Piers, cheerfully sitting down and holding up his plate to Maggie for food. 'If you think your father treated you badly, you should have seen what mine did to me. Anyway, you're over eighteen now, and supposed to know the difference between right and wrong.'

Maggie sent worried glances in Oliver's direction, but cleared plates, and handed out yoghurts to those who'd finished their first course.

'The thing is,' said Oliver, 'that I really like seeing what I can do on computers. One of my friends' fathers taught me all sorts of tricks. Actually, I don't think he should have taught me some of the things but it was, like, academic. Just seeing how to get round things. It wasn't for real. We were never going to do those things, except that . . . well, eventually, I suppose, I did. Then one day,' Oliver shuffled his feet again, 'I turned on my Dad's laptop, just for fun.

'I found some hardcore porn. I couldn't believe it. I'd heard of such things before, but I'd never actually seen any. He caught me at it and went ballistic. We've never really got on, you know, he and I. I thought he was going to hit me, so I threatened to tell Mum. He said I'd completely misunderstood what I saw, that he'd only been doing some research. He said I had a dirty mind and was probably into porn myself, though of course I'm not.'

'So that's why he threw you out?' asked Bea. 'Because he was afraid you'd spill his guilty secret?'

Oliver nodded. 'He wanted me out of the house before Mum came back from shopping. He said he'd tell everybody that it was I who was into porn and not him. He said he'd tell them that was why he'd thrown me out, and that they shouldn't speak to me if I did phone up. He didn't beat me up exactly. I tripped and fell down the stairs and got a nose bleed when he swung at me. So I ran away.'

Maggie slammed a dishcloth down on to the table and everyone jumped. 'Oh, Oliver, you told me he beat you up!'

'He would have, if I hadn't got away. Then you rescued me, and brought me here and that was all right, but Mr Abbot told us we had to be out at the end of the week, and I didn't know what to do. I'd kept in touch with my friend from school and he told me it was up on the notice board that I'd got all my As. So I emailed Dad asking for my certificates, and he replied that I should go to hell and that if I tried to contact him again, he'd tell the police that I was into porn.'

'He probably wouldn't,' said Piers, 'because then it would come out about his own misdeeds. Go on, Oliver. Tell them what you did next.'

Oliver took a deep breath. 'I've had my own bank account for about a year, for birthday cheques and what I earned cleaning cars at weekends. Only, I'd just bought a new sound system for myself, so I was down to a few pounds. I knew my father's credit card number and banking details. I can remember numbers, only have to see them once. So I . . . I bought stuff over the phone, tickets to pop concerts and football matches and stuff that I knew would sell out quickly.'

He gulped. 'I used my father's bank details to pay for them. Then I sold the tickets on ebay. That way I thought that when Maggie and I left here, I'd have some money to give her and we'd be all right. Dad won't find out till the middle of next month when his bank statements go through.'

Bea brought her eyebrows down from her hairline, and managed to close her mouth, which was agape. She smoothed out a smile and tried to frown but didn't quite make it. Coral choked on her yoghurt. Piers hid a grin behind his fist.

Maggie's expression passed through astonishment and horror to reluctant admiration. 'You'd do that for me?'

'Well, and for me, too.'

Bea knew she'd sound prissy but felt she had to say it. 'You do know that using someone else's credit details is wrong, don't you, Oliver?'

He met her eyes steadily. 'What would you have done, Mrs Abbot?'

'Found someone to get your certificates from your father, I suppose. If you'd gone to your friend's father, wouldn't he have helped you?'

'Yes, he might. But I'd have had to say what I'd found on Dad's computer, and he might or might not want to believe me. If he did believe me, he'd have to do something about it, wouldn't he, because he's on the board of governors for the school. Then Dad would lose his job. I don't care about him, but I do care about Mum, even though she's a bit of an idiot sometimes. She'd have to divorce him, wouldn't she? They'd lose their house and then what would Mum do? And if my friend heard that I was supposed to be into porn, he probably wouldn't speak to me, anyway.'

'No, I see that. You haven't tried to buy things on anybody else's account, have you?'

Oliver shook his head. 'You mean on Mr Abbot's account? No, I wouldn't. Even though I don't think he treated Mrs Payne right.'

Piers pushed his plate forward for second helpings. 'Eat up, lad. What you did was wrong, of course. But, well, perhaps

Mrs Abbot can get you those all-important certificates in due course. If she can't, then I will. Right?'

Oliver gave Piers a look of such gratitude that Bea was taken aback. He'd never earned that look from his own son. She wasn't sure that Piers even liked Max. Perhaps that was the key to it, that he liked Oliver and would put himself out for him? For a lad who ought by rights to be handed over to the police for retribution? Well, if not for retribution, he ought perhaps to be given a caution. No, he didn't deserve to be given a police record for what he'd done. Or did he?

She was too tired to think straight, and it was only half past two in the afternoon.

She said, 'Well, I'm glad that's straightened out. I don't know about you lot, but I'm bushed. I'm going up to my room to have a little rest. After that, we'll have a chat about what we do next. Agreed?'

She didn't wait for their agreement but set off up the stairs. At her age she oughtn't to be needing a nap after lunch. But there it was. She shucked off her outer clothes and her shoes, slid under the duvet, wriggled about a bit, and tried to drift away from all her problems.

She woke slowly. Bars of sunlight were finding their way through the window and making patterns on the carpet. There was a scatter of videos on the floor beside the collapsed cardboard box. She'd put them back later.

The room was warm. High summer in London can be rather too hot for comfort. She found a white cotton top and chinos that didn't look too creased, made a face at herself in the mirror, tidied her make-up and went down the stairs slowly. She didn't feel particularly refreshed by her nap.

The house was very quiet. Had she heard Maggie's high-pitched laugh while she was dragging herself back to consciousness? She rather thought the phone had rung a couple of times. Well, if it had, Maggie would have dealt with it. She stifled a grin, thinking of the cleaning woman trying to get into the House of Commons to see Max. What a laugh! The woman must be off her rocker.

Tea. Hot. Strong. She made herself some in a mug, and took it out through the sitting room and down the outside stairs into the garden. The sycamore tree provided shade there, and on one of the loungers lay Piers with a glass of wine at his elbow. He'd opened the bottle of wine he'd brought. Naturally.

He said, 'You're up, are you? Still feeling jet lagged?'

Which meant she must be looking her age and more. She let herself down on to the other lounger, and sipped tea. 'Where are the others?'

'Playing cops and robbers. You'll have to watch young Oliver. Got an imagination that shocks even me. Playing detective's keeping Coral off the booze. No news from the hospital, which is good news, I suppose. Wouldn't a glass of wine do you more good than that stuff?'

She shook her head. The tea was just right. How she'd longed for a really good cup of strong English tea while she was abroad. It was one of the last things that Hamilton had asked for. *Oh, dear Hamilton, I miss you every minute of the day.*

Piers sipped wine. 'I'm amazed at myself, I really am. There I was, thinking I could drop in on the grieving widow, pat her hand a few times and perhaps conduct a light flirtation before going on my way. Instead I find myself encouraging a caterer to flout the tax laws, coming the heavy father over a computer fraudster whose activities will undoubtedly land him in jail some time, and consoling a runaway bride that I don't even want to get into bed with. Old age has suddenly overtaken me.'

'Is Maggie a runaway bride?'

He snorted. 'Who knows? Who cares? They're your problem, not mine.'

'Then why are you still here?'

'Because Maggie promised to cook supper for us and then book me into a hotel. I want to do a couple of quick sketches before I leave, if my wrist doesn't pack up on me.'

Bea wondered if he would want her to change before he sketched her, and if so, what she should wear.

He said, 'That flaming hair against bilious green. Pure rag doll. Maybe I can work it up into something.'

He wanted to sketch *Maggie*? Not Bea? She swallowed tea, and calmed her heartbeat. Luckily she hadn't said anything to reveal the fact that she'd thought he meant to paint her.

Maggie came bustling down the garden with a tray of sausages and kebabs. 'Thought we could eat out here. Max often had a barbecue here in the evenings. Eat it with our fingers. No washing-up. Mind if I light up now?' She pulled the cover off a gas barbecue, and started it up.

'That's new,' said Bea.

'I expect they'll want to take it away, but we might as well use it while it's here.' She fiddled with controls. 'Can the others come out now? We've got something to report.'

Bea nodded. 'I'll watch, if you like.'

Maggie gave her a doubtful look, clearly wondering whether Bea could be trusted. Then went off, calling to the others that it was safe to come out now.

'Are we such ogres?' Bea wondered, shifting her chair so that she was nearer the barbecue.

Piers poured himself another glass of wine. 'If you want to play cops and robbers, it's nothing to do with me.'

Maggie chivvied Coral and Oliver out into the garden, bringing a bowl of tiny red tomatoes and some fresh bread rolls with her. Coral carried pickles and her mobile phone, but Oliver carried a sheaf of papers.

'Any news of June?' Bea asked Coral.

Coral shook her head. 'Jake rang. No change. They're putting her on bed rest to try to stop the contractions. Jake'll let me know if anything happens, and in the meantime, playing detective takes my mind off things.'

Bea nodded. 'So, Oliver. What have you found out?'

'It's all three of us, working together, Mrs Abbot.'

'Call me Bea, please.'

He blushed. Couldn't quite manage it. 'Well . . .'

Bea wondered if the generation gap really was so great he couldn't manage to call her by her first name.

Maggie produced a barbecue fork which looked as large as a trident, and started to lay food out on the grill. She nudged Oliver. 'Go on. You start.'

Oliver said, 'I thought the first thing to do was to make a list of everything we knew about them, which is quite a lot, really. We've got their letterheads and their brochures for a start.' On the table he placed a folder. 'This is all the stuff Coral kept.' He extracted some returned cheques and several pieces of paper, some of which had been folded in three to act as fliers, and others which looked like covering letters.

Piers languidly reached out to feel the quality of the paper.

'Not quality paper. Laser printed. Not embossed.' He held one piece up to the light. 'Common watermark. Home-produced, I'd say.'

'That's what I thought,' said Oliver, eagerly. 'Given a quarter of an hour I could turn out a copy of that letterhead on any computer with a scanner and laser printer attached.'

'A forger in the making, eh?' said Piers, removing his attention.

Oliver flushed.

Maggie shot Piers a dark look, but nudged Oliver to continue. 'Go on. Tell them what else we found out.'

Oliver addressed himself to Bea. 'It was a false address. Coral, you tell it.'

'It's a good address, just north of Notting Hill Gate,' said Coral. 'Most of the houses have been turned into flats with speakerphone entry, but there's one or two businesses as well. Discreet plates beside the door, that sort of thing. That particular address had two flats above a convenience store, on the corner of the main road but not actually on it. I looked for the name of the charity, but it wasn't there. I rang the bells for the two flats, but no one had ever heard of them. So I gave up. Oliver tried a different tack.'

'I looked the address up on the Internet,' said Oliver. 'The ground floor is a corner shop and newsagent and I wondered if they might act as an accommodation address for a fee. So I primed Maggie with what to say and she rang them on her mobile.'

Maggie flourished her trident, turning sausages over. 'I gave a false name, said I'd let my flat and was going away for three months on business. I said I needed someone I could trust to look after any letters that might come for me in my absence. They quoted a price, and I agreed to it. I think the shop acts as an accommodation address for the charity. Letters sent there would be held till . . . whoever . . . came to collect them. That's how the charity manages to fool people into thinking they've got offices in a decent street.'

'What we could do,' said Oliver, 'is write a letter to the charity and try to deliver it by hand, see if they accept it. If they do, we'll know I'm right.'

'Good for you,' said Bea, surprised at how thorough he'd been.

'I expect he can do crosswords as well,' said Piers, looking bored.

Oliver decided not to hear him, though his ears went pink. 'Next, the phone number on the letterhead. If you look closely, you'll see that the original number has been crossed out and a mobile number put in its place. I rang the original number. It's the Bolivian Embassy.'

'Someone has a sense of humour,' said Piers, sitting up and taking notice.

'What about the mobile number?'

'Out of service. I've heard that it's easy enough to get a mobile. You steal it or buy one in a pub or at a car boot sale, or in fact just go to Woolworths and buy a pay-as-you-go phone. You use it for a short while and then throw it away so it can't be traced back to you.'

'What about the charity number at the bottom of the paper?' asked Bea.

'Bogus. Yes. By one numeral. That's clever, that is. If challenged they could always say it was a misprint.'

'What about the names of the people who were supposed to be on the board of the charity?'

'All well-known names, celebrities of the older generation, people with titles, that kind of thing. You can't speak to them except through their secretaries, or agents or whatever. I only managed to speak to two, but neither of them had ever heard of this charity. I left some messages on the websites for two more, and they may get back to us or they may not, but I think we can assume their names were taken in vain.'

'Particularly,' said Maggie, triumphantly, 'since Oliver worked it out that one or two of the names have been misspelled. Coral agrees with him. *They* can both spell,' said Maggie, with the awe of one who couldn't.

'That's true,' said Oliver, eyes shining as he got into his stride. 'Once we saw that, it showed me the way forward. You see, the eye glances over a misspelling. The brain records what it expects to see. I read down that list of names and at first I was impressed. Then I began to check up. Coral helped here.'

'I read all the glossies,' said Coral, looking embarrassed. 'Who's having whose baby and stuff like that. I see these people from time to time when I'm catering, and it's nice to know who they are.' She pointed out a name on the letterhead. 'This man here is not a Sir but a Lord. This woman spells her name without an "e" at the end. There should be a hyphen between this double-barrelled name. Do you see?'

'And the well known comedians who were supposed to supply the cabaret?'

Coral said, 'Never turned up. Either time. They got substitutes in at the last moment. Not much cop.' Her enthusiasm ebbed away, and she looked tired. 'I don't see that this gets us any further on.'

'Oh, it does,' said Oliver, full of enthusiasm. 'I'm beginning to get the *feel* of how these people think. There's one last thing; the letters were signed by a man calling himself Graham Briggs. There's no-one of that name in the phone book, but I tried Directory Enquiries and they didn't know of one either. Of course, he might be ex-directory.'

'Supper's ready,' cried Maggie, and they all gathered around, eating with their fingers, saying 'Mm,' and 'This is good.' Even Coral perked up with food inside her.

The French window upstairs was thrown back against the brickwork, and the newcomer said, 'So there you all are!'

Wednesday, early evening
For all her pretended calm, Lena was ready to bite someone by the time Noel returned in mid-afternoon.

'Noel, wherever have you been?' she demanded.

Noel took a seat, leaning back, hands in pockets, not a care in the world. 'Am I late? I took the receptionist to lunch, didn't I? Nice place, you'd like it.'

'Noel!' She tried to keep calm. 'We were worried sick!'

He examined his perfect fingernails. 'I thought it could go on expenses. The little chick was all over me. I didn't give her the cheque for the hotel until I dropped her off, so they can't get it into the bank today. There's been no hue and cry yet. The barman had only just started work at the hotel, and no one knew much about him. They were livid when he didn't turn up this morning. Short staffed, it seems. They haven't even got round to reporting him missing yet. In a couple of days we'll be out of here, with different names. There's nothing to worry about.'

He drew a stack of envelopes out of his breast pocket. 'I called round the shop in the Grove on the way back. The usual. More requests for tickets for Saturday, cheques, dunning letters.'

He held them up, just out of Richie's reach. Richie tried to take them, and Noel pulled his hand back, laughing.

Lena said, 'That's enough, Noel. You're such a child, some-times.' But her tone was indulgent, and both men understood what that meant.

Seven

Wednesday, evening

Down the steps from the sitting room came Max, dressed in a suit despite the heat of the summer's evening. His eyes looked anxious, but he dispensed approving smiles all round before bending over Bea to give her a hug and kiss her cheek.

'I see you've found the domestic staff. Mother, I must speak to you.' His eyes were on Piers, who looked as if he were wishing himself elsewhere.

Bea hoped Max wasn't going to make a scene as she didn't think she could cope. She said, 'How long is it since you two met?'

Max said, 'He used to come to school to watch me bat, the year I was captain of cricket, but he never spoke. Hamilton pointed him out to me.'

Piers got to his feet. 'I was in the House of Commons when you made your maiden speech, too. Do we shake hands, do you think?'

Max coloured up, but put out his hand to shake.

Bea tried not to grin. 'Too, too British, both of you. Max, have you eaten? Piers, pour him a drink.'

'Not wine,' said Max. 'I have to go back to the House soon. Mother, may I have a word in private?'

'Of course, dear.' She handed him a sausage in a roll and led the way up the stairs to the sitting room, cool and shadowy in the early evening.

Max followed, holding the hot dog as if it were burning his

fingers. 'Mother, it's so good to have you back, you've no idea how much I've missed you and Hamilton. I keep thinking that I can ask him something and then remembering that I can't. And now there seems to have been some sort of misunderstanding about the house, which is quite ridiculous. Poor Nicole doesn't know whether she's coming or going.'

Oh yeah? thought Bea.

'I don't know what to say to her. I thought it was all settled, and I still think it's the best solution for all concerned. Not least for you. Hamilton was so worried about how you'd cope without him. He asked me to look after you, to see that you didn't fall to pieces . . .'

As if I would! thought Bea. And then, Well, maybe I could, if I allowed myself to.

'. . . and so we arranged, he and I, what should happen if, when, well, you know. He did hope to get back to England, but he knew he'd never be able to run the business again. I said I'd do whatever he wanted . . .' He looked around for somewhere to put his hot dog, and deposited it on the mantelpiece next to Hamilton's photograph.

Piers came into the room and sat by the window with his glass of wine.

Max gave Piers an uneasy glance, but continued. '. . . And that's what I did. I went down to the South Coast on three separate occasions and looked for the sort of accommodation Hamilton had in mind near to a golf course, and I got Nicole to come with me the last time and we selected a couple of places which were just what Hamilton said he wanted, and now—'

Bea interrupted. 'Dear, dear Max. You've been to such a lot of trouble for me, but my dear boy, you should have talked to me about it first. Those nice quiet places on the South Coast aren't at all my thing. I'm a city girl, Max. I'd die of boredom down there.'

Max swallowed. 'I hear what you're saying, and of course I respect it. But as Nicole says, it's come as a bit of a shock to learn that you're going to throw out everything Hamilton wanted for you.'

'Wanted for himself, dear. Not the same thing. If he'd lived, I'd have gone along with it because he was very dear to me and I knew he was on his way out. I never said I didn't like

the idea when he was alive because I wouldn't have hurt him
for the world, but now, I can.'

Max rubbed his eyes. 'I can see that. It's just that when I
mentioned it to Nicole she thought it solved all our problems.
She's been so excited, making plans for the future. It still seems
to me that . . . though of course I see your point of view . . .
but I don't like to disappoint Nicole. It's going to be so hard
for her if she has to start looking for another place, and what
we could afford wouldn't be anything like this. You do see how
I'm placed, don't you, Mother?'

'Nicole must find you a place that she can do up to her
own taste. I love this house and I can afford to live in it for
the time being, so that's what I'll do. Long term, I really don't
know.'

'You know Hamilton thought the world of you, and was
really worried that you'd be taken for a ride when you were
all alone, and lonely.' He didn't actually look in Piers' direction, but Bea got the message.

Piers snorted into his drink. 'Hamilton asked me to look
after her, too. And here I am, rather against my better
judgment, I must say. To be frank, Bea, I'm almost of the
same mind as Max. Are you sure this big house with all its
memories, isn't going to be a burden to you, rather than a
pleasure?'

Bea thought about that. The house had four bedrooms, and
she'd be occupying only one of them in future, with a creepily
dark basement below. She'd arrived home to a houseful of
people but in a few days' time it would be just her, rattling
around in a too-quiet house, with all its memories of Hamilton
still in place. How long could she stand that?

Then a house needed constant maintenance. The garden
would need caring for; that sycamore tree ought to be lopped
again. The basement needed redecorating. Possibly rewiring.
Wouldn't she be better off, not have so many cares, if she
moved into a little flat? Not on the South Coast, of course, but
somewhere else in Kensington?

Coral had come to stand in the doorway, unseen and unheard.
She said, 'What about me? If you two have your way, I can
say goodbye to my money, my daughter will be homeless, and
Oliver and Maggie will be thrown on the street.'

Max shook his head. 'Coral, it's sad but true that you've

made your bed and must lie in it. My mother couldn't possibly take Hamilton's place in the agency.'

'I second that,' said Piers, downing the last of his wine.

Bea didn't know what to think. She was annoyed that Max believed her incapable of running the agency, even though the thought of the effort involved gave her indigestion. If Hamilton had been here, would he really have wanted her to move into a happy retirement home? And if she did, what would she do with herself all day?

Well, what was the alternative?

What she wanted more than anything was to go to bed and lie there watching television, with someone bringing her drinks and tasty foods every now and then. She could afford it, couldn't she? Hamilton had made sure of that, what with investments and insurances and pension plans, and so on and so forth.

She didn't want to move to the seaside and play golf. Not her scene at all. Besides, if she did that, she'd lose touch with all her old friends. Like Coral, who knew her better than any of the people in their social circle. Coral had known her since she was a bedraggled divorcee with a small child in tow, desperately trying to make ends meet by cooking and waitressing while taking an IT course in the evenings.

She didn't want to let Coral down. Or those two awkward children, Maggie and Oliver, who had now joined Coral to look at her with wide, beseeching eyes. Where would they go, and what would they do, if she turned them out? Did she have the strength to fight their battles for them? Wouldn't helping them out only be one way of staving off the loneliness which threatened to overwhelm her the moment she stopped thinking about something else?

Well, Maggie would land on her feet. But Oliver? No, probably not.

'Max,' she said, 'I'm really touched that you've been worrying about me so much. It makes me feel much less lost. Since Hamilton . . .' She stopped for a moment, fighting a desire to burst into tears. 'Since he died, I've concentrated on getting back home in one piece, and I've made it. I'm not sure what I do want to do with the rest of my life but I do know that I don't want to go and live by the seaside and play golf. Perhaps I will want to one day. I don't know. I can't see into the future. So for the time being, I think I'd better just stay here and tidy up the remains of the agency and just give myself time. Right?'

'Hear, hear,' said Piers, emptying the last of the bottle into his glass. 'You always were a sensible little thing, Bea. Is there another bottle somewhere?'

That made her laugh. She, sensible? She didn't feel it. Out of the corner of her eye, she saw Coral make wafting movements to Maggie and Oliver, edging them out of the room.

Max stood with his legs slightly apart, head forward. Max was thinking up his next argument. Max was not going to give up easily.

She went on tiptoe to kiss his cheek. 'Dear Max. What would I do without your support? You always were a kind, loving little boy, and you've grown into a fine man, a real prop and stay for your poor old mother, who doesn't know what she'd do without you. Now I want you to stop worrying about me for the moment, and concentrate on finding somewhere for yourself and Nicole to live. Oh, and . . .' she'd just remembered. '. . . some woman came here to see you about a cleaning job. She said she was going to try to track you down at the House. I hope she isn't going to be embarrassing.'

'They don't let people in that easily.' He put his arm around her in a fierce hug and then, probably feeling he'd demonstrated too much affection, let her go. Glanced at his watch. Busy, busy. I'm late, I'm late, for a very important date.

Bea's tired mind, continued, No time to say hello, goodbye, I'm late, I'm late, I'm late.

He said, 'I have to go. I'll try to explain everything to Nicole. I do understand what you're saying, and perhaps you're right and you ought not to do anything in a hurry, but . . . when Nicole's got an idea in her head, she's not the easiest person to . . . no, no. I'm sure she'll understand, too. In the long run. I'll try, anyway.' He aimed a kiss at her forehead, missed, and left.

Only after he'd gone did Bea remember she'd meant to ask him about her car.

'Anyone for coffee?' Maggie came into the room bearing all the paraphernalia for coffee for five people. The coffee table which had been used to stand before the cream leather settee, had vanished. As – Bea realized with a frown – had the good table in the window on which Hamilton had been accustomed to play patience. She felt another surge of fatigue.

Piers took hold of her elbow. 'Do you want to go back to bed, or call a conference?'

A conference? Was he mad? Or was she?

Prompted by him, her mind cleared. 'Maggie, let's take the coffee downstairs, shall we? Into the office. We'll keep all the paperwork there.'

She half expected Piers to make some excuse and disappear but he helped Maggie carry the tray down the stairs, and settled himself into a corner of the settee. Bea seated herself in Hamilton's chair, noting with pleasure that his computer was now back where it used to be. Or rather, a newer model now sat on her desk, which gave her bad vibes. Would she be able to cope with it?

Coral sat opposite Bea – as client-in-chief. Oliver sat, warily, with some files on his knees. Maggie usurped Bea's function as hostess, poured coffee and handed it round. Bea had to admit that Maggie made an excellent cup of coffee. She irritated Bea no end, but she had her uses.

Everyone looked at Bea, whose mind became completely blank. What on earth was she doing, chairing a meeting on something she knew nothing about?

She stirred a sweetener into her coffee. Maggie nodded at her, giving the cue for her to start the meeting. Bea couldn't think what she was supposed to say. Only a small part of her brain seemed to be in working order.

She said, 'What I don't understand is . . . no, let me put it another way. Coral, you know that these people have pulled off a scam twice, using roughly the same format. Do you think they could have tried it on before?'

Piers had managed to acquire paper and pencil and had started to doodle. He said, 'Doubt it. There's only so many people you can fool into buying tickets and giving money for charity in any one area.'

Bea tried to concentrate. 'But this is London, and London is enormous. If they target a slightly different audience every time, the number of different people they could reach is huge. Coral, did you recognize any of the same people at both functions?'

'I'm not sure. Yes, perhaps.'

'How about if these people don't know they've been fooled, and actually think it's a good thing to throw some money in the way of charity? From their point of view, they had a good night out, ate some decent food and drank some reasonable wine. I assume the wine was drinkable, was it, Coral? Yes? Anyway, they had a good night out, so why shouldn't they turn up again at a similar function?'

Coral tested out this theory. 'Y-yes, I suppose that would work. The first event wasn't so big. There was no headliner for the entertainment, just a singer who wasn't much cop and a man tinkering on a piano, though he was quite good, I must say. Golden oldies, that sort of thing. Oh, then there was a DJ, very capable but turning the volume up as they do.

'The second time they'd scheduled a cabaret and it was a much bigger do, only of course the star didn't turn up. Done a sickie. They had some sort of rap singer instead. Garage, do they call it? Couldn't make out a word he said, but then perhaps that's just me. People seemed to like it, though of course some said they were disappointed. Then the DJ, the same one as before. He was quite good, not the tops, but handsome enough to turn heads. Making eyes at all the older women. You know. Oh, and an auction.'

'If the customers had been well wined and dined, they were probably in a mood to forgive the star not turning up for the cabaret. At least, they'd forgive it once, but not twice. Who was it supposed to be?'

Coral said, 'Can't remember, someone who's had chart toppers in his time but not recently. Isn't it on the flier?'

'No, it isn't. "Cabaret: to be announced." That covers a multitude of sins.'

Bea checked that Oliver was taking notes. Which he was. 'They wouldn't try that on twice with the same customers, would they? I wonder who else they didn't pay? The hotels? Maggie, didn't I ask you to check the hotels?'

'I thought you'd never ask,' said Maggie, beaming. 'I couldn't get anyone to talk to me about them at the two places Coral was stung, but then it occurred to me that maybe they were making a habit of doing it. Well, not a habit, exactly, but—'

'We get the point,' said Bea. 'You've come across them somewhere else?'

Maggie was so pleased with herself at being able to contribute that her words tumbled out almost too fast to follow. 'I've just discovered that these people, at least, I think it's the same because the name's nearly the same only not quite, and Oliver says he thinks that's what they do, change the name slightly each time, so nobody realizes. Anyway, they've got another do on in a couple of days' time, Saturday, at the function room at Green's, a hotel not far from here.' Her voice died away. 'Only, of course Oliver pointed out that it may not be the same people and they may be absolutely kosher, and I didn't know how to check.'

'Oliver?' said Bea.

'On to it,' he said, leaving the room at a fast lope.

Coral wasn't convinced. 'Hotels always ask for references and a deposit when they take a booking.'

'References can be forged,' said Piers, from the depths of his chair. 'I'm sure Oliver could tell us how.'

Maggie made an inarticulate noise but, having taken Piers' measure, made no other protest.

'How do they get round the deposit?' asked Coral.

Bea said, 'The best scams, surely, are those which pay out something in order to get something back. If they give a genuine deposit which is cleared by the bank, then when it comes to paying the balance, why, that's when they're just not there. Like Macavity.'

'What?' said Piers.

'Sorry. My mind's wandering. In the *Cats* show. When any mischief occurs, he's never there. Macavity.'

Oliver returned, holding his clipboard in front of him, but with a sparkle in his eye. 'I think Maggie's on to something. The charity is calling itself The International Emergency Fund for Aid to the Far East. A really big charity ball, cabaret, auction, late-night DJ. The contact person is a Mrs Amanda Briggs. I enquired for tickets, and they said I could phone her direct. It looks like a mobile number. Or write to their address which – wait for it! – is the same as the one they used earlier, the shop.'

'Briggs!' shouted Maggie, waving her arms around. 'It was Briggs before, wasn't it?'

'If Oliver's right and they just change their names a little each time,' said Bea, 'then it's definitely the same people. The continued use of the accommodation address confirms it.'

Piers' eyebrows peaked. He was going to say something outrageous, Bea knew. She wondered why she wasn't throwing him out. The problem was that although she knew he could be as unreliable as quicksand, there were times when he'd proved trustworthy. Maybe this was one of those times. He said, 'Well, shall I get us some tickets, Bea? Oliver, get on the phone and magic them up for us, there's a good boy. But don't charge them to your father this time, right? Use this.' He held up what looked like a platinum card for Oliver to take.

'Righto, sir,' said Oliver, only too eager to obey.

'Stop!' Bea clapped both hands over her eyes, to help her to think more clearly. Then removed her hands so that she could check on Oliver's reactions. 'Oliver, from the depths of your experience, is it a good idea to let a dodgy concern have access to your card number?'

'Er, no.' Oliver reddened. 'Not really. They could use it to buy all sorts of things and sell them on ebay. Shall I use my father's number, then?'

'No!' shouted Piers and Bea together.

'No,' said Bea, more quietly. 'Let's think this through. I agree that it might be a good idea for Piers to go to this shindig—'

'I'm not going alone, my girl. You come with me, or nobody goes—'

'—and I'm strongly of the opinion that if anyone goes, it should be Coral—'

Coral had gone off into a corner to use her mobile and didn't hear this. Presumably she was ringing the hospital.

'—because she's the only one who can recognize the people who are running the scam. If we can only make some kind of identification, we can . . . oh, I don't know. Piers, could you do some sketches of them?'

Piers looked at the sketch he'd been making, pulled face, and tore it into tiny pieces. 'Not unless my wrist makes a miraculous recovery.'

'What about taking photographs of them on a mobile phone?'

'I hate those things,' grumbled Piers. 'I can manage the ordinary sort of mobile when I have to or in an emergency, but you need an engineering degree to make these camera phones work, unless of course you're under twenty-five.'

Oliver said, 'I've got one, and I know how to use it.' They all looked at him, and he reddened. 'Well, I bought it for Maggie, but she wouldn't take it when she knew how I paid for it.'

That silenced everyone; could they square their consciences enough to allow Oliver to use a phone which he'd bought on stolen information?

'Then it belongs to your father, not you,' said Bea, but didn't sound too sure about it. 'Oliver, you really must sort yourself out with your father, confess what you've done, make restitution and so on. Now about paying for the tickets, since we don't want to give them a card number I think we should pay them by cheque.'

'One that will bounce?' asked Oliver, hopefully.

'I don't know how to write a cheque that will bounce,' said Bea, between amusement and shock.

'Let me write it out for you,' said Oliver. 'You don't need to know anything about it, just sign it. We'll deliver it by hand to the address at the corner shop, and they send us the invitations by return. Before the cheque bounces.'

Piers said, 'I hate to throw cold water over what promises to be an enchanting evening, but what do we do when – if – we get to the ball, and Coral does recognize these people? We can't summon the police and say, in lordly fashion, "Lock these miscreants up!" There'd be a riot. We'd be thrown out into the street as drunken revellers, or worse.'

No one had the answer to that. Bea tried to think, rubbing her forehead, wishing that Hamilton would beam down the answer to her from wherever he was now, heaven, probably, if you believed in heaven, which he had done, bless him. Now and then she believed in heaven herself, but not always, not all the time.

Maggie was frowning at Oliver, who was biting a fingernail, disgusting!

Coral was still busy on the phone, staring at the wall, oblivious to what was going on behind her. Worrying about her daughter. This was, of course, only right and proper, but Bea felt like slapping her. And all of them. Why? Because they weren't Hamilton, that's why.

Piers had finished his coffee. Any minute now he'd ask if there were another bottle of wine going. Bea stood up, wanting to be out of there, wanting to be sunning herself on a palm-fringed beach, in a five-star hotel in France, anywhere but here. Wanting Hamilton. She'd been too abrupt. Their shocked faces proclaimed that they'd been prepared to go on talking all night. Well, she wasn't.

'I'm sorry, but I'll have to throw you all out,' she said. 'It's just hit me, jet lag or something. Sorry, sorry, but I'll be no use to man nor beast till I've had a good night's sleep.' Even as she said it, she knew she wouldn't sleep tonight, either. She was too tired, too sad, too far over the hill and down the other side.

Coral clicked off her mobile. 'Jake says they're keeping June in tonight, but the contractions have stopped, which is good, isn't it? Ready for bed, Bea? I should think so and all. It takes days to get over a long flight and months, sometimes years, to get over losing your best friend. So I'll be on my way. I'll check back with the hospital first thing tomorrow, and if there's no news I'll come on in, see what's on the menu, right?'

'We need more information,' said Piers, grumbling to himself, but getting to his feet. 'The hotel is the logical place to start. Where am I sleeping tonight, does anyone know?'

Bea was so tired, she ignored him. She tried to close the French windows that led on to the garden, but couldn't seem to make the catch work.

'I'll do that,' said Maggie, predictably taking over.

It seemed for an instant as if Bea were back in the plane, hearing the drone of the engines. She shook her head to clear it. What nonsense. She put on a smile, and made her way to the stairs. She was aware of someone following her. If she concentrated hard enough, she'd get up the stairs to the first floor. There, she'd made it. And now the second set of stairs. She was floating up them, how very odd.

Someone came into the bedroom with her and closed the windows, drawing down the blinds, talking to her in a soothing monotone. *Here's your dressing gown, that's right, this arm first. This way to the bathroom, I'll wait outside, shall I?* She stood in the shower, thinking how absurd this all was. She was being treated like a small child.

Here's a nice, big towel. There you go. And I found this nightie for you, isn't it pretty? Where did you get it? Well, never mind all that now. Look, I've turned down the bed for you, and all you have to do is pop yourself in and I'll turn off the lights as I go out, right? See you in the morning.

Bea lay on her back on 'her' side of the big bed, and resolutely closed her eyes. She told herself she was tired enough to sleep through the night and half of the next day, and feared she wouldn't sleep at all. She ached all over. She wanted to get up and find her reading glasses and open Hamilton's Bible and read something soothing. A psalm, maybe. But she hadn't the energy to get out of bed.

After a while she found herself staring up at the ceiling. As dusk drew on to night, the edges of the room faded into darkness. She only realized that she'd been crying for a while when the pillow beneath her head became sodden.

She made herself move over to Hamilton's side of the bed.

When he couldn't sleep, he used to get up and go downstairs so as not to disturb her. He'd sit and play a game of patience at his table in the window. Sometimes he'd pick up a book of puzzles, and work through several until he felt relaxed enough to come back to bed. She'd heard him crying in the night, once, when he thought she was asleep.

She stared at the ceiling. Willed her eyelids to shut. Lay still, still, still. Did she doze off? She rather thought she might have done. Eventually the first of the birds began their chorus. Just before dawn, and not at dawn as the poets said. The night would end sometime. She had to believe it.

What she couldn't believe was that the dawn would come and Hamilton wouldn't be there to see it. It just wasn't possible that life could go on, that people would whistle in the street, go about their business, get on buses and Underground trains and go to work and come home and have supper and switch on the television and go to bed. Without him.

She'd be no use to anyone tomorrow. Hardly able to help herself, never mind anyone else. She dozed and woke and dozed again, falling properly asleep at four.

Thursday, morning
Noel let himself into the flat at dawn. His mobile rang. The little receptionist, wanting to make sure he'd got home safely, and that when he'd said he'd loved her, he'd meant it.

He couldn't think why he'd bothered with her. She hadn't been able to tell him anything of interest, except that the missing man had played both ends against the middle, had even asked her out for a drink. Not that she'd accepted. She wasn't at all bothered that he hadn't turned up yet, though the management was beginning to fret.

Noel found his mother's handbag and lifted some fifties from it. What a wonderful woman she was, to be sure. Never a word said, but a supply of petty cash always on hand. It was lucky she didn't know about the other incident. She might not be so forgiving if she knew this wasn't the first time he'd killed.

Eight

Thursday, morning

B ea rose at ten. She usually got up at seven, but had over-slept. She could hear people moving about the house. If only she'd had the gumption to throw everyone out last night, she could have had the house to herself, and slept as long as she liked. She hated herself and everybody.

She showered, dressed and dragged herself down the stairs, thinking that there was something she ought to be thinking about, doing. The black dog sat on her shoulder.

'Morning!' said Maggie, clashing pans together. 'What would you like for breakfast?' The girl was wearing a turquoise tank top over a skirt so short it looked like a pelmet. Her legs were far too thin for a short skirt. She'd pulled her hair into a topknot and fastened it with a silk orchid on a band. Too chirpy to be true.

'Morning!' said Piers, seated at the table already with a cup of coffee in his hand. He was wearing a white towelling robe over nothing much.

Bea was shocked. 'You never spent the night here, did you?'

'Who helped to put you to bed, right? I said I'd better sleep across your door like a squire of old in case you started sleep-walking, but Maggie insisted I took the spare room instead. I'll find somewhere else today. Did you sleep all right?'

What a ridiculous question! Besides, Bea knew very well that it was Maggie who'd talked her into getting undressed and into bed. She ignored Piers, and accepted the mug of coffee Maggie put in her hand.

Oliver popped up with a sheaf of papers in his hand, looking wide awake and bushy-tailed. Bea snarled at him that she didn't want to know about anything.

He treated her to a forgiving smile. 'Of course. My father's like that in the mornings, too. There's not much been happening, anyway. That cleaner woman's been on the phone again, nearly got arrested at the House of Commons trying to get in to see Max, would you believe! Then there's the usual; a couple of people who've heard you're back and want you to ring them back. Oh, all right. I won't bother you with the details till you feel better.'

'I feel fine!' Bea spat the words out. 'Just go away and leave me in peace.'

'Okey-dokey,' said the irrepressible one, shoving a pen and a letterhead into her hand. 'Just sign here, and the cheque here, that's right. Maggie or I will take it round to the shop this morning and see if they accept it, right?'

Bea signed, knowing with one part of her mind that she was probably committing a felony because the cheque would bounce though she couldn't see why since it looked all right to her admittedly bleary eyes. Where were her glasses?

The coffee was working. A bit. Caffeine did kick-start a lousy day into touch. Not that the sky looked lousy. It looked pellucid blue, forewarning of another hot day to come. How come it was going to be another beautiful day when Hamilton was not there to see it?

She was going to dissolve into tears again. No, she wasn't. She sought for something else to grumble about. 'Anyone know what's happened to our cars? Max said something about using Hamilton's, but what about mine?'

'Further down the street,' said Oliver. 'We've got residents' parking now and Max applied for a space for you. He's taken Mr Hamilton's car and I suppose he's parked it somewhere near wherever he's staying at the moment. Mrs Max was using yours but she had a puncture a couple of days ago, and I took it round to the garage and had it mended. It meant a new tyre, I'm afraid, so I paid for it with my father's . . .' His voice faded, and he blushed.

Piers gave a very audible sigh.

Bea still felt disagreeable. 'Are you old enough to have a licence?'

He swallowed. 'Provisional. I was taking driving lessons, getting on really well, until . . . you know.'

'I sat in the car with him when he drove it to the garage,' said Maggie, polishing glassware till it shone. 'He's going to be a really good driver.'

Bea shook her head to clear it. 'So, Maggie, you've got a licence?'

Maggie ducked her head between her shoulders. 'Well, actually, no. Failed my test three times. But—'

Bea held on to her head. 'I'm going mad. Get out, all of you. And that means you, too, Piers.'

They whispered their way out of the room. Bea drank her coffee and tried to put her brain back into working order. It was absolutely no use wanting to turn the clock back. Life was never going to be the same as it had been before Hamilton became ill. So why didn't she make a clean break with the past and move out of this house with all its memories of him? Find a flat somewhere, take up bridge, shop at Harrods, have rendezvous with old friends who'd come up from the country for the day?

The house phone rang. There was an extension in the kitchen, so she answered it without thinking. A voice quacked at her but she couldn't make out what they were asking. She cradled the phone.

No sooner had she put the phone down than it rang again. Bea shuddered. She couldn't cope with one more person asking her to do something for them. She was finished, washed up, and put out to grass. If it were urgent, the caller could leave a message. She muted the bell so it didn't disturb her again.

Piers came back into the room, fully dressed and carrying his mobile. 'I know you only want to be left alone, Bea, but I'm not sure that's the right thing to do. I keep asking myself what Hamilton would have done.'

She turned her shoulder on him, thinking he'd leave her, but instead he sat down at the table. 'Yes, I'm going in a minute. My agent wants to see me, and then I'll check into a hotel and get back to one or two people who've been trying to get in touch. I'll leave my mobile on in case you want me for something.'

The phone rang again downstairs, and Maggie's high-pitched laugh assaulted the ears. Bea closed her eyes and sank her head into her folded arms on the table. How long before Piers took the hint and went away?

'Those two young things,' he said. 'They make me feel like the Ancient of Days. Do you want to tackle Oliver's old man for him? Or shall I?'

Bea shrugged.

A pause. 'Maggie's dusting everything in sight down there, even under the computers, getting under Oliver's feet. She's threatening to come up here and give the oven a good clean, so be warned.'

Bea half lifted her head. 'That laugh of hers drives me crazy, and she talks down to me as if I were a small child.'

'You need her at the moment. I suspect there's a shrinking violet somewhere beneath all that bravado. I'd like to know how her marriage ended. With a bang and not a whimper, I should think. Perhaps her husband knocked her about?'

'I can hardly help myself, and you're asking me to take those two social misfits on board?'

An exclamation from the doorway, and Bea turned her head long enough to catch sight of a turquoise top disappearing from view. She bit her lip. Oh dear. Now what had she done?

'Oops,' said Piers. 'Well, what is it to be? Are you going to sink into a nice, destructive bout of self-pity, or get your skates on and tackle the baddies?' He sighed, got to his feet. 'Hark at me, playing the wise guru, sorting everyone out while unable to get my own life straight.'

He left the room, humming. Bea heard him shout down the stairs to Maggie that he was leaving now, and that there was some post on the doormat. She heard him drag his suitcase to the front door. It opened and closed.

He'd gone. Bea relaxed, laying her arms on the table before her, stretching them out, resting her head on them. Somewhere in the house, Radio Three announced a change of programme. What would Hamilton have said, if he'd been here?

Well, Hamilton had had a coping mechanism for the times that he felt life was getting too much for him. He'd say, 'I know I can't do it on my own strength, but I know someone who can. I'd better go and ask Him to take over.'

If it were fine, he'd go out into the garden and sit under the tree, hands on knees, palms facing upwards, head down-bent. And hand everything over to his Lord to deal with. If it were raining, he'd shut his office door on everyone and do the same thing. Then in ten minutes or thirty, he'd come back looking relaxed and cheerful, ready to kick ass or negotiate or console or . . . whatever was needed.

She'd never tried doing that. Her way was to go on worry, worry, worrying away at things till she was exhausted and hadn't really sorted anything out. Yes, she'd tried prayer every now and then, but had always felt self-conscious about it. She'd been brought up to think that you always had to use the words of the prayer book when you talked to God, and had been scandalized that Hamilton didn't always bother to use words, never mind words that other people had written. Oh, of course he'd liked to repeat certain prayers, but he'd also believed that you could pray without words, not even asking Him to grant a petition, but just opening yourself up to God. This morning she was in such a tizzy that she couldn't remember any 'proper' prayers all the way through. Perhaps she ought to try it Hamilton's way?

She sat upright, closed her eyes, laid her forearms on the table with the palms uppermost, and tried to relax. Failed. Allowed herself to slump a bit. Said, 'Please Lord,' over and over in her head, not being at all sure that He would be listening, but hoping against hope that someone was out there and cared enough to help her on the next stage of the journey.

Oliver came into the room with the soft footsteps of someone visiting an invalid. 'Mrs Abbot?' He'd muted his voice, too.

She opened her eyes, and straightened her back with an effort.

'Mrs Abbot, would you like us to clear out? We could go to the park or something, the weather's fine. Just say the word and we'll be off and leave you in peace. If that's what you want.'

She shook her head. She didn't think she'd had any direct message from God but she did at least understand what she had to do next. The thought of being left alone in peace and quiet in her house was attractive, but she couldn't throw the children out yet, especially after calling them social misfits.

She tried to sound as if she were back in control. 'No, of course I don't want you to go yet, Oliver. Now, what have we got on this morning?' She tried to think. 'Oh yes, we have to get that cheque in, don't we? It's local, shouldn't take long. Then I suppose I might have a go at the hotel where the function's

being held on Saturday. What's it called? Green's Hotel. I think
I know where it is. Not far away, but just too far to walk.' She
couldn't take Oliver, looking like something out of a refugee
camp. 'I'll take Maggie with me, shall I? Maggie, if that's you
lurking behind the door, do come in.'

Maggie banged open the door, looking as if she'd rather like
to hit someone, preferably Bea. Should Bea apologize? Better
not; that would be to make too much of what had been a
moment's thoughtlessness. But how to restore harmony?

'Maggie, you can be my social secretary. I shall say that I'm
enquiring about facilities for a party I want to give in the
autumn.' She sought for a reason why she would be giving a
party. 'It will be a sixtieth birthday party for my famous ex-
husband Piers, the well-known portrait painter. I shall enquire
about catering, and drinks and silver service and a band, and
you will take notes for me. I shall boast, in a deprecating
manner, about the pictures he's had hung in the National Portrait
Gallery.'

Maggie's mouth hung open. 'A social secretary? Me?'

'I shall drop the information, carelessly, that I'm attending
the ball at the hotel on Saturday and will need to compare
prices with what is being provided then. I'm sure they'll tell
me what I need to know.'

'Brilliant,' said Maggie, grudgingly. 'But—'

'I know what you're going to say,' said Bea. 'You aren't
dressed like a social secretary, except perhaps for the Bubble
character in *Ab Fab*, and that's not quite the impression we
intend to make, is it? I'll find you something less obvious to
wear. Does that pink colour wash out of your hair or is it a
dye?'

'You don't like my hair?' Maggie's arms went akimbo again.

'Very trendy,' said Bea, realizing that she'd said the wrong
thing, yet again.

'*I* like it,' said Oliver.

Maggie tossed her head, unplacated. 'Yes, but if *she* doesn't,
I don't know what—'

'No need to make a song and dance about it,' said Bea,
losing patience. 'You're dressing up to play a part to help Coral.
I'll find you a longer skirt and . . .' Bea looked with dismay at
the tatty flip-flops the girl was wearing '. . . and perhaps some
better shoes.'

'I've got awkward feet,' said the girl, pointing out the obvious.

Bea could see that. Maggie's feet were long and slender and needed expensive shoes to show them off. 'We'll buy you a pair before we do anything else.'

The girl went bright red. 'I've got shoes of my own, if you don't mind!'

'Of course,' said Bea, telling herself that it was like walking through a minefield, trying to talk to this child. 'Now if you can help me move some of Max's stuff out of my dressing room, I can get at some clean clothes and we'll be on our way. Oliver, you've got plenty to get on with?'

As she went up the stairs with Maggie, Bea looked across at the mirror over the fireplace in the living room, and clutched at the banister, feeling as if she'd missed a step. There was the silver photograph frame, but there was no picture in it. The photograph of Hamilton was missing.

Bea was spooked. Could a photo disappear when the subject of it died? She couldn't breathe properly. Was she so short of sleep, so swayed by grief, that she saw his likeness one minute and the next, it was gone? She told herself that there must be a rational explanation. She'd think of it later. Perhaps the sun had caught the frame at such an angle that it blanked out the picture.

She followed Maggie up the stairs, feeling unreal. Maggie helped Bea pull various bits and pieces out of the dressing room, till she could edge in far enough to rescue some clean clothes. It had been summertime in the Antipodes, and it was summertime again now back in London. Her clothes, bought in good boutiques and in Harvey Nichols, were mostly subdued in colouring, classic rather than ornate. She picked out a knee-length swishy skirt in a soft grey-green for Maggie, with a darker green top to match. Bea could see that Maggie thought the clothing dull, but in fact on her spare frame they looked well.

'Fancy dress,' said Bea, making herself smile. 'You look the part now.'

'And my hair?' The girl stuck her lower lip out.

'Drop the dead orchid, and it'll be fine. Find yourself a pad and pen, and the keys to the car. Then we'll be off.'

It was better to do something rather than sit down and howl, which is what she wanted to do. The mess in her bedroom offended her tidy soul. She couldn't bear to go into the living room and take down the photograph frame for a closer look. She was sure she'd been mistaken. The light, her poor sight, the hours she'd spent in sleepless misery.

She was sure the photograph of Hamilton would be back where it always had been, when she went into the room again. Sure of it. She found her reading glasses and put them in her handbag. Money, keys, cards, notebook. She was ready.

Her car was sitting in a parking space down the street, just as Oliver had promised.

Maggie said she hadn't even got a provisional driving licence at the moment, so Bea backed the car out and edged into the traffic, turning north. It was strange and yet familiar to be driving her car again. Kensington was gridlocked, of course. It usually was. They crossed Notting Hill Gate and continued north and west. The houses in these roads were rather grander than Bea's, with no garden in front but some expensive shrubs in fanciful containers under columned porches. They turned into a quiet side street. The shop they were looking for lay on the corner. The sunshine lay heavily over all.

'Where can we park?' Bea spotted a place some way down the road, and manoeuvred her car between a 4x4 and a toy boy's sports car. 'It says "No Waiting", so I'll stay in the car. If there's a problem, I'll keep circling the block until I can pick you up again.'

Maggie smoothed her hair up into the topknot – now without the orchid – and set off for the shop. Bea angled the mirror to watch her. If the shopkeeper accepted their letter, they'd have solved one part of the problem.

Ten minutes later there was still no sign of Maggie. Bea was getting hotter by the minute and beginning to worry. What could be keeping the girl? Had she been kidnapped by white slave traders – ridiculous notion – or got into a row with the shopkeeper or what? The shop was popular. The postman dived into the shop and came out a moment later. It was probably the only outlet for newspapers, sweets, instant meals and booze for half a mile.

A young man had been hanging around the doorway of the shop for a while, talking, laughing, chatting to someone standing inside.

Bea looked up and down the street. Was it safe to leave the car? Most of the other cars in the street had parking permits on them. The fines for illegal parking were horrendous.

Then Bea spotted a greenish skirt, brushing the young man's legs. She gawped. Was that idiot Maggie actually chatting up a young man, leaving Bea to sit in the car and fry in the sun?

Finally the young man – a personable-looking lad in expensive, casual clothes – lifted his hand to Maggie and went into the shop, while she bounced back to the car, grinning.

'Mission accomplished. I went in all innocent, asking if they knew where these people lived, and the woman behind the counter said the charity were in the process of moving to another address and they were forwarding stuff, so it would be all right to leave my envelope with them. The postman dumped some mail on the counter for them as well. Luckily I can read upside down.'

'And the young man?' Bea was feeling waspish as she edged the car out on to the road.

'He was just hanging around, at a loose end. He was nice.' Maggie turned her blushes away from Bea. 'He wanted to know if I lived locally. He's just visiting, did I know the best pubs and eateries, had I any free time to show him around, that sort of thing.'

'A good chat-up line.'

Maggie sighed. 'He said he'd ring me, but I don't suppose he will.' Now she was fiddling with her watch strap, mouth turned down. Was the cocksure Maggie not so sure of her appeal to the opposite sex?

'Where's this hotel?' Bea took a right turn, checking street names. 'Along here, somewhere? Parking in the square opposite. Good. Cheer up, child; on with the game and all that.'

'He said he liked longer skirts on tall girls. Do you think it looks all right? I mean, it's not exactly trendy, is it?'

Bea sought for something to say which would help the girl. 'Graceful girls can pull it off. Gawky girls can't.' Who'd have thought it? The tiresome girl was begging for reassurance, wanting to know if Bea really thought she was graceful. 'You look good in that rig-out,' said Bea, feeling older than Time but only half as lively as the man with the scythe. 'Ready to take notes? Prompt me if I forget to ask anything important, won't you?'

Bea led the way into the hotel, deciding it would be a good idea to have a cup of coffee, suss out the strengths and weaknesses of the place, before asking to speak to the manager. She turned into the coffee room – panelled, leather-clad chairs, lots of framed cartoons on the walls – a trifle old-fashioned but solid. If that was their clientele, then they'd caught the right note with the décor.

'Let's sit here for a bit,' said Bea. 'Have some coffee before we talk business.'

Maggie sat, but didn't know what to do with her legs. Bea set her feet side by side, and swung her knees slightly to the left. She leaned back in her chair. Maggie tried to copy Bea. Not a bad attempt.

The coffee was reasonable and the milk was hot. There were three different kinds of sugar. Shortbread biscuits came with the coffee, plus thick paper napkins. So far, so good. Bea consulted the waitress, asking if the manager were free to discuss a possible booking. Maggie tried crossing one leg over the other. Bea tried not to raise her eyebrows. Maggie uncrossed her legs. She pouted, fiddled with her hair. Oh dear.

A smooth-looking middle-aged woman came to join them. Black business suit, good haircut, discreet make-up, unusual jade earrings. Oh dear, Maggie was nibbling skin at the side of a fingernail.

Bea launched into her spiel about hosting a party for her ex-husband. Maggie got out her pad and made notes. Costings, food, size of rooms. The manageress was called away to the phone. Maggie refilled their coffee cups and spilled some in the saucer. 'Leave it,' said Bea, holding back irritation.

They waited for the manageress to return. They could see her behind the reception desk, talking to someone on the phone. At length she returned to them, with a professional smile. 'Staff problems. So sorry. Now, may I show you the room I think would be best for your purpose? This way.'

Maggie was staring at someone who'd just come into the foyer. She dropped her eyes and smiled, looking coy, then mumbled something about needing to visit the ladies'.

Bea might need reading glasses but her long sight was good. The young man who'd just entered was the same person who'd been chatting Maggie up in the shop. The girl was obviously smitten. Easy meat, thought Bea. He can see she's easy meat.

All that aggressive behaviour, and she rolls over and dies for a man who pays her a compliment. Who'd have thought it?

I suppose I can manage without her for a few minutes. She followed the manageress down a corridor to the function room.

Thursday, noon
Noel kissed the back of his mother's neck. 'Darling Mummy, don't scold, I know I'm late. I spotted this girl delivering to the shop – her aunt wants some tickets for Saturday – and she was delivering the cheque by hand to make sure they got the tickets in time. Quite a coincidence. Then I took the menus into the hotel, and had a word with the receptionist, who says the manageress is in a snit, holiday times, shortage of staff, man gone missing. They're thinking of reporting his disappearance to the police, but they hadn't done it by the time I left.'

Lena shrugged, stuffing tickets into envelopes. 'Good luck to them.'

Noel caressed her neck, deciding not to tell her he'd arranged to see the girl Maggie that evening. No confidence in herself, that one. Should be a pushover; a little flattery, a bunch of flowers, a glass of wine too many. He'd turn her inside out tonight, find out if she had money. Well-heeled girls were always eager to give him a present.

Nine

Thursday, afternoon

Bea feared she'd made a mistake. She oughtn't to have taken Maggie with her to the hotel or anywhere that a randy young man could get at her. The girl was in a happy dream; she answered questions at random, tripped over a chair, forgot to warm the plates at lunchtime. She was humming something which sounded remarkably like a carol. *Noel, No-el?* Oh dear. Was Noel the name of the young man who'd been chatting her up?

Bea hadn't lived to sixty without recognizing the type who'd got Maggie circling the kitchen, smiling to herself. He was handsome enough; granted. Well-dressed and polished, probably university, though not Oxbridge. Streetwise rather than studious. Job? Bea guessed he probably worked in advertising or the media, but he wouldn't work too hard at whatever it was.

Bad news for Maggie, who might act hard-boiled but who seemed to have a soft centre, despite her marriage . . . if she really had been married, which at that moment Bea doubted. Bea told herself that she had no right to interfere. Maggie wasn't her daughter, luckily. Maggie was a temporary employee, who would be leaving the agency next week.

Oliver was trying to make sense of the pages of information Bea had gathered, but raised his head long enough to stare at Maggie. 'Aren't you eating?'

Maggie didn't hear him. She'd put the machine on for some coffee, though Bea didn't like drinking proper coffee at lunchtime if she was planning to have a nap afterwards. Which she was. She'd been drinking too much coffee this past couple of weeks, anyway. It might partly be what was stopping her having a good night's sleep.

Oliver switched his eyes to Bea. 'What's up with her?'

'Love's young dream,' said Bea, thinking that she was being a sour old puss, and maybe the young man would turn out to be someone who saw through the aggressive exterior to recognize Maggie's true worth. 'Six foot two, works out, looks like a model complete with obligatory five o'clock shadow.'

Maggie was smiling. 'He's gorgeous, isn't he? Mrs Abbot, do you think I could have the afternoon off to have my hair done?' A troubled look. 'Oh, but I forgot. Are you going to pay me any wages, or does my living here till next week mean that I don't get any?'

Bea wondered if it wouldn't be better in the long run to deny the child her wages, if it meant she wouldn't appear at her best before her new man. Though precisely what Maggie's 'best' might be, was an awkward thought. What hairdresser would she patronize, and would that hairdresser turn Maggie out like Kate Moss or Strewwelpeter?

Bea hesitated too long. The child's arms had gone akimbo. Bea said, 'Of course you get paid. You've looked after me very well, I couldn't have had anyone better. You'd prefer cash, wouldn't you? How much has Max been giving you?'

Maggie and Oliver consulted one another without words. Oliver said, 'He didn't pay me at all, but that was all right. He gave Maggie a pittance in cash every Friday, plus a hundred for household expenses. Mrs Abbot used to order the food and drink on the Internet from Waitrose, and they delivered. That's how the food and drink for the party came. Everything else Maggie gets from Marks and Spencer's on the High Street. Mr Abbot kept a float in the safe in his study, but I don't think there's much there now.'

'Do you know the combination?' Of course Oliver knew the combination. 'Then let's look, shall we?'

Before they set off on their round the world trip, Hamilton had left his dress watch and studs in the safe together with Bea's mother's jewellery – which she rarely wore – plus the usual birth and marriage certificates, family papers, and a couple of thousand pounds in twenties. There was a wad of notes still there. Whose money was it, Max's or Bea's? How much had Hamilton left in the safe? Bea hadn't a clue; he'd always dealt with such things himself.

She wrote out a receipt for the money, gave Maggie five hundred, saying they'd sort out who owed what later, and told her to go off and enjoy herself. She set a new combination for the lock once Oliver was out of the room, and hoped he wasn't planning to become a safe-breaker. She did trust him. On the whole.

Coral arrived as Maggie left. Bea had been hoping for a little nap on her bed but clearly it was not to be. So Bea took Coral up into the sitting room, asking Oliver if he'd mind trying to make sense of all the information she'd got from the hotel that morning.

'So, Coral. How do we stand? We've applied for tickets for Saturday, and I've got some details out of the hotel about outside catering. They prefer to do it themselves, but sometimes they have people come in for it. Ditto for the wine.'

Her sitting room was not as tidy as she liked it. The photo-graph frame was not at the right angle. She picked it up. A bland brown surface was the only thing to be seen inside the silver frame. No picture of Hamilton.

Coral was speaking, something about the wine.

Bea looked towards the window where Hamilton had been accustomed to sit, playing patience. He'd always used a rather good Regency card table for the purpose, and it was missing. That table had been handed down from his parents, who'd been given it as a wedding gift by *their* parents. When the top was folded over, it looked like any other side table, but underneath was a drawer in which you could keep packs of cards, dominoes, or a chess board. When the top was opened out, its baize-covered surface would accommodate four players, each with their own built-in 'dish' intended for gaming chips. Not that Hamilton was a gamester. Far from it.

The table had disappeared, just as Hamilton's photograph had done. Bea put the silver frame face down on the mantel-piece. She told herself that Max had taken the photograph and had the table moved for some reason. Except that the photo-graph had been in its place all the time she'd been talking to him last night and when she went to bed. So Max couldn't have taken it.

'What was that you said, Coral?'

Her old friend was concerned for her. 'Didn't you sleep well?'

'Can't fool you, can I? But it's best to keep on. How's June?'

'The contractions have stopped but they want to keep her in one more night. I'll go in to see her later on. I've been thinking. Maybe I could get a second mortgage on my place to pay for June's.'

'How could you ever repay it?' Bea forced herself to concen-trate. 'We'll track them down somehow, never fear. Now, I've been thinking, too. I understand from the hotel that the people who are doing the food on Saturday night – Oliver's got the details – are new to this sort of operation. I wonder if you'd like to ring them, go to see them, warn them. If they've been paid up front then of course it's all right, but if not—'

'They'll be looking for a second mortgage, too.' Coral was grim. 'Do you know who it is who's supplying the wine?'

Bea tried to remember. 'The hotel is doing the wine. They charge so much corkage per bottle that it's not worth anyone bringing it in from outside. That first time, at the Garden Room – that's attached to a public house, isn't it? – presumably they did the drinks themselves.'

'I think so. I'm trying to remember who did the drinks the

second time round. They'd have been stung too, I suppose. But unlike me they weren't stupid enough to do it again.'

'Or if they were such a small firm, it drove them out of business.'

'Ouch,' said Coral. 'I wish I could remember the name but there are lots of small firms in the wine business, plus shops here and there. I thought he gave me his card but I can't find it. An odd little man, but he knew what he was doing. He runs wine-tasting evenings. I should hate to think he's been driven out of business.'

Bea pressed buttons on the phone, which had an extension to the agency rooms downstairs. 'Oliver, have you managed to make any sense of my notes? We'll come down and discuss them, shall we?'

Muffled shouts came through the phone. 'Sorry, sorry,' said Oliver. 'Just seeing someone out.'

Bea and Coral exchanged amused glances, and went down the stairs. Oliver appeared in the doorway from reception, flushed. 'Sorry about that. It was the cleaner, the one who tried to get into the House of Commons. She says we owe her some money, but honestly I can't find any record of us giving her a job. She must be trying it on, knowing that we're closing down and hoping, I suppose, that we're a bit chaotic with our system, which of course we are.'

Coral was sharp. 'Give her Max's current address.'

Bea held back a grin, but Oliver didn't. 'Will do. Now what was it you wanted to know?'

'We need a list of all the people who might have been stung. I was wondering about a photographer, surely there must have been one, and the cabaret people as well as those who provided food and drink. Could we start ringing round, trying to find other people who might have been involved? Get a clear picture of who is owed how much?'

Coral followed Bea into reception, hitting her forehead with the heel of her hand. 'He wrote a column on wine for the local newspaper. I'm sure that's what he said.'

'The freebie newspaper?' Oliver dived into the wastepaper basket.

'Maybe. Would they have a column about wine in the freebie? Wouldn't it be in the Friday *Gazette*? That's got much more in it.'

'The papers all get recycled,' said Bea. 'We keep the box for them in the hall.'

Oliver ran up the stairs – How fast the young do that, thought Bea – and returned with last week's paper. He gave half to Bea and half to Coral, reaching for the phone which rang at that moment.

Bea put on her glasses and shuffled through her half, noting that some messy person had been reading the paper, dog-earing pages, folding some back untidily. Hamilton had always been a neat person, but he'd been messy with papers. Just as he never put a towel back on the rail properly, but kept it bunched up. How could you get a towel dry if you bunched it up like that?

'Not in here,' said Bea, flapping the paper to open it out and refolding it.

Oliver was jotting down notes on his pad, saying, 'Yes, yes. I quite understand, and I promise I'll tell her you rang. No, I'm afraid she's not available today. No, I'm not quite sure when she will be. Have a good day.'

'Got it!' Coral laid the paper open on Maggie's desk. 'Leo's wine column, Wines for the Week. Leo's Wines and Spirits, with an address and telephone number. He's just off Notting Hill Gate. I'll give him a ring, shall I?' Without waiting for permission, she reached for the phone.

Bea raised an eyebrow at Oliver, who gave her the gist of his phone calls. 'There's quite a list. Do you know a Mrs Weston, or Westin? No? Someone called Smithson? Something about an outing for her grandchildren which she wants us to arrange. I said we don't do that any more, but she insists she's got to speak to you about it. She's rung before.'

'Smithson?' Bea shook her head. 'Can't recall anyone of that name. Nor Weston.'

'Some people Max knew, I suppose.' He drew a line through his notes.

Coral was talking on the phone. 'Is that Leo of Wines for the Week? We met some time ago. Coral, of Coral Catering . . . Yes, yes. That's it. Do you think I might drop in to see you sometime? What time do you close? . . . Right, I'll be there.'

Coral dropped the phone back on to the hook, and punched the air. 'Bingo. I'll pop round to see him now, shall I?' She was halfway out of the door before Bea could say yea or nay. And disappeared, letting the outside door bang to behind her.

Oliver was consulting his notes again. 'Mr Max rang. He's arranged for you to have a tour of the House of Commons tomorrow at eleven, will take you for lunch afterwards. Then Mrs Max rang to say she's picking you up at ten thirty tomorrow morning to take you out for the day.'

'Also tomorrow morning?'

Oliver made a clucking sound. 'They haven't synchronized their watches, have they?'

Bea shrugged. 'Either way, I can't spare the time. Is that it?'

'Some of your old friends leaving their numbers; the list's on your desk. A few people still wanting to know if we can take on jobs for them, someone selling stationery, nothing of importance.'

Oliver disappeared behind his computer screen and Bea wandered through into Hamilton's office. Her office now, she supposed. For a short while only, of course. Winding an agency down was bound to take a little time. The sky had clouded over. Was that rain hitting the window? No, probably not. Should she do something useful like watering the containers of busy Lizzies in the garden? Or just stand and stare as she was doing?

There really wasn't anything she felt like doing, anyway. She supposed she ought to tackle the ever-growing pile of post. There were people to see, return calls to make. The phone was ringing next door. She didn't move.

Oliver popped his head around the door. 'That was Piers. Said you must have turned your mobile off. Said he'd got a rush job on but if you needed him, he'd come round for supper, late. I said you'd ring him if you got back from wherever it is you're supposed to be at the moment.'

Sensible boy. 'Thank you, Oliver.' She was touched by his thoughtfulness. She remembered that he was working just for bed and board. 'Oliver, shall we pay a visit to your father, ask for your certificates? It shouldn't take long.'

She could hear him swallow, even though she had her back to him. He stammered, 'I-it's holiday t-t-time. He's p-probably n-not there.'

'Wouldn't he have to go into school for a few days at least to talk to parents about their children's exam results?'

Silence.

'I'll come with you,' said Bea. 'Let's get it over with. I've thought of a line you could take. Tell him you've used his card illegally, but that if he gives you your certificates, you can get a job and earn enough to start paying him back.'

More silence.

Bea turned to face him. 'You have told me the whole story, haven't you? There is nothing else?'

He shook his head, shifting from foot to foot.

'You need to pick up your belongings, as well. You have your own laptop, clothes and so on?'

He nodded.

'Then let's go and get them.'

Mr Ingram, Oliver's father, was headmaster of a small private school for boys aged eleven to eighteen, in a tree-lined Kensington square. The school itself occupied two four-storey terrace houses. Next to it was the house which he and his family occupied.

'It's sort of grace and favour,' explained Oliver, taking his time about getting out of the car. 'The Trust owns the school and the house next door, and they let Dad live there as long as he's head.'

'Is he a good headmaster?'

Oliver shrugged. 'His results are OK. He gets a lot of kids whose parents have come from overseas on short-term contracts, so they can afford the fees he charges. Most of those can't speak English very well.'

'Mixed ability?'

Oliver nodded. Fidgeted with his collar. His breathing had sharpened. 'Dad's ultra keen on sports, which impresses some parents no end. My elder brother and his wife are already working for him at the school. I'm the runt of the litter, very much an afterthought, don't really fit in anywhere, never have. I suppose we'd better try the office in the school first.'

He mounted the steps to the front door rather as if they were the steps to the scaffold. Rang the bell. A disembodied voice asked for a name. Bea – following close on his heels – gave her name, thinking they would take her for a prospective parent. The voice said that the head was not there that day, and could they call back tomorrow.

Oliver looked relieved. He would have returned to the car, if Bea hadn't done an about-turn and marched up the steps to the family's house next door. She pressed the doorbell. Chimes rang out. Not an appropriate sound for an early nineteenth century house.

An over-thin fifty-ish woman with sculptured fair hair opened the door. She had a face like a well-bred sheep – if you could have a blue-eyed sheep – and was expensively if unimaginatively dressed. On seeing Oliver she gave a little scream, and clapped both hands over her mouth.

'Mrs Ingram, I assume?' said Bea.

'It's all right, Mother,' said Oliver. 'Really it is.' She didn't make any move to touch him, and he didn't make any move to touch her. 'I've just come to collect my things and have a word with Dad if he's around.'

'No, he . . .' She looked back into the house, and lowered her voice. 'He's out, but your brother's here.'

A hefty looking young male appeared behind her. Much older than Oliver, possibly in his early thirties. Big, blond and blue-eyed. Tie neatly centred. 'You! How dare you come here after what you've done!'

Oliver seemed to shrink. He was a foot shorter than his brother, anyway. 'Look, I can explain—'

Bea decided it was time to intervene. 'May we come in for a moment? My name's Abbot, by the way. Oliver is working for me at the moment.'

Oliver's mother was reaching out to him, but not actually touching him. 'What are those clothes, Oliver? They're not very nice.'

The older brother yelled back into the house. 'Daffy! Come and see what the litter louts have dropped on our doorstep!'

Oliver set his jaw. 'Is my father in? I really need to speak to him.'

'Out to you,' said his older brother. 'For good. Get going, or I'll call the police.'

'That's enough!' said Bea, exercising authority. 'Will you tell Mr Ingram that his son needs to speak to him on a delicate matter. If he doesn't want to meet Oliver here—'

'He's not entering this house again—'

'—then he must appoint a meeting somewhere else. Urgently. And now, Oliver needs to collect his things.'

Oliver's mother began to weep. 'Oh, why did you do it, Oliver?'

'Do what?' said Oliver through his teeth. 'If he says I was accessing porn, well, I wasn't.'

'Why would he lie about it?' An intense-looking, thickset woman joined her husband at the door. 'What, has that cretin dared to—'

'That's enough!' said Oliver, and if his imitation of Bea came out as a squeak, it was enough to hold the tirade for a moment. 'He was – was mistaken. There's no porn on my laptop. If you let me in, I can show you all the sites I've visited.' He looked from one implacable face to the next. 'I know you don't want me around. I don't want to be around, either. I'm happy to move out. I've found a job and a place to stay, but I need my clothes, my laptop and my exam certificates. Also I need to speak to my father about, well, business.'

His mother was crying into a paper tissue which she'd fished out of the pocket in her jacket. 'Oh, Oliver, he's so angry with you, you've no idea, and he won't speak to me about it at all, and if it wasn't the porn then—'

'He's a lying little toad,' said the elder brother. 'He's not coming in here again. That's what *he* said and that's how it's going to be. We're well rid of him, I say.'

His mother held out her hands to Oliver, but only a little way, not far enough to touch him. 'We're giving your room to a new teacher at the school, so everything's been packed up and put out for the dustmen, only they don't come round till tomorrow, so it's all still here if you want it.'

Oliver was vibrating like a plucked string on a cello. 'Oh, Mother! Don't cry. I didn't do it, honest. At least, I didn't do the porn. But you know how it's been, I don't fit in and it's best I leave.'

She gulped, and wept. 'But where are you going? Do you really have a job? Will you give me your address?'

'Fantasy,' said the elder brother, brutally. 'He's too much of a wimp to go for a job, or to hold one down.' He eyed Bea up and down. 'Got him as your toy boy, have you, love?'

Bea spurted into laughter, shaking her head, but Oliver fired up, red in the face. 'How d-dare you! Mrs Abbot is not that sort of—'

Bea said, 'If you've packed up Oliver's stuff already, we'll take it away with us. My car's just there. But it would be a good idea for you to contact his father and arrange when they can meet, preferably on neutral territory, right? Here's my card. You can contact him at that address. Come, Oliver.'

She touched him on the arm, and he went with her to sit in the car. He was shaking. He put both his hands between his knees and clenched them tight.

'You did well,' said Bea, putting sincerity into her voice.

He said, 'I know his PIN numbers. I could empty his account in five minutes.'

Bea tried not to smile. 'I've no doubt you could, but you won't, will you? You will "rise above it" as Noel Coward used to say.'

'Who's he?'

Bea felt tired. 'An actor, writer, entertainer. Before your time. Remember that phrase, though. "Rise above it." It's useful when things get you down.'

'I'm all adrift, don't know where to put my feet, what to do next. Poor Mum. She always used to say I take after her younger brother, he was a businessman, very successful by all accounts, only he got killed in a car accident a couple of years back, or I might have gone to work for him. If I'd wanted to be a teacher and work for Dad it would have been all right, but that's not the way I am.'

'Do you want to go to university? With those results, you could.'

'I want to work with computers, but above all, I want to get away from home.'

'Don't make up your mind yet,' said Bea. 'You could get away from home by going to university.'

'Couldn't afford the fees and Dad won't pay up for me, will he?'

Not after he'd stumbled across his father's secret. Unless he blackmailed his father into paying the fees. But would that be a proper use for blackmail? It was a puzzle.

The front door of Oliver's home opened and several bulky black plastic bags were thrown out. Oliver went to retrieve them. Clothes and books, judging by the way he either picked them up or dragged them along to the car. Then he staggered over with a large cardboard box contained stereo equipment, and a printer. Lastly his mother came out with a laptop which she laid carefully down on the steps before waving to Oliver and retreating into the house. The front door closed behind her.

Oliver brought the laptop to the car and opened it up. 'I've been wondering if my father might have tried to put some porn on my laptop, to bolster his case against me.' He booted up, set his fingers to work and sighed with relief. 'It's OK. Nobody's touched it.'

'No one else in your family is bright enough to work out what your password might be?'

'Mixed up numbers and letters, some uppercase, some lower. They wouldn't ever get that. Plus I change it frequently.'

Bea turned on the ignition. 'Home, then?'

He nodded but didn't speak. She was annoyed with herself. He didn't have a home, nor any chance of getting one for months, maybe years. She'd be glad to see the back of noisy, bossy Maggie, but if Oliver could cut the umbilical cord that bound him to the girl, maybe she'd let him stay on after next week. Provided he paid her rent for his room. Which meant he'd have to get himself a job, and he still hadn't got his certificates. But perhaps she ought to be arranging for him to go to university?

No, no, she couldn't take on all the woes in the world. She needed to get her own home straight, tackle the mail on her desk, reply to phone messages from friends, clear out Hamilton's clothes, perhaps arrange a memorial service for him, wind up the agency. She wished she hadn't said she'd go to this function on Saturday.

Oliver said, 'I wonder what colour Maggie's hair is this time?'

Maggie had treated herself to the golden look, all long flowing curls. She'd also had a facial and a manicure. She was wearing one of her micro-skirts, plus a skimpy, spangly top which left nothing to the imagination. This was a pity, because she really didn't have enough of a bosom to wear that kind of thing. Being charitable, Bea said she thought Maggie looked stunning. Close to, Bea noticed for the first time that Maggie's eyes were those of an anxious child.

'Bravo,' said Oliver, carrying his laptop carefully up the stairs as Maggie descended, treading with care in extra high heels. 'You look amazing.'

'Well done,' said Bea, following with a bag of Oliver's clothes.

'Do you think I look like a model?' Maggie tried to pirouette on high heeled sandals, but had to clutch at the banister to save herself from falling.

'Indeed you do,' said Oliver. But when he and Bea had reached the top floor, he voiced his concern. 'Is she going to be all right, Mrs Abbot? She says she despises men, but I don't think she knows much about them.'

Bea was beginning to think the same thing. 'She's been married. Presumably she's had some experience.'

'Not sure she has,' said the schoolboy-turned-elder-brother. 'She married someone who was on the rebound from a long-term relationship. After a couple of months he went back to his old love, leaving Maggie stranded.'

Bea sighed. Was Maggie yet another burden to take on? No. She couldn't cope. 'She's free, white and nearly twenty-one. I'm sure she'll have a perfectly lovely time.'

Thursday, late evening
'Where have you been?' His mother had stayed up for him, apparently. Watching television, flicking channels.

He kissed her cheek. 'Clubbing. You'd like the girl. Pots of money in the background, big house in Kensington.'

'Paid for the evening out, did she?' His mother could be very acute.

He shrugged. 'She can afford it.'

'I hope you gave her satisfaction?'

He grinned. He'd taken her every which way but up, in the club, the cloakroom, in his car. And then on the settee in the office of some house that her aunt owned. She'd hardly been able to stumble to the door to let him out afterwards. Yes, she'd been given satisfaction all right. 'She's coming on Saturday with her aunt and various hangers-on. Mrs Abbot, Kensington.'

'Don't get too close to her. Remember that after Saturday we'll be off and away.'

He smiled as if he agreed, but it did occur to him that there was no necessity for him to disappear when his mother and Richie did. He could take his cut and say he needed a spot of holiday and would join up with them later.

Suppose he did hang around London for a bit? It would do no harm to keep seeing a biddable young girl from a wealthy family. Unsophisticated, naïve, but anxious to please. A man

could do worse than string her along. Her family would prob-
ably pay him well to leave her alone in the long run.

He didn't need to tell his mother all that was in his mind.

'Dearest,' he said, kissing her goodnight. 'Sweet dreams.'

Ten

Friday, morning

B ea didn't sleep well that night either, though better than
before. She forced herself to get up at eight, had a shower,
dressed and went downstairs. There was a fresh stack of mail
on the hall table. She made coffee and took the lot downstairs
to Hamilton's – to her – study, to add to the pile already there.
Someone had already sorted the previous day's post into junk
mail and correspondence.

For an hour she sorted mail, binning most of it. She tried
to boot up the computer and had to call Oliver in to help her
as this new one operated in a slightly different way from the
ones she'd been used to. He was a nice boy, she thought. He
hid his contempt for older women who weren't up to date with
computers pretty well. She settled down to her correspondence.
She decided to get some cards printed for answering letters of
condolence – or could Oliver contrive some for her?

Oliver tapped at her door again. 'Mrs Abbot, may I . . .? The
thing is, I'm a bit worried about Maggie, and I wondered if
you'd like to check on her.'

'Mm? She came in late, didn't she? I must have dropped off
by that time. Let her sleep.'

'Two o'clock. Yes. But . . .' He clung to the door handle,
then let it go and the door banged back, making them both
jump. 'I can't be absolutely sure but when she dragged herself
up the stairs, I think she was crying.'

Bea swung her chair round to face him. He was nervous, but
standing his ground. He was wearing a maroon sweatshirt over
jeans, trainers. His own clothes, obviously. He was heavy-lidded,

as if he hadn't slept well, either. She wondered if he'd lain awake waiting for Maggie to return, and if he'd then stayed awake worrying about her.

'I'm sure she's perfectly all right,' said Bea, failing to convince either him or herself. She glanced at her watch. Nearly ten. 'But perhaps I could take her up a cuppa.'

He nodded. 'And you haven't forgotten that Mrs Max is coming round?'

Bea set the printer going – yes, it worked! Good – and stood up. 'I haven't time for outings at the moment. See if you can get hold of her, tell her I'm too busy today. Now, let's see if Maggie's all right, shall we?'

She made some more coffee and took it upstairs. Oliver padded after her. Bea tapped on Maggie's door. A mumble from within enquired what time it was. Bea went in. This had once been Max's games room, an untidy cave for an untidy adolescent. It was clean, neat and tidy now, all Maggie's garish clothes hidden in the built-in cupboards and shelving along one wall. The outfit Maggie had worn the night before was on the floor. With her pants and bra. Both torn.

Maggie was sleeping on Max's old settee with one arm let down to make a bed. On hearing the door open, she lifted a heavy head from her pillow, and pulled the duvet over herself. Bea shut the door in Oliver's face, and set the coffee down on the floor beside the bed. Maggie's bright blonde hair trailed over the pillow but that one glimpse of her face told Bea that Oliver had been right to call her.

Bea forgot that the girl had ever irritated her. She pulled Maggie into her arms, saying, 'There, there.' Maggie hid her face in Bea's arm. Her eyes were puffy, and so were her lips. There were dark marks on her wrists.

'Let me see,' said Bea, pushing the covers back.

Maggie moaned. 'I'm all right.' But let Bea look. More bruising. Bite marks.

Bea drew in her breath. 'You must be very sore. Was it just rough sex, or rape?'

Maggie spoke through gritted teeth. 'He said I was loving it, and in a way I suppose I did like it at the beginning, but he wouldn't stop.'

Bea rocked the girl in her arms. 'I must ask. Did he use any contraception?'

Sniff, sniff. 'Yes. I'll be all right. I had a shower and then a bath, and it was my own fault, anyway. He said I'd asked for it, and of course I did only I didn't mean him to go on and on. I'm sorry if I overslept. There must be lots to do. I'll get up in a minute.'

Bea thought that it had been near enough rape judging by the bruising, but date rape was notoriously difficult to prove. 'Take it easy today. It was a shock to the system, whichever way you look at it. I'll get you some painkillers, you go back to sleep for a bit.'

Maggie struggled to sit up. Her pale skin was blotched. He'd bitten her lower lip – or she had. 'I'll be all right. I can't stay in bed, just because . . . I'm not letting that man upset me. Just don't tell Oliver, will you?'

Bea held the girl tightly. 'Oliver knows. It was he who told me.'

'Oh! I can never face him! I've been so stupid. I ought to have seen what he was like. It's all my own fault.'

'No, it isn't, Maggie. You might have given out the wrong signals, perhaps, but no nice boy would take advantage of you like that.'

'I ought to have realized that such a handsome man could have his pick of beautiful women and that if he picked on me, it meant he expected more than a kiss at the end of the evening. All he saw in me was a cheap night out!'

'You're worth more than that, Maggie.'

She sniffed. 'He didn't think so, did he? It's just as my mother says, and my husband that was. I'm just too ugly and awkward to attract a real man.'

'No, you're not, and to prove it, you're going to put this down to experience and get on with your life, make something of yourself, show the world what you're made of.'

Maggie sniffed again. 'Yeah. Sure. Aim for Prime Minister, why don't I?'

Someone tapped on the door. Oliver said, 'Look, I don't want to come in or anything, but the phone in the sitting room has been ringing almost non-stop but if I rush to answer it, there's no message been left on the answerphone. The agency phone keeps ringing as well, Mrs Max has arrived downstairs, and Coral's here with a strange little man in tow. Shall I tell them to go away?'

Bea said, 'I'll come down.'

Maggie found a tissue and snuffled into that. 'I'll get up, too. Maybe I can help, clean the kitchen floor, fetch the dry-cleaning, get some lunch going.'

Bea patted her shoulder. 'Good for you.' She exchanged a roll of the eyes with Oliver as they went down the stairs together. Even from there they could hear raised voices in the sitting room.

Nicole was standing by the fireplace with her little dog in her arms, telling Coral to get lost. The dog was yapping.

Coral was red-faced. 'I'm not going till I've spoken to Bea.' She had an odd-looking man in tow, who looked at first sight to be wearing a navy blazer with gold buttons on it. Bea automatically thought 'ex-squadron leader', because he had swept-back grey hair and a moustache. She looked again, and saw that he wasn't wearing a blazer but a navy blue suit, and his moustache – though it existed – was minimal. A survival from an earlier age. She wondered if he really had been a squadron leader in the dim and distant, or just liked to act the part.

'Bea!' Nicole was almost spitting with rage. 'Tell this woman, and her whatever he is, that we have an engagement to—'

'Madam, I was invited here. Were you?' asked the ex-squadron leader.

'We're not moving,' said Coral in tones which would have wobbled if she hadn't been so wound up. 'Or anyway, not till Bea has heard what—'

'Oh, spare me the sob story!' said Nicole, casting up her eyes. Her little dog continued to yap, screwing everyone's nerves up a notch.

Bea told herself to stand up straight and deal with the situation. 'Nicole, I'm so sorry you've been bothered. I was going to ring you to say I couldn't make this outing, whatever it is you've so kindly arranged. As you can see, I'm up to my neck in business, but—'

Nicole tapped her little dog on the nose to stop it creating. 'You don't understand. It's taken me ages, but I've managed to set up appointments with three estate agents for you to view the properties—'

Bea injected some metal into her voice. 'Wouldn't it have been better to consult me first? I'm sorry to disappoint you, but I am not free today.' This had sounded a bit harsh. She didn't want to show Nicole up in front of Coral. Bea tried to soften her tone. 'But now you're here, Nicole, would you care for some lunch?'

The squadron leader was not enjoying this. He touched Coral's arm. 'Look, if it's not convenient to—'

Coral thrust out her jaw. 'If you're going to accept the loss of your business lying down, well, I'm not. Bea, we were right and Leo didn't get paid for the International Relief do either. He tried to go to the small claims court, but as the phone numbers and addresses the charity have given are false, he can't find anyone to sue. But if you're going to their event on Saturday night—'

Nicole allowed herself a frown. 'You don't mean the International Rescue appeal for the after-effects of the tsunami? This Saturday at Green's Hotel? What about it? I wouldn't have thought you'd be going to that. The tickets cost—'

Bea said, 'Are you going, Nicole? I thought you said you had a constituency function on this weekend and that's why you couldn't invite me over.'

Nicole reddened, shifting the dog from one arm to the other. 'I was mistaken, got the dates mixed up. Yes, we're taking a party to it. What's wrong with that?'

Bea tried not to dislike her. 'I think that we'd better sit down and bring one another up to date with what's been happening. Nicole, tell us how you got to hear about the event, will you?'

The phone had been ringing downstairs for some time, but everyone had ignored it except for Oliver, who now popped his head around the door. 'Sorry, but Mr Abbot's on the line downstairs. He tried ringing on the line up here but couldn't get any reply, and he wants to know where you are because you didn't turn up for the tour of the House that he'd arranged for you, and are you going to be there for lunch or not.'

'What?' cried Nicole. 'He didn't tell me.' She subsided, looking put out.

Bea tried to be conciliatory. 'This is getting complicated. Nicole, everyone . . . we shouldn't be discussing business up here. Let's all go down to the office and then we'll be on hand for phone calls, right? Oliver, will you give my son my excuses, say I'll ring back later? And see if Maggie's up to making us some sandwiches?'

Coral raised her eyebrows. 'We wouldn't want to be any

trouble.' Coral had been ruffled by Nicole's manner and wasn't going to make it easy for Bea.

Bea felt like smashing their heads together and only desisted because it would take too much trouble to clear up the resultant mess. 'Fine. Shall I lead the way?'

Downstairs, Nicole took the big chair – the client's chair – and set her little dog on the floor. To Bea's horror, he immediately lifted his leg against the desk. Bea opened the doors to the garden, and he shot out to bark at a squirrel who had been exploring in one of the big flowerpots.

Bea closed her eyes momentarily, told herself that the day would end at some point, that every minute that passed would never come again. Eventually she would have the house to herself in peace and quiet. She would make herself some smoked salmon sandwiches on white bread with the crusts cut off. She would take the sandwiches and a glass of chilled fruit juice to the card table in the window upstairs and, perhaps, soothe herself by learning how to play a game of patience.

Except, of course, that the table was no longer there.

'Nicole, a small mystery. Do you know what's happened to Hamilton's card table that used to be in the window upstairs?'

Nicole shrugged. 'It got moved, I suppose. Things did. Parties, and so on.'

'I'll ask Max. Leo, would you and Coral like to sit on the settee? That's lovely. Now, Nicole—'

Nicole was consulting an expensive wrist watch. 'Five minutes and I must go. I had all those meetings set up so I'll have to ring and apologize.'

'Thank you, Nicole. Now, can you tell us how you got your tickets?'

'From my cousin, of course. She's always going to charity dos. She's on the board of the local one for animals, at least I think that's the one she's on, and they tap into the corporate entertainments market, highly lucrative. She introduced us to this woman and suggested we take tickets for one of their functions. You remember my cousin, don't you?'

Bea remembered, all right. Not just a double-barrelled but a triple-barrelled name and a voice that would disgrace a corncrake. Married three times – or was it four? – heavily bejewelled, excellent alimony, which she spent on being seen at all the right places with the right kind of people. Not Coral's sort at all. Nicole might well end up with much the same sort of life.

Nicole peered over her shoulder, trying to see where her little pet had gone. 'Hamish, come here! Hamish!' Hamish paid not the slightest bit of notice. He'd seen off the squirrel and was now rooting under a bush at the bottom of the garden.

Nicole consulted her watch again. 'I really must go. You've been out of touch for so long, Bea, you don't understand how these things work. We have to dispense a certain amount of hospitality, it's expected of someone in Max's position, so these charity dos are invaluable. We take a table and fill it with our guests, everyone has a perfectly splendid time and the money goes to charity.'

'Or not, as the case seems to be,' said Bea. 'At least, I suppose they might send some money overseas eventually. The problem is that at the moment they are taking the money from the punters without paying for the wine and the food. They may not be paying the cabaret, the venue, the DJ or the people who supply party favours, either.'

Nicole shrugged that it was none of her business. She stood up and went to the window, calling, 'Hamish, we have to go now! Where are you, Hamish?'

Coral exchanged an eye roll with Bea, while the ex-squadron leader pinched at the knees of his trousers and stared ahead.

Bea said, 'Nicole, doesn't it worry you that Max might have paid for an evening out under false pretences?'

'He got his money's worth.'

The ex-squadron leader gave a little cough. Everyone looked at him, including Nicole. He continued to stare straight ahead. 'I suppose you invited lots of important people for these charity events, Members of Parliament and so on and so forth? I don't suppose they'd be very pleased if they knew the charities were fake and that you'd invited them under false pretences. I don't suppose they'd like that titbit of news to get into the papers.'

Nicole clutched at the back of her chair, breathing hard. 'What, what? I don't, you wouldn't, you couldn't! It would ruin Max!'

Bea and Coral, exchanging glances, saw that it would, indeed, hurt Max's reputation. Nicole stumbled back into her chair. She plucked at her neckline. 'No, no. Impossible. We acted from the very best motives.'

'Ignorance,' stated the ex-squadron leader, 'is no defence, in law.'

Nicole began to hyperventilate. Bea felt sorry for her. Almost. 'Calm down, dear. I'm sure we can find some way to work round it. For instance, if Max were instrumental in exposing the fraud, wouldn't your guests be grateful?'

'Hoo, hoo . . . yes, I suppose. But . . . hoo, hoo . . . how?'

'Tell us everything you know about the people who ran the function you went to before, and the one you're going to this Saturday.'

Nicole found her handbag, dug out an inhaler and used it. Was she really asthmatic? Possibly. Bea told herself that she must be kinder to her daughter-in-law.

Nicole's breathing eased. She shook back her hair, crossed her legs. Decided to cast in her lot with Coral and Leo. 'The woman who runs it is called Briggs. Hyphenated. Briggs something, or something Briggs. Very well dressed, a widow, I think. American? Or an American ex-husband? Over here because . . . I can't remember why. Son in university here?

'She'd been devastated by the news of the tsunami, wanted to do something about it, which is where my cousin came in. They'd met . . . now where did they meet? She did say. Covent Garden, some committee or other? I'm not sure. Anyway, we chatted about it, and I saw straight away that we could return a lot of hospitality by taking a table at her next function—'

'Did she suggest it, or did you?'

'She did, I think. Max agreed and we got up a table, and it was fine, except that the cabaret artist couldn't make it for some reason. But there was a darling little man who played the piano awfully well, got everyone going, and then a really good disco with a young man, a real knock-out. He was making up to one of our guests' daughters, even asked her for a date, would you believe. Luckily she was going back to the Sorbonne the following day.'

'Do you have any names for the piano player and the DJ? We really need to contact the other people who helped them, to see if they got paid or not.'

Nicole fidgeted. 'They were introduced, I suppose. Yes, I'm sure they were, but who remembers the name of somebody like that?'

'You say the DJ was making up to a girl on your table. Didn't you hear his name?'

Nicole shook her head. 'If I did, it's gone. You know what these occasions are like. So noisy. I was concentrating on our guests.' She glanced again at her watch. 'You must excuse me, the estate agents will be waiting for me, I must phone them, apologize, though what I'm going to say I don't know. And where is my naughty little poppet? He always disappears when I'm in a hurry.'

Bea nodded at Oliver, who'd been hovering in the doorway. 'Oliver, do you think you could phone the estate agents, if Nicole gives you the numbers? Apologize, say the prospective buyer is staying where she is.'

'Oh yes, much better if you do it,' said Nicole, delving into an enormous bag for the estate agents' details.

Bea stood up to ease her back and knocked the waste-paper bin over. A used condom spilled on to the floor in a pile of junk mail. Ah. So Maggie had brought her handsome boy into this room last night? Tacky. Bea made a mental note to see that her office was locked up every night in future.

She tried to think straight. 'Now who's going to tackle what? Leo, could you write down everything you know about these people, what names they used, their phone numbers, addresses, everything? And compare your list with Coral's? Nicole, let's you and me go to look for Hamish, and think who we know who might help us.'

'Lunch, anyone?' Maggie appeared in the doorway with a tray of sandwiches and iced fruit drinks. She was wearing Bea's skirt and a long-sleeved blouse to hide her bruises. And oversized dark glasses. She'd tied her bright hair back and altogether looked most unlike her usual self.

'Splendid,' said Bea. 'Thanks, Maggie. Let's all help ourselves and then get down to work. We'll pool what we know in an hour, say? And Oliver, any ideas that may occur to you . . .? Absolutely splendid.'

Bea thought she was beginning to sound like an infant-school teacher. 'Always praise, never blame.' Well, if they would act like children, why not? She wondered whether she would ever again feel emotion. She couldn't remember feeling anything much since Hamilton died. She was going through the motions of this absurd enquiry to pass the time, really. She didn't really

care about it. She wondered how many long years of life she
had left to her.

Friday, noon
Noel picked up a copy of the Metro *freebie on the Tube, and*
glanced through it, yawning. It had been a good night as far
as he was concerned. Maggie hadn't been particularly gifted
in the art of pleasing a man, but she'd put up a pretty show
of reluctance, which always spurred him on. And on.

He smiled. And then stopped smiling, because on one of the
inner pages there was a news item about Shirl, an earlier . . .
er . . . problem. A man was being questioned about her death.

Noel had thought Shirl's death would have been passed off
as accidental. He'd only banged her head against the tree a
couple of times to make her stand still, and had been really
surprised when she'd gone all floppy on him.

Well, so long as it wasn't him who was being questioned.
He shrugged, turned to the sports section.

Eleven

Friday, afternoon

B ea went out into the garden with Nicole to retrieve one
dirty but happy small dog, minus tartan bow, from the
undergrowth. Nicole washed him in the kitchen sink while Bea
made them some herbal tea – so much more digestible than
coffee – which they took outside to sit under the tree. Bea half-
closed her eyes while Nicole droned on about the difficulties
of being an MP's wife.

Finally, Bea shook herself into action, and asked Nicole to
ring her cousin and find out what she knew about this Mrs
Briggs-whatsit.

Nicole grimaced but did as she was bid, handing the phone
over to Bea.

Nicole's cousin had one of those penetrating voices you

could hear even on the Tube. 'You want to know about Mrs Somers-Briggs? She's very well-connected, pots of money, has lived abroad for some time, America, diplomatic service, something like that, but returned to England without her husband who seems tragically to have disappeared somewhere en route. Not divorced, something to do with an upset in a South American country – not Peru, dear, at least I don't think it was Peru. Did I hear Brazil? Yes, probably.

'Anyway, plenty of money in the background. Mrs Somers-Briggs is looking for a base in Kensington at the moment, while staying in some friend's flat somewhere down near the river . . . the address? I should have it somewhere, but it will be out of date, because she's moving this weekend – or was it last weekend? Into a rented flat. I think she said it was in Dolphin Square. Really it's best to phone her if you want any more tickets . . . a phone number? Yes, I think so, wait a minute, I'll see if I can lay my hands on it. It's a mobile number, of course.'

'I have that,' said Bea. 'Does she organize these functions by herself?'

'No, no. Far too much for one person to do. She has some kind of helper, not exactly our type but useful, you know? And her son, or maybe it's her nephew, who helps out. That's how we came to meet. He knew my godson from somewhere, the one who's gone into the Foreign Office. Such an asset at parties, my dear. Can always be relied on to spend time with the girls who aren't perhaps quite as pretty as they might be.'

Bea said, 'Didn't he ask one of the girls in your party out?'

'The DJ did, but she's seeing one of a friend's boys, merchant banker in the City, so she wasn't interested.'

'This is the son or nephew?'

'Now you're confusing me. Wasn't it the DJ? Or maybe not. Nice-looking lad, from her first marriage, of course. That's why the name is different. Charming, totally charming. What's so nice about him is that he throws himself into making his mother's charity evenings work. And always so protective of her, which comes from his losing his father so early, I suppose.'

'What's his name?'

'My dear, I haven't the slightest. What I do know is that they all work themselves ragged to make these affairs successful, no expense spared. I got my husband to take a table at their last function, and we would be going to this next one if we hadn't got tickets to Glyndebourne, yes, it is a pity, isn't it! But I told my husband that if we couldn't go, we should still send them the cost of the tickets and he's spread the word through the office and at the golf club so they'll be capacity, I should think. Are you going, then? I'm sure you'll enjoy it.'

Bea handed the phone back to Nicole, who was not a happy bunny. 'I ought to have warned her, oughtn't I, if her husband's got all those extra people to buy tickets. What is Max going to say? He'll kill me!'

'No, he won't,' said Bea, thinking how unlikely it was that Max would turn on his wife. The other way round, now? Bea pulled her thoughts back from that one.

'Nicole, you've done nothing wrong. In fact, you're doing your best to help him. Let's see if we can get a clearer idea of what these people are like and how they operate before we tell anyone. We don't want to start a panic and have people cancel their plans to attend on Saturday. If we don't have their address and they're only using mobile phones, we've no means of tracing them until they turn up at the function. That's when we nab them.'

Nicole frowned and used her fingers to smooth her forehead. 'Do you know, I think she was introduced to me by another name, but I can't think what it was. Somers? Saunders? It might have been her first husband's name, and she could have added the Briggs later on. As one does.'

'Briggs might have been her maiden name, or perhaps her first or second husband's name. I wonder what the boy's name is. Can you ask your cousin what name she knows him by?'

Nicole rang her cousin back, but the answerphone was on. Nicole left a message, and switched the phone off. She said, 'It's Friday afternoon. She'll be at the hairdresser's, getting ready for her trip to Glyndebourne tomorrow. I wonder if they can fit me in, too, since I'm not spending the afternoon on the South Coast. I really must have something done about my nails.' She rose to go.

For the first time Bea kissed her daughter-in-law with warmth. 'You've been great about this, Nicole. You'll let us know if you hear from your cousin, and we'll let you know how we get on, right?'

'To tell the truth,' said Nicole, 'I'm half thinking it would be best to tell Max what we suspect and get him to cancel, even at this late stage.'

'And disappoint your guests?'

Nicole was perturbed enough to let emotion show on her face. 'Can you promise me you won't make a scene at the hotel?'

'What would be the point? The guests pay for their tickets and get good value in return. It's the suppliers and the charities that get stung. We need to trace these people and then, bang! Get them to pay what they owe.'

Nicole wailed, 'Yes, but how are you going to do that?'

'I'll think of something.'

Nicole wafted herself away with her little dog yapping away under her arm.

Down in the office there was confusion. Coral was sulking, the ex-squadron leader was pontificating in a loud voice while Oliver was crouched over the phone, trying to listen to what a caller was saying. Maggie had seated herself in a corner with a notepad on her knee. She was still wearing her dark glasses, and every now and then she blew her nose into a tissue.

Bea forced her back to straighten. 'Now, then; where were we?'

Oliver put the phone down and said, 'That was Mrs Westin again. I think it's Westin, rather than Weston. She's insistent you call her back.'

'What else?'

'I've been trying to find out if the Garden Room got paid for the first charity function, but all they'll say is "no comment". As for the Country Club, the manager's out but I got some girl on the phone who says they insist on a deposit two months before the event, and that's all she will say. I suspect they got a deposit but the cheque for the balance bounced. I think it's as you said, Mrs Abbot; they spend some money in order to rake in the rest.'

The squadron leader cut through Oliver's report. 'Dear lady, this is not helping me to get my money back. I can see nothing for it. I shall have to sell my Rover, my faithful friend. It would almost cover my losses.'

'We haven't exhausted all the possibilities yet, Leo,' said

Bea, gently pushing Oliver away from her desk so she could sit down. 'Coral, any news of your daughter?'

'They're sending her home this afternoon. They want her to keep quiet for another seven days until the baby's officially due. Jake's fetching her and I'll take some supper over later.'

'That's good.' She had been going to ask Maggie to take notes, but although the girl was physically present, mentally she seemed lost in misery, staring vacantly into space. 'Oliver, will you take notes, please? I'll recap what we know and if anyone else can add to it, or thinks they know something different, then they must speak up. I'll start.

'Some months ago a woman appeared on the London social scene, calling herself Somers, or Briggs or Somers-Briggs, twice married, husbands both mislaid, plenty of money, wanting to do something for charity. Her introduction into society is eased by a son or nephew, who's been mixing with the young moneyed crowd and has lots of useful contacts. Her real name might be just Somers, or Briggs, or something else entirely. Anyone heard her first name?'

Coral said, hesitantly, 'Helen, or Helena. Ellen?'

'Lena,' said the squadron leader.

Bea checked to see that Oliver had got all this down. 'She mixed in the best society, was seen in all the right places, got her name out and about as a charity fund-raiser. No known means of support. Moving from one address to another, possibly now renting a flat down near the river. Oliver, what have you got on her?'

'The function room for this weekend is booked in the name of a Mrs Amanda Briggs. This time the charity's name is The International Emergency Fund for Aid to the Far East. Mobile phone number only. Nobody seems to have any publicity material left. I asked. The only contact address they have is that of the shop.'

'It's interesting that they keep on using that address,' said Bea, 'because they've been so careful about everything else. I wonder if there's a reason for it. Ideas, anyone?'

They all shook their heads, except for Maggie, who didn't appear to be listening. 'So,' said Bea. 'Back to Mrs Briggs. Let's try to get a picture of her. Coral?'

'Nice looking without being a beauty. Late forties, though she tries to look younger. Speaks well, British accent, upper class rather than middle. Good figure, expensive tan. I thought at first that her hair was dyed blonde, but it might have been a wig. She wore long black both times and diamonds, the real thing.'

'All right, Oliver?' Oliver nodded.

Bea said, 'Now for the son or nephew, who I suppose must be in his early twenties. He might be called Somers, or Briggs or something quite different. Coral, you mentioned a DJ who circulated among the guests and made a pass at one of the guests. Nicole also mentioned him. Was it the same man both times? How did he react with Mrs Briggs? Did you hear his name?'

Coral put a finger to her cheek. 'There was a DJ, right enough, a real heart-breaker. Good value for money, worked the crowd well. She must be much older than she looks, if he's her son. And then there's the pianist, of course.'

'Pianist?' Bea checked herself. 'No, let's finish with the DJ first. Do we have a name for him?'

Coral hesitated. 'I think he called himself "The Don" when he was acting DJ. He introduced the records in the third person, "The Don likes this one because . . .", "The Don says he's giving this one a twirl . . ." That sort of thing.'

The squadron leader agreed. 'The Don, yes. Stage name.'

'Description?' said Bea.

'Tall, dark and handsome,' said Coral. 'Wonderful teeth, expensive casual clothes. Works out. Possibly a gym freak. Very sure of himself and of his appeal to women.'

'Squadron . . . sorry, I mean, Leo? What did you think of him?'

He blinked. 'I don't use that title nowadays, Mrs Abbot. Occurs to me, had a lad like that up before me once. Beaten someone to pulp, argument over a girl. Seemed to me he thought himself above the law. Nasty piece of work.'

Bea's eyes switched to Maggie, who was fingering her mobile phone and staring into space. Was she listening? Did she see the similarity? At least her date hadn't beaten her to a pulp.

Coral was tapping her cheek. 'That pianist, now. Not what you'd call classy, was he, Leo? Not like her. She was classy, all right. But could he play the old Joanna! He reminded me of my husband's mate who used to play all night long Fridays and Saturdays down at the old Red Lion. Never used sheet music. You set up the drinks for him on top of the piano, and he was off. We don't see his like nowadays.'

'Was the pianist there both times?'

'Yes, he was. I don't know how to describe him, exactly. I mean, he was more than just hired help, because he acted as MC and ran the auction, as well as playing the piano in the cabaret. He knew Mrs Briggs but they weren't lovey-dovey. More like,' she lifted her shoulders and let them drop, 'I can't describe it.'

Leo crossed one leg over the other and gave his trousers a little pinch at the knee. 'My guess is he used to be a turn at an end-of-the-pier entertainment.'

'Y-yes,' said Coral. 'He was a bit more than that, because his eyes were everywhere and when one of my girls dropped something, he was on to it quicker than I was.'

Bea wondered, 'My information is that Mrs Somers-Briggs has a partner or aide. Was this man part of her team, do you think?'

Coral nodded. 'Could be.'

Leo patted his own slender figure. 'He was fifty-ish, older than her. Putting on weight, ought to watch it. Balding but still enough dark hair to go round. Looked good-natured, but nobody's fool. His evening dress was off the peg.'

Coral agreed. 'He's the type you'd see in the pub and he might try to chat you up, but he'd stop if you told him not to.'

'Name?'

Coral and Leo exchanged glances. 'Richard? Rickie?'

'Don't think I ever heard.'

Bea made eye contact with Oliver, who was scribbling away, biting on his lower lip. 'I think we can make the following assumption; the team consists of three people, two major players and one minor. Mrs Somers-Briggs appears to be the moving spirit with this older man as her aide, and her son or nephew who acts as DJ. Now, is anyone else involved, do you think? What about the cabaret?'

Coral and Leo shook their heads. 'A different man on each occasion. They scrounged food and drink off us, chatted a bit, didn't have anything much to say to Mrs Briggs or whatever her name is. The pianist looked after them, saw the mike was switched on and at the right height, that sort of thing. The singers brought their own ghetto blasters with backing tracks.'

'Do we know their names? Can we contact them, find out if they got paid? Or indeed, if they have an address for the team?'

Leo shook his head. 'I don't think I exchanged more than a couple of words with the man. I was busy at the bar.'

Coral was trying to remember. 'Was one of them called The Mad Hopper, or maybe it was Bopper? They both had stage names. I didn't take much notice, too much going on.'

Bea tapped her teeth with her pen. How could they find out?

Leo smoothed his hands over his knees. 'What I think is, they've been very careful but they've made one mistake which you, Mrs Abbot, have spotted, and that is in keeping the same accommodation address throughout. I vote to stake it out. We know they're still using it, so one of them must visit it every day to pick up the mail. I hang around, I spot one of them, I follow him, see where he goes. Right?'

'There were people going in and out of that shop all the time I was there, weren't there, Maggie?' Maggie was gazing into space and didn't reply. 'What's more, it's residents' parking only.'

'I have my trusty steed,' said Leo. 'My velocipede.'

Bea blinked, mentally picturing him on an ancient motorbike, wearing flying goggles and leather gauntlets. And a helmet. Did he really go out dressed like that?

'Suppose he's on foot?' said Oliver. 'It's more likely, isn't it? Around here most people walk, there's plenty of buses, the Tube's not far away. If they did choose that shop for a reason, then my guess is that they live nearby.'

'They ought,' said Leo, severely, 'to have found another accommodation address for each event.'

'Granted,' said Bea, hiding a smile, 'but maybe Oliver's right. They think they've covered their tracks, they don't know we're hunting for them, and they've kept that place on because it's close to where they live.'

Satisfied, Leo nodded. 'I'll get on to it, then.'

'Wait a minute,' said Bea. 'If they spot you, they'll know you're on to them. And then what? Do you try to make a citizen's arrest? The rest of the gang would disappear and we'd be left no better off. Do you have a camera? If you do spot one of them, do you think you could take a photo? But only if you can do it without their realizing.'

'Point taken, dear lady. The last thing we want is for them to disappear before we've got them where we want them. I'll buy a disposable camera. If I see them, I'll go snap, snap! And then follow them, right?'

Coral said, 'Aren't they supposed to be living somewhere down near the river?'

Bea shook her head. '*Supposed* to be isn't the same as actually doing it. Can we believe a word they say? The shop accepted our letter with a cheque in it yesterday, and why not? From their point of view, the more the merrier. Let's recap . . . yes, Maggie, what is it?'

Maggie was playing with a tissue. 'I was thinking about food for the weekend. We need to get some in. Could you spare me some cash?'

Their concentration had been broken. The phone rang again in reception. Presumably the answerphone was taking messages. Had it rung before? Perhaps it had. 'Yes, of course.' Bea dipped into her purse. 'Remember some of us are going to the function tomorrow evening, so will eat there.' Maggie took the money and left.

Coral eased herself off her chair. 'About tomorrow. I don't think I'd better come with you. The moment they see me in your party, they'll take fright.'

'We need you there. It's only you and Leo who can identify them.'

Coral persisted. 'Do we know who's doing the catering tomorrow? Is it the hotel?' She leaned over to look at their notes.

Bea found the reference first. 'A company calling themselves A Passion for Food is doing it. I've got the address and phone number. The hotel people said it was a small concern, just starting out.'

'Poor things,' said Coral. 'I hope they know what they're doing.'

Bea rubbed her forehead. 'Do you think we should warn them?'

Coral shook her head. 'They may cancel at the last minute, and then the villains might take fright and scarper. Can we risk that? No, what I was thinking was that I'm pretty well known in the trade. If I can get hold of these people, I might be able to talk my way in as an extra waitress for the night. Then I can tip you the wink if I spot them.'

'What if Mrs Briggs spots you?'

'That sort don't look at the paid help. Give me the number of these people who are passionate about food, and I'll see what I can do.'

'So who's going to go as guests?' asked Oliver.

The phone rang again. Bea ignored it to count on her fingers. 'Me. You to take pictures in case Leo doesn't get lucky. Piers, if he troubles to surface again. That leaves one spare. We'll take Maggie. Cheer her up.'

Coral was getting ready to leave so Leo stood, smoothing his moustache to left and right. 'That's all very well, but supposing we do get to confront them. Has anyone the slightest idea what we do next?'

They all looked at Bea, who stared back. Well, what were they going to do?

She hadn't a clue. If they couldn't go to the police – and they couldn't because of Coral's problem with the wages – then what could they do? 'I'm working on it,' said Bea.

'The phone, Mrs Abbot,' said Maggie, popping her head back through the door. 'Mr Max has left two messages, also Mrs Winson – or whatever her name is – and they both asked you to ring back.'

The front doorbell rang. And rang. There was a general exodus from the office. Bea said, 'I'll take it,' to no one in particular, and climbed the stairs to the hall.

She opened the front door and said, 'You stole the photograph, didn't you?'

Piers slid into the hall, and shut the door behind him. 'You guessed why? I cadged a corner of a studio from a friend and started straight away, worked most of the night, bar a couple of hours when I dossed down on his couch. Got to have a break now or I'll go crazy, but it's coming on.'

Anger had replaced her first feeling of loss. 'Did it occur to you that I might not want Hamilton done in oils?'

'Pastels, dear. Not oils.'

She shrieked, 'Pastels? How cheap!'

He was laughing, steering her into the sitting room. 'Come off it, ducky. Oils it is. It's a gift so once it's done, you can smash it up and burn it if you like. Although I'd have you know that my portraits command a very respectable price these days.'

'Yes. No. I'm sorry. No, I'm not!' She clenched her fists and closed her eyes. 'I'm so angry I don't know what to, how to . . . I thought I loved him mildly, as a friend, but it seems I loved him wildly as well.'

Piers investigated the side table. 'Shall I open a bottle?'

'The photograph going missing, that almost did me in. Why didn't you tell me? I couldn't think what had happened to it. His table's gone missing, too, that he always used to sit at and play patience, and I've still got his clothes to sort out.'

'There's a good-looking antique table in the shed in the garden. I spotted it when we were hunting for Oliver. Would that be it?'

'The damp! Cobwebs! How dare Max put it there!'

'I expect they needed the space for entertaining.' He pressed a glass of something into her hand and guided her on to a chair. 'Sit down, drink up, and relax. I suppose you've been letting Coral wind you up.'

'I could scream!'

'All right then, scream.'

She took a sip from the glass. Brandy. She set it down. 'No, thanks. I'd rather have coffee. No, I wouldn't. I'm not sleeping properly, and coffee only makes it worse. What have I got myself into, Piers? I've said I'd try to help these poor people, but I haven't a clue how. Even if we find out where they live, what can we do? Camp out on their doorstep, begging for the money? The police would move us on. Coral can't take her case to the police because her son-in-law fiddled the books, and as for the squadron leader—'

'The what?'

Bea was overwrought. 'Don't try to make fun of him. He may be an anachronism but he's lost a packet, too. He went to the small claims court, but without a genuine name and address to give for them, he didn't get anywhere and neither will we. We've hardly any proof of their existence, even.'

'Then get some, ducky. If they've done it before—'

'Twice that we know of.'

'—then they must have left a paper trail somewhere.'

'The squadron leader is all for staking out their accommodation address but hundreds of people go through that shop every day. Even if he did recognize someone and follow them, he'd be spotted, for sure. He doesn't exactly blend into the background.'

The phone rang at her elbow. She glared at it and turned her head away. 'I've had enough. I want out. Out of here and out of everything.' That came out as a whisper.

Piers picked up the phone. 'The Abbot residence . . . Well, hello, Max. Yes, it's me, propping up your mama, who is in dire need of support at the moment. She's worried about Coral. I'm going to advise her that Coral sues you personally for her money since—' He clapped his hand over the telephone while Max went ballistic at the other end. At length, 'Yes, but you must admit it's a reasonable solution, Max. No doubt you are covered by insurance, and obviously your mother can't be expected to pay . . . yes, I daresay it would be a tidy sum and no, I don't suppose the Party would be best pleased if you were dragged into a dispute but . . . well, yes, you might have to settle out of court if—'

Max slammed the phone down, and Piers cradled the handset, laughing.

Bea was forced to laugh, too. 'Now, now, Piers. Don't wind him up. I suppose Coral could make out some kind of claim on us, though she wouldn't.' Or would she? If the worst came to the worst, she just might. 'Well,' she said, 'whether Coral could or couldn't, the squadron leader can't because he wasn't introduced through Max.' A thought struck her. 'I wonder. We used to find clowns and magicians for children's entertainments in the old days, using a theatrical agency in Soho. I wonder if Max asked them to supply singers for those two functions.' She hesitated, wondering whether to ring Max back. 'I'd better go downstairs and see if Oliver can trace them.'

Piers wriggled his wrist. 'I'll need some help getting your table back up, so let me have first crack at Oliver. Then, duty done, it's back to work. I think you'll be pleased with the portrait when it's done. It's the best I can do to make up for his loss.'

'I reserve judgment. Oh, and you'd better get your dinner jacket ready for tomorrow night. You're squiring me to the ball, remember?'

Friday, early evening
He was – just slightly – put out. In his experience, girls never ignored his phone calls and text messages. Of course, he had to admit that Maggie was different from the type he usually

went for. Sexually practically a virgin, which was also unusual. Apparently her ex-husband had been unable to rouse her in bed. What a prick!

He'd even considered that he might do worse than get serious about this one. He'd phoned and left a dozen messages. Texted her again and again. No reply. Odd. Girls were usually hanging on to the phone waiting for him to ring.

Like the little slag of a receptionist. Like Shirl. Like, well, others.

Still no reply. Perhaps her battery had run down. He'd have to phone the house if she didn't get back to him soon. He'd been thinking about her all day. Unusual for him. Perhaps it was because she was so childlike? Expected nothing from him? Yet her body had excited him as few others had done.

Abbot. Kensington. He knew the road. He could find her, no sweat. He wasn't planning to see anyone else that evening. And definitely not the little receptionist whose calls and texts he'd been deleting all day.

Twelve

Friday, evening

Bea put aside all her worries in order to restore her table – Hamilton's table – back to its original glory. Luckily Max had thought to swathe it in some plastic sheeting before stowing it in the shed. True, once Piers and Oliver had manoeuvred it up the stairs into the sitting room, it did take up a bit of space by the windows, but it was an elegant piece and anyway, it was only in high summer that it was warm enough to leave the French windows open.

A slurp of vinegar in a bowl, some warm water, a soft cloth. Greasy finger marks and dust disappeared. Another soft cloth, and the surface burnished up nicely. The high-backed chair that Hamilton had been accustomed to use was too low for Bea, but one from the dining-table was just right.

She slid the top of the table round and discovered several packs of playing cards inside, including two packs of patience cards, with an instruction booklet. Hamilton had got through a double pack every six months. She'd bought them from Harrods for him; one at Christmas, and one for his birthday in June. The last pack hadn't even been opened.

She pushed the tabletop back into position and opened it up. She tore the wrapper off the virgin double pack of cards, and checked that they were all there. She replaced one pack back in its box, and shuffled the other. Hamilton could do this with a flick of his wrists. Shrrrrrim. She couldn't do it as quickly as him, but she didn't do badly, either.

As a beginner, she used only one pack of cards in an easy game. She dealt out the cards, face down, in the Clock patience. One o'clock, two o'clock, rock. Right round to the queens at twelve o'clock. Four times. Then four cards face down in the middle in the king's space. Turn the last card of the middle pile face up. A two. Slip the two under the cards at two o'clock, take the top card off that pile. A queen. Tuck that under the pile at twelve o'clock, take the top card off that pile and put that under the pile at nine o'clock. Here we go round the mulberry bush. King. Eight. Two. Ace. Three kings were up. If a fourth one came up, the game would be over. We're nearly there. Bother. Four kings up and a lot of cards still face down. The game was over but hadn't worked out.

She shuffled, and stirred the cards, face down. Dealt again.

Hamilton hadn't played the Clock patience. He'd liked several double patience games, all of which looked complicated. She wouldn't attempt one of those. Two kings came up quickly. She slipped cards under and moved them around the clock. Four kings came face up before half the cards had been revealed. Finish.

Hamilton had played patience a lot when he was stressed. He'd said it calmed him down, let his subconscious deal with the problem while his hands moved the cards around. She dealt again. One king came up straight away.

Some people were superstitious about cards, thinking that the queen of spades meant death. There was the queen of spades, not quite smiling up at her from the table. Bea swept the cards to one side and leant on her arms, looking out over the garden to the tree beyond, and beyond the tree to the sky which was clouding over, and the spire of the church. Up in the sky some birds were circling. She didn't know what they were. House martins, perhaps? Perhaps she should set up a bird table and get a book to learn the difference between a sparrow and a starling.

Playing patience hadn't done anything for her. It had been a waste of time and energy. What she needed to do was make a list, build a folio of facts, a pile of presentations. Why, she'd really no idea how much money these con men had managed to accumulate so far, or how long they'd been doing it, either.

Oliver had managed to trace a few names of people and organizations who'd been used by the con men, but as for evidence . . . forget it! She'd been all woolly and sympathetic and not at all businesslike, and did that get you anywhere? No.

Where was Oliver, anyway? And was Maggie fit for work yet?

The afternoon was clouding over so Bea went to shut the French windows, noting that Maggie – really the girl was too thin for perfect health – was watering the tubs below. Bea told herself that Maggie was coping all right, wasn't she? And then thought that if it had been her who'd been abused like that, she wouldn't be out watering the garden, but be tucked up in bed, crying. Bea had to admire the girl's grit. She went down the steps to talk to her. 'How are you feeling? You ought to take it easy today.'

Maggie held up her mobile phone. 'He won't take "no" for an answer. Wants to see me this evening. I don't know what to do.'

Bea was brisk. 'It's your call, love. Tell him "yes", tell him "no". Get on with your life.'

'He doesn't frighten me. Not really. I mean, it would be silly to let him scare me, wouldn't it?'

Bea sat on irritation. 'Then text him "no".'

'I did, first thing this morning. He's tried to get through to me umpteen times since, and sent me lots of texts. I keep texting him to get lost and he takes no notice. He knows where I live because I brought him back here last night. I said, sort of implied, that you were my aunt and now he thinks . . . I don't know what he thinks.'

Bea set her teeth. 'Swap phones with me. I'll put a flea in his ear, if that's what you want.'

The girl was not far from angry tears. 'Would you? You've been pretty good to me, all things considered, and I know I'm hopeless in the office and you've no need of me there, and I'm not afraid of him, I'm not. But what will happen if he comes to the door here?'

So she *was* afraid of him? Bea was brisk. 'He won't, not after the earful I intend to give him. If he does, we call the police, right? Because that's stalking.'

'Oh. Yes, I suppose it is.' Maggie passed her phone over to Bea. 'I suppose when you're old, nothing upsets you, does it?'

Doesn't it? thought Bea, suppressing a desire to hit the child. The phone felt slightly sticky. Yuk. She put on her glasses. 'Now, how does this phone work? Oh yes. I see. Maggie, will you go and put the kettle on, there's a dear? Herbal tea for me, not coffee.'

Maggie disappeared and Bea walked around the garden, composing a text. Something off-putting was required. Something to make the man feel small but not to humiliate. Voicemail might be easier for what she had to say. The phone vibrated in her hand, and another text message appeared.

Bea grimaced. The young had no sense of decency, had they? So he'd enjoyed Maggie's body and wanted a repeat? Had he no idea what he'd done to Maggie, was doing to her?

She returned his last voicemail call. An eager voice said, 'At last! What have you been—?'

Bea broke in. 'Young man, I don't know you and you don't know me, but this is Maggie's aunt speaking. She borrowed my phone last night, so I've been getting all her messages this afternoon, which is rather annoying. I understand you'd like to see her again, but she tells me it was just a one-night stand as far as she was concerned, and she's not interested.' Bea killed the call over his protest.

There. Done. The phone upstairs was ringing now. Someone was leaving a message. Bother. She thought it might rain and the French windows were still open, so she climbed the stairs and pulled the windows shut. The caller hadn't left a message, which was fortune as Bea didn't feel up to civil chit-chat.

She went down the stairs to her office. Oliver was clattering away at his computer in the middle office, so she called out to him to join her.

'Oliver, we have to get ourselves organized. We need to get

statements from all the people who've been conned out of money. Let's make a list and divide it up. The first two venues, for a start.'

'I've tried ringing the managers but they'll neither confirm nor deny that there's a problem.'

'If they'd been paid what was due, they'd not be cagey but quite open about it. Probably boast that they'd never been caught. Give me their names and addresses and I'll go to see them.'

Oliver extracted a couple of sheets of paper and handed them over. Bea put on her glasses and saw that she'd have to use the car to reach them. 'Fine. Now when Coral gets back to us, ask her to write us an invoice for each of the functions she catered for. A detailed one. Tell her we're not taking it to the police, but we do need to know exactly what she's owed. The same for the squadron lea— for Leo. Got that?'

He nodded. He was proving to be an excellent PA. Bea reminded herself that he was still very young and shouldn't, perhaps, be pushed too hard. All work and no play, etcetera. She said, 'Have you heard from your father yet?'

He shook his head, eyes on his notebook.

'Well, if you don't hear by tomorrow we'll write him a letter suggesting a meeting. Perhaps you'd like to draft one while I'm out? Now, I'd like to get a line on the singers who appeared at the Garden Room and the Country Club. In the old days we used to recommend entertainers from a theatrical agency called Stars Unlimited, in Soho. Can you trace any recent recommendations from them? In other words, did Max give their name to Mrs Briggs, and if so, did they supply the singers? And if so—'

'Did they get paid? I'm on to it.'

'You're something of a star yourself, Oliver. I hope I'm not giving you too much to do.'

'I like it. It's like a hunt, better than a computer game.'

'It's not a game.'

'No, I know that.' He glanced at the door. 'What happened to Maggie's not a game, either. He ought to be shot.'

'No fisticuffs, please.'

He tried on a grin. 'I wouldn't be much good at that, anyway, would I?'

'No karate skills?'

'I wish. Maybe I'll take lessons, sometime.'

Bea nodded, smiling, dismissing him. Thinking that if he didn't grow another couple of inches, it might indeed be a good idea for him to take some form of self-defence classes.

She gathered up her papers and looked down to see if she was wearing sufficiently business-like attire. She wasn't. She hurried up the stairs, checking the time by her watch, slid into a silky suit in palest grey-green, checked that her make-up looked reasonably intact, found her car keys and some of the agency business cards, and set off for, what was first on the list? The Garden Room.

The Garden Room was a huge conservatory added on to the side of a busy arterial road pub. There were hanging baskets around the perimeter, a fair number of vehicles in the car park, and a general air of prosperity. Bea noted that there was no litter wafting about the place, and passed through double doors into the bar. There were a number of customers inside, and through a glass door at the back she could see more sitting at tables on the patio outside. A board advertised the menu. There was also a sign pointing to the Garden Room, asking that customers be appropriately dressed.

At Bea's request, the barman produced the manager, a solid-looking individual with enormous hands and watchful brown eyes. A toughie, who'd know how to care for his beer. 'Tommy Banks,' he said, introducing himself. 'How may I help you?'

Bea said, 'I may be interested in hiring your function room for a party. Would it be possible for me to see it?'

He led her through double doors into the room beyond. There were pretty blinds at the window, bamboo furniture, glass-topped tables. Everything was sparklingly clean. There was a small stage at one end and a second bar, currently shut off behind a grille. It would be a pleasant place for functions, seating about 150 people.

That day about half the room had been screened off, and Bea could see the tables had been laid out for a birthday party with balloons and favours beside each plate. The sun was setting but it had been a warm day and shades had been drawn over the windows in the roof. Bea approved the place. She also took a liking to the manager, who showed her to a seat and asked if she'd care for a drink.

She declined, not wanting to mislead him about the reason for her visit. 'I may well be interested in a venue for a party later on, but just at present,' and here she laid a business card on the table, 'I'm looking for information about a charity function run by a Mrs Somers-Briggs.'

The manager's vast hands clasped together, though his facial expression never altered. 'I told your man on the phone, No Comment.'

Bea persisted. 'We know that she ran a function here some weeks ago. The caterer got paid with bum cheques, but foolishly believed their assurances that it was all a mistake, and went on to cater for an even bigger event at the Priory Country Club. She got a bum cheque for that, too.'

Did his eyelids flicker? Bea went on. 'You may remember her, Coral Catering?'

'She did a good job. I said I'd recommend her for other functions in future.'

'She hasn't got a future,' said Bea, in a flat voice, 'unless we can help her to get her money back. She's relying on us to do something because the introduction came through our agency . . .' She explained how she'd come to take an interest in the matter, and what she'd learned so far. 'We are currently trying to compile a list of what everyone is owed. I wondered if you'd like to come in on this.'

His eyelids flickered again. 'The management says, "No comment."'

Definitely, they'd been stung. Bea considered her options. 'Do I take it that the management doesn't wish to go to the police in the hypothetical case that they have made a loss on this event?'

'The brewery runs a tight ship. The manager, in such a case, might well expect to lose his job.'

'Ah. Still talking hypothetically, would the manager be prepared to give me a quote for a similar function? This would give me some idea of how much you are – correction – you *might* have been out of pocket.'

He nodded. 'I could give you a quote for the function you are thinking of staging, yes.'

'Also, hypothetically, could you confirm how you might first have heard of a team similar to the one we're talking about?'

'She – Mrs Briggs – had been having a drink in the garden,

noticed we did functions, asked if she could book one herself, for victims of the tsunami. Talked a lot about how much good it would do the pub if we went into raising money for such causes in a big way. We've always held the odd evening for charity, quizzes and the like, but yes, this would be a step up-market. She gave me a brochure for a similar event that she'd run out of town and it looked OK. Lots of well-known names on it. The cheque for the deposit arrived late but it cleared OK, no cause for worry. The cheque for the rest bounced and, as you say, the charity doesn't exist.'

'A familiar story. What did the team look like?'

Mr Banks gazed over her head. 'A rich bitch with a salon haircut and a smart-ass accent. A trendy youngish man acting as DJ; he was first-class. Then there was the photographer, her son or gigolo, can't be sure which; film-star looks, had the girls swooning for him. And a sidekick, MC and auctioneer, who was a barrel of laughs, and a talented barroom piano player, probably from the East End.'

'That's them,' said Bea. 'So there are two young men involved? I thought there was only one. You haven't a photograph, have you?'

He went back into the main bar, and returned with a photograph of himself and a buxom woman – his wife? – on either side of a slender Asian girl with large dark eyes, wearing the headscarf and trouser suit of Pakistan.

'I suppose the girl was in on it. She gave a spiel about how she'd lost her whole family in the disaster, a real tear-jerker. The organizer suggested we get photographed with her rather than with them. We thought they were being modest. We paid fifteen quid for the photo and that's all we've got to show for it.'

'What was the girl's name? Do you know where we can find her?'

He shook his head. 'It wasn't a name I'd remember, went in one ear and out the other.'

Maybe they could track her down through the photographer. Bea turned the print over to look for the photographer's label, but there wasn't one.

'I thought of looking him up, too,' said Mr Banks. 'But it was one of those Polaroid cameras that spits out the print straight away. I thought it was a bit amateur because professional photographers have digital cameras nowadays, but he said it was easier and quicker with a Polaroid. He took the photos, showed us the print, we paid him cash there and then. He said it was a good way of dealing with it, saving all that bother of ordering prints later on, and I agreed with him. Of course it also saved him from giving us a name and address.'

'They think of everything, don't they?' said Bea.

'I'm not sure how much the girl was involved, because she didn't go off with the others at the end, but had a hire car come for her. The driver came into the bar and said he'd come for the Asian girl, I went and got her from the function room, and she went off with him and that was that. I don't remember which cab firm it was. An Asian driver, that's all I can tell you. But then, they're mostly Asians who drive for the cab companies around here.'

'Clever,' said Bea. 'So, no photo of them, no evidence. What about the singer?'

'The real thing didn't show up. A lookalike came, stand in, what have you. Stupid name, Mad Man? No, not that, but something like that. A rapper. Not bad, if you like that sort of thing. He went down all right with the crowd.'

'Was he part of the team?'

He thought about that. 'No. In fact, there was a bit of a barney in the car park at the end of the evening. Him and the auctioneer, the one that played the piano. I know because I had to sort it out.'

'The rapper didn't get paid?'

'He said he was supposed to get cash at the end of the evening, and they put him off with a cheque. He didn't want a cheque. He was almost weeping. I thought maybe he'd needed cash to get drugs and that's why he was so upset.'

'What cars did they drive?'

'The rapper? A white transit van, five years old. The DJ had his own van, of course, because of all his equipment. I'd say he was doing pretty well because it was last year's model. The Asian girl, you know about. The others? A BMW, last year's model, tax disc up to date. All three went off in that.'

Bea sighed. 'What a lot of misery these people leave behind them. I won't bother to tell you the grief they've caused the caterer, and the man who supplied the wine at the next event is probably going to have to sell his car to cover his losses.

Then there's you, with your job under threat. If I could get some of the money back for you, would that help with the management? Hypothetically, of course.'

'It might. The wife and I like this pub and don't want to shift. It all looked so good on paper, too. I was properly taken in. When I checked, afterwards, I could have done myself an injury for being so stupid.'

'Have you heard of them doing this kind of thing before? She showed you a brochure saying they'd run a similar event somewhere else? Do you have it?'

'She kept it, saying it was the only one she had, but that she'd send me another. Which she didn't. Cheltenham? Bath? Some place in the West Country.'

Bea leaned forward. 'We think we know where to find these people tomorrow night. Now we could bring in the police, but we won't because the caterer doesn't want that – it's a long story – and I can see you wouldn't want it, either. What I want to do is confront them, say that they must pay back what they owe or we hand them over to the police. It's a bluff, I know, but it might work.'

He flexed his fingers. 'Need any help with persuasion?'

Those fists of his! Yes, Mr Banks would be very 'persuasive', but was that sort of persuasion legal? Wouldn't it get them into more trouble than they were in already? 'I hope it's going to be sufficient to present them with the facts and demand a cheque. No, not a cheque, come to think of it. Oh, they probably do Internet banking and I've got someone who's good at that. Then I'll say that we'll give them twenty-four hours to scarper before we hand the file over to the police.'

'I wouldn't mind hanging around, playing the heavy, make sure they pay up.'

She thought that one punch from his enormous fist would probably be fatal, rather than gently persuasive. 'It's Saturday night,' she said, soothingly, 'you'll be busy here, won't you? If I'm successful, I could give you a ring Sunday morning and let you know how we've got on.'

He grinned, revealing a set of beautiful teeth. False? 'Hypothetically?'

'Definitely. So if I could have a quote?'

'How about a photocopy of the original invoice, and another of the cheque that bounced?'

'You are brilliant!'

He nodded. 'Hypothetically. Would you like a drink, some food, while you're here?'

'Do you know, I rather think I would. A soft drink and a sandwich?'

He nodded, was getting up to go when he stopped and said, 'Baby on board.'

'Unh?'

'Sticker on the back of the car. Baby on board. I remembered because it didn't match the passengers. Unless, of course, it referred to the grown-up baby, that pretty boy that the woman doted on. Nah, that doesn't make sense, either.'

'You think the car might have been stolen?'

A shrug. 'Tell you one thing, though. The playboy wouldn't be seen dead driving a saloon like that. He'd want the full Monty, the sports car with a soft top, E-type or similar. And a personalized number plate.'

She smiled. She was getting a very good picture of these people, now. It all helped.

Friday, evening
Noel couldn't concentrate. Richie hadn't noticed; all he could think about was checking over the goodies they'd extracted from different companies for the auction. His mother was busy with the table plan, but she could see he was distressed and came to sit beside him.

'What's the matter, my pet? Tell mummy.'

He reverted to childhood in his grief. 'There's this girl, and I really thought she might be the one, she was just as keen. Now she's dumped me, and I can't stop thinking about her. She didn't even dump me herself, but got her aunt to do it for her. Oh, what am I going to do, Mummy?'

He fell across her, his head in her lap, real tears on his lashes. She soothed him. 'There, there. If she could do a hurtful thing like that, she's not worthy of you.'

'No, she isn't, is she?' His lower lip came out. 'She's a slag, that's what she is. I can't think why I didn't see it before. She's coming to the do tomorrow night, and I'll show her then.' He smiled, thinking how he might punish her for dumping him.

Richie pushed aside his lists and yawned. 'Think I'll go and pack. *Might take some of my stuff over to my brother's tonight, get it out of the way.'*

'*What's the rush? We've got the flat till the middle of next week.' She followed him into his bedroom, which he always kept clean and tidy, something to do with his old army training. She knew she was a bit of a slut, but there, did it matter if the place wasn't cleaned up till they were ready to leave? She said, 'Losing your nerve?'*

'*We've never done more than one event in any one town, before. Granted, this is London, but I think we should have called it a day after number two.'*

'*We've never pulled in so much money before, either.'*

He packed socks into shoes and placed them in linen bags at the bottom of his case. 'I've got a bad feeling, that's all.'

She snapped a frown at him. 'You're jealous of Noel.'

He shook his head. 'Jealous? No. It's not as if you and I have ever had anything but a professional relationship, but . . . him and his girls, him and the barman; that makes me nervous. What I'm thinking is that after this, I might drop out for a bit.'

'*Richie, no! What would I do without you?' But she knew he'd been thinking along those lines for some time, and maybe she had, too.*

Thirteen

Friday, evening, continued

Bea was locked into slow-moving traffic in her car, fuming at the waste of time, wondering if she dare use her mobile phone while driving. Everyone said it wasn't safe to do so, but a lot of people did it all the same. She decided not to, and pulled into a garage forecourt to fill up with petrol. Afterwards, parking by the free air hose, she got out her mobile. Only this was Maggie's mobile, and the battery was low.

There were no more messages from lover boy, thank goodness.

She rang home. Oliver answered. 'Lots of messages. Mr Max popped in, but has gone again. There's been two or three other calls, people wanting you to ring back. The theatrical agency has changed it's name to Superstars. I found them in the files, but there was nothing about recommending any singers to Mrs Briggs. Of course that didn't mean Max didn't recommend them to anyone, because as you know, there's a nice gap in the book-keeping about that time. So I rang them and spoke to someone called Sylvester—'

'That's the man.'

'—and he says to welcome you back and he's missed you. He says he hasn't had any calls from Max for a long time, but he's going to see if someone called Briggs has been in touch with them.'

'Can you call him back if he's still in the office, and ask if he knows about a rapper calling himself Mad Man, something like that? Even if Mad Man is not with Sylvester, he might know where he could be found.'

'Will do. Maggie's wanting to know when you want supper. She says she's all right, but to tell the truth, I'm a spot worried about her.'

'I'm trying to get to the Country Club before I head back, and it's some way out. Tell her not to bother with supper for me. Now Oliver; I've been thinking. This scam has spread so much misery around, much more than we realized at first. People are losing their jobs, their cars, their houses. How much did you take off your father, and what will the loss do to him? Don't you think you ought to contact him, pay him back what you took?'

Silence. Oliver put the phone down.

Bea was shaking. She hated having to tell people off. She was no good at it. Hamilton had always played the role of tough man when it was necessary for someone to do so. Oliver would probably turn round now and say it was none of her business. Her interference had probably confirmed him in his plot to fleece his father. She'd been amused when she'd first heard of it, thinking it served Mr Ingram right. Well, it did and it didn't. Two wrongs didn't make a right. No, definitely they did not. But she could understand that injured feelings and a sense of injustice might push Oliver into crime.

She checked in her *A–Z* and continued on her way to the

Country Club. This was not all that easy to find, being at the back of a private golf club in outer suburbia. It was in a modern building, nicely landscaped with plenty of parking. The cars were what you might call resplendent, nothing costing under thirty thousand, at a guess. The function room was off to one side, all lit up, busy with a wedding reception.

Bea walked into the bar, very pleasant, lined with trophies. One wall was covered with photographs taken at various evening-dress functions. Perhaps there was one there from Mrs Briggs' charity event?

Bea looked around. A few eyebrows were raised as she wasn't recognized as a member. Bea wondered how Mrs Briggs had managed to get in here? Through her son?

A girl was serving behind the bar. Was she the one Oliver had tried to get information from on the phone? A buxom lass, not too many brains. Bea picked up a couple of leaflets from the bar. One advertised the prices for hiring the function room. Her eyebrows rose. Expensive, very. She asked to have a word with the manager, and the girl indicated a man sitting at the bar.

This manager was a very different type from Tommy Banks at the Garden Room. This was a smoothie with a middle-class accent and a smile that came and went in a flash. Good teeth, probably his own.

She said, 'Might I have a word in private?'

'Not a member, are you?' His tone indicated he didn't think she was the kind of person he'd want to accept as a member, either.

'No,' said Bea. 'The name is Somers-Briggs. Mrs Somers-Briggs.' She saw the name register with a shock but he flashed his smile nevertheless. 'Come this way.'

He led her into a small office, very businesslike, equipped with the latest computer. His dark hair was very smooth, thinning on the top at the back. He wasn't as tall as she was, but tried to make up for it with a fussy manner designed to impress.

He took the big chair behind the desk, and waved her to an upright, opposite. He flashed his teeth at her, steepling his fingers and touching his chin lightly with his fingertips. 'You are Mrs Somers-Briggs?'

'You know very well that I'm not.' She put one of her agency cards on the desk. 'My name is Bea Abbot of the Abbot Agency.'

'A private eye?' He was amused, patronizing even.

'Certainly not.' She went into the spiel of what the agency did – used to do, concluding, '. . . the agency is now being wound up, but there is one last case outstanding, which concerns an event held here a couple of weeks ago, arranged by Mrs Somers-Briggs. Apparently she's been arranging functions for charity and vanishing without paying her bills.'

Again, that flash of a smile, as insincere as a meringue. 'So why come to me?'

Bea leaned back in her chair, trying to understand him. If he hadn't been stung, then he'd have thrown her out before now. If he had been stung, then why wasn't he being more helpful? Was he, too, in danger of losing his job over the unpaid bill? 'May I ask how you came to know Mrs Briggs?'

'We are very particular about who we accept as members.'

'In other words, she was introduced by a member?'

He neither confirmed not denied this.

She said, 'We are trying to find out exactly how much they owe everyone before we arrange a confrontation.'

He pulled on his earlobe. 'You know where to find them, then?'

'We know where they'll be tomorrow night. Hosting yet another function for charity.'

'We insist on a deposit of twenty-five per cent, two months before the event. Naturally.'

Bea inclined her head. 'Naturally. To give you plenty of time for the cheque to be honoured.'

'Yes. Of course, we are usually booked up a year ahead. This is a very popular, exclusive venue, but earlier this year we had to close down for refurbishing the kitchens. It cost us a great deal. So when a charity asked if we had a date for them at short notice . . .' He spread his hands. 'Naturally we agreed.'

'Was the cheque for the deposit honoured?'

A hesitation. 'Yes. Eventually it was honoured.'

'But the balance?'

His eyes snapped to the door, which he'd shut behind them. Firmly shut. 'Only a couple of people know about this. The club is being very generous. The short-fall will disappear with some clever accounting, and a hike in prices for the rest of the year.'

'It must have been a considerable amount.'

A flashing smile. 'They value my services and the good name of the club. We are fully booked from now till after Christmas. We'll recoup our losses, one way or the other.'

'Would you care to let me have a copy of the outstanding invoice? I can't promise anything, but if I were able to get some of the money back . . .?'

'What percentage would you take?'

She blinked. She ought to have thought of that. Hamilton would have thought of it. The labourer was worthy of his hire, etcetera. 'We'd charge a fee to cover our time, wages bill, that sort of thing, but it would be minimal.'

He'd caught her momentary hesitation. She could see him lose respect for her. His smile morphed into a sneer. He accessed a file on his computer and worked on it for a couple of minutes before printing off a sheet of paper and handing it to her.

She looked at it. 'More creative accounting? Surely they didn't owe this much?'

'Naturally I added a little to cover interest, our wages bill, that sort of thing.'

'Naturally,' she said, thinking that she neither liked nor trusted him, and that if she did succeed in getting any money back from the con men, she'd discount his bill by a good fifteen per cent. She folded the sheet and put it in her handbag. 'By the way, do you happen to have a photograph of the team?'

He opened a drawer, extracted a photograph and spun it across the desk to her. The photograph showed the same Asian girl, flanked by the manager and another round-faced, self-satisfied looking man, possibly the club president. Bea turned the photo over. No label. It was another dead end.

'Polaroid?'

'The photographer said it saved time and hassle. A bit amateur, but . . .' He shrugged.

She rose to her feet. 'Well, if anything comes of this, we'll let you know.'

He flashed his smile again. Hamilton would have called him 'a slimy cove'.

Bea flashed an equally insincere smile back.

On the way home, Bea began to think about Maggie, who was superficially a capable woman but inwardly an insecure teenager, despite her bossy front. The sooner Bea was shot of

her, the better. What a relief it would be to have the house to
herself at last! She suppressed the memory that Oliver had been
worried about the girl.

Bea found a parking space just down the road from her
house, and let herself in through the front door. All was quiet.
No phones ringing. No drinks clinking. No visitors. The aroma
of spicy cooking hung in the air if she sniffed hard. Perhaps
the filter over the cooker needed changing?

Oliver appeared from the basement, looking worried. He
gestured towards the closed kitchen door. 'Mrs Abbot, I'm glad
you're back. She told me to get out, to leave her alone. She's
been banging pots and pans around, and shouting a lot.'

'Thank you, Oliver.' Bea straightened her shoulders and went
into the kitchen, shutting the door in Oliver's face. Maggie was
sitting at the table with her head in her hands. She had cut off
all her long golden curls. Tufts of hair stuck out on her head
in all directions. Had she been punishing herself for being
raped?

Bea made an inarticulate sound, thinking she ought not to
have gone to the Country Club, but to have come straight back
when Oliver told her he was worried about Maggie. But then,
was Maggie really her responsibility?

At least the child hadn't cut her wrists, which Bea had heard
young girls sometimes did when they got into despairing mode.
Bea thought, I am *not* a professional counsellor. I don't know
what to do. What I do know is that I'm tired and cold and
thirsty and hungry and could do with being looked after, instead
of having to look after someone else. She investigated the
contents of saucepans on the top of the oven. Soup? Just the
thing.

'Soup?' she asked Maggie. 'Looks good.'

'Courgette and brie.' The girl wasn't crying. Not at the
moment, anyway.

'Want some?' Bea pretended everything was normal. She
poured herself out a liberal helping, and some for Maggie.
Hooking up a stool, Bea sat opposite the girl and started on
her soup.

'The thing is,' said Maggie, 'I realize it wasn't all his fault
last night. I was giving him the wrong signals. I was trying to
be glamorous, which is really not me at all. My mother and
my husband were always on at me to "make the best of myself",

which meant looking like a brainless bimbo with long blonde hair and big boobs. But I'm not beautiful and sexy and I'm not going to kill myself trying to look like that any longer, right?'

'Mmm,' said Bea, rather surprised to hear Maggie showing insight into her problem.

'I was the girl next door. Three doors away, anyway. Our mothers were great friends. He was, is . . . I looked up to him, always. He's much older. Brainy, wonderful job, friends everywhere, models and television people and minor royalty and a long-term girlfriend whose father owns a yacht and a country house and ponies, and, well, everything. Everything I wasn't. Only the girlfriend went off with someone else and suddenly he was all over me. I was so surprised!

'I mean, what did he see in me? Working as an assistant in a school for children with special needs, helping at the local soup kitchen, that was me. Not done anything much, or been anywhere, never even dreamed of it. Then suddenly he was saying how shallow his life was and how I'd got all the right values. Why did I believe him? Because he was the first man who'd ever told me I was beautiful. Even though I knew it was a lie, I believed it. Isn't that stupid? My mother was thrilled, wouldn't you know? Big wedding, lovely big flat, parties, parties.

'Only, once we were married, he wanted me to change, to be more like his ex, and of course I couldn't. Bed wasn't what I'd expected, either, though I tried . . . how I tried! He kept saying I should make more of an effort. I dyed my hair and bought mad clothes and tried to like his friends and remember who was important and who wasn't, but it didn't do any good. One evening we were at a party and *she* was there. He sent me home in a taxi and never came home himself. She was married by then, of course, not that it made any difference to her, or to him. I hoped I might be pregnant, but I wasn't.'

'Dear me,' said Bea, reaching for another helping of soup. 'I hope you got a good solicitor.'

'I wouldn't take a penny from him, no way!' Maggie tried to shake back what was left of her hair. 'He's supposed to give me some money when he sells the flat, but he hasn't even put it on the market yet. No, I went back home to Mummy – who was horrified to have her ugly duckling back on her hands – and tried to find another job.'

'Ah, the perfect victim. Now I had hoped you'd kicked him in the goolies at the very least.'

A snort. 'Well, actually, I did get my own back a little. We met in a restaurant to have "a civilized discussion". I tipped the curry over into his lap and left. I wish it had been scalding water from a kettle!'

'Good girl. You're well rid of him, of course. You'd had a boyfriend before, I trust?'

'Not really. There was someone who seemed to like me at work, one of the teachers at the school I was working at. But then I left to get married. I haven't been back. Too ashamed.'

'And yesterday, there was love's young dream?'

'Come to think of it, he had much the same line of patter. "How unusual you are, Maggie." That sort of thing. Reminded me of my ex. Am I stupid, or what? I've decided; in future, I'm done pretending to be what I'm not. I'm just plain old Maggie. Good for cooking and cleaning and hopeless in bed.' She ran a comb under the tap and tried to make her tufts of hair lie down.

Bea resisted an urge to help.

Maggie pulled a face at herself in the mirror. 'Do you think the agency could find me a job as a housekeeper?'

Bea thought Maggie deserved something better. 'We'll get you a good haircut in the morning. Something sleek and shapely. And one or two good outfits, also sleek and shapely.'

Maggie dragged the bowl of soup towards her, and began to eat. 'Sleek and shapely. I don't think I could do sleek and shapely. Not enough up top.' She indicated her skimpy top.

'You've got a model's figure, girl. You could do anything you set your mind to. Is there anything else to eat?'

'Oh, you poor thing,' said Maggie, reverting to her Mother Earth role. 'You must be so hungry and tired. Would you like a piece of quiche and some salad? Quiche Lorraine, or Mushroom?'

'Either. Thanks, Maggie. I could do with something to eat.'

Maggie bustled around between fridge and microwave.

Bea lifted her voice. 'You can come in now, Oliver.'

'Listening at the door, was he?' said Maggie.

Oliver inched his way in, looking embarrassed. He gave Maggie's haircut a sideways look and scuttled to a stool. Maggie ladled out soup for him, and put a huge slice of warmed quiche in front of Bea.

'This is nice,' said Bea. 'The Three Musketeers, or something.'

'There were four, after D'Artagnan joined them,' said Oliver.

'Oh, don't let's include Piers for the moment. Too much trouble.'

The doorbell rang, and Bea cringed. 'Not Piers, please! I can't cope.'

'I'll tell him you've gone to bed early,' said Oliver, and disappeared. Maggie made another attempt to flatten her hair, and sighed.

Oliver had left the door ajar. They could hear him exclaim, and a man's voice raised in anger.

'Not Piers,' said Bea.

The voice in the hall went on and on. Bea and Maggie guessed who it was at the same moment and made for the hall, Bea leading by a short head. Like his elder son, Darren's father was big, blonde and blue-eyed. He wore a good suit and an authoritative manner. His lips barely moved as he scolded his son.

Oliver was trying to speak, hands raised to try to stem the tirade.

'Mr Ingram, I presume,' said Bea, advancing on him with her shiniest smile. 'I'm delighted to meet you. I've heard so much about you from your son, who's been doing a perfectly splendid job helping me out in the agency. Will you come into the drawing room? A sherry, perhaps? Coffee?'

'Mrs Abbot, I presume?' He radiated barely controlled anger. 'All I need is five minutes with my son.'

'No trouble, I assure you.' She led the way and after a moment's hesitation, father and son followed her. She waved them to seats, but Mr Ingram preferred to stand.

'I wish to speak to my son in private.'

Bea continued to smile. 'I daresay, but this is my house, and you are my guest.' She seated herself by the fireplace, wishing that Hamilton had been here. He would have known how to deal with this pompous prat, while she was just muddling along and probably saying the wrong thing. 'I'll just sit on the sidelines and be umpire, shall I?'

Oliver's colour had risen, but his voice was steady. 'Dad, I had to tell Mrs Abbot what I saw, but I promise you no one else knows. I haven't told Mum, and I won't unless . . . I mean, No, I won't tell her. She wouldn't be able to cope.'

'I don't know what you think you saw. You've always had a vivid imagination.'

Oliver swallowed. 'What you said about me being into porn, well, I understand that you were trying to stop me telling Mum, but you didn't need to say that, because I wouldn't.'

'Naturally that's what you *would* say.'

Oliver made a helpless movement with his hands. Bea lost the next bit of conversation because it had suddenly struck her that two blue-eyed parents couldn't produce a brown-eyed child, could they? And there was the small matter of a slightly dusky tinge to Oliver's skin, and his very dark, almost black hair. Had the boy been adopted, or was he the result of a side-slip on the part of his mother? Either way, if he had grown up not conforming to the family image, then he would indeed be the odd one out. Which explained a lot about his treatment at the hands of his family.

Did Oliver realize it? Probably not. What a tangle!

Bea tuned back into the conversation to hear the headmaster saying, '. . . and if I ever hear that you've been telling lies about me, saying that I've accessed certain sites, sites of which I can assure you that there is absolutely no trace, then you can never return home.'

'Oh, Dad.' Oliver held his head in his hands. 'You may have deleted the sites but they're still there on the hard drive, and any expert could retrieve them. Likewise there is no porn on my computer and never has been, and any computer expert could confirm that.'

A slight flush rose to the headmaster's cheeks. 'In any event, you realize there is no place for you now at home.'

'I didn't expect anything else,' said Oliver, bracing himself. 'Before you go, there's something I need to tell you. I was pretty angry when you threw me out, plus I was skint. So I used your credit card details to buy some stuff on the Internet, and sell it again. To give myself some cash.'

'What! You did what? I don't believe you! Not even you!' His blood pressure was visibly rising.

Oliver took a chequebook out of his pocket. Bea could see that his hands were trembling but he wrote out a cheque and handed it to his father. 'This covers what I took out. I'm sorry.'

'You . . .!' Mr Ingram raised his hand to hit his son, and Oliver ducked. Both men were breathing hard. It looked to Bea as if Oliver were accustomed to having punches thrown at him. She wondered if his father only became physical with his family. Did he treat the children in his charge the same way? Because if so, he was going to lose his job pretty soon.

Oliver laid the cheque on the mantelpiece and took a couple of paces back. 'Take it. It's all there.'

'Why, you thieving . . .!'

'You stole my reputation,' said Oliver. 'I don't expect you to apologize, but—'

'I should think not!' Mr Ingram stowed the cheque in his pocket. 'You . . .! If I catch you anywhere near—'

Oliver said, 'I won't. Provided you let me have my A level certificates.'

The headmaster ground his teeth. 'I don't want you contacting your mother. I don't want to hear from you, ever again.'

Oliver shrugged. 'I'll make my own way in life, thank you.'

Bea said, 'That's all very noble, Oliver, but what about going to university? How many places have you been offered? I'm sure your father will agree that you should go.'

The headmaster was breathing hard, nostrils flaring, head bent forward. 'He's eighteen now. He doesn't get a penny more out of me.'

'Well,' said Bea, 'at least you can let him have his birth certificate, passport and so on.'

The man's head snapped round. He stared at Bea, who stared back. She thought, I've asked for Oliver's birth certificate and that's made him stop and think. Does that birth certificate show that Oliver was adopted? And how does that affect Oliver's future? She held Mr Ingram's eye till he looked away, smoothing back his fair hair. Bea risked a glance at Oliver, who looked puzzled.

Oliver didn't know? Best not to say anything.

Mr Ingram said, 'Look at the time. I must go. Meetings. I'll put those papers in the post to you, Oliver. I'll see myself out.'

He blundered out of the room. The front door crashed to behind him. Maggie slunk into the room. She'd obviously been listening at the door and now she was worried about how Oliver was taking things.

He was showing signs of strain, but tried to grin at her. 'Well, that's torn it. No going back. Not that I want to, of course.'

Maggie threw back her head. 'We'll be all right. We'll go

down the Job Centre, find somewhere to live, maybe move out
of London, even. '

'Oliver may have fooled you, Maggie,' said Bea, 'but he
didn't fool me. Oliver, you borrowed your father's money to
trade stuff on ebay, fine. I'm sure you made a good profit,
which I'm equally sure you didn't pass on to him? Am I right?'

Did he blush? 'I wouldn't ever try to fool you, Mrs Abbot.
Maggie, there's enough to give you and me four weeks' leeway
when we leave here.'

'May I remind you,' said Bea, 'that you've both agreed to
stay on here for another week, to help me clear up the mess
that the agency is in? Now I've got some thinking of my own
to do. Oliver, will you put all the information we've got so far
on my desk downstairs? I want to go over everything, see what
we're missing, try to sort out a plan of campaign before I go
to sleep.'

Oliver nodded. 'Oh, by the way. Coral rang. June went into
labour properly this morning. She's had a baby boy, they're
both fine but the hospital's keeping them in overnight. Coral
also said to tell you she's not been able to get herself a job for
tomorrow night. Does that make sense?'

'I'm afraid it does. Without her or the squadron leader on
board, we can't be a hundred per cent sure of identification.
I'll have to think of something, though I don't know what.
Anything else?'

'The usual.' He rubbed his forehead, trying to think straight.
'That Mrs Weston or Mrs Westin, getting really annoyed that
you haven't rung her back. The cleaner came round again. I
didn't let her in. Mr Max wanting to know if you need a lift
tomorrow.'

Bea was also tired, but tried to sort out her priorities. 'Maggie,
I've an appointment at my hairdresser's tomorrow which you
must take.' It cost Bea a pang to forgo her appointment, but
Maggie's need was greater. 'Which reminds me; Oliver, do you
have a suit or other garb suitable for this event?'

Oliver, deflated, said he didn't think so. Maggie fidgeted.
Clearly she didn't have anything suitable, either.

'All right, both of you,' said Bea. 'Dress hire, first thing
tomorrow. DJ for you, Oliver. Maggie, I want you to wear
something subdued and slinky, black or some other dark colour,
ankle length, no pattern, no glitter. Right? I'll sub you. Now

let me get at that paperwork before I decide I'm too tired to do anything more than crawl into bed.'

Because there was a problem she had to solve, wasn't there? She believed the police often had the same dilemma. Do you allow a crime to take place, so that you can catch the villains in the act – which may mean the victims get thumped financially or physically before you can step in to arrest the baddies – or do you warn the victim beforehand, and risk tipping off the villains? Which was best? Prevention or cure?

And how on earth was she going to extract the money from the con men? What weapons precisely did she have in her armoury?

What about Tommy Banks' huge fists? Could she risk bringing him in? He'd be a force to be reckoned with, but did she approve of fisticuffs? Well, no. Not usually. But in this case . . .?

If only they'd been able to trace the villains back to their lair!

When Oliver and Maggie had disappeared, Bea went to close and lock the French windows. With her hands on the catch, she thought, Hamilton, I need you. Advice, please. She went down the stairs into the garden and sat where her husband had been accustomed to sit and pray.

She rested her hands, palm upwards, on her knees and bent her head. She didn't know what words to use. Perhaps none were necessary. Perhaps all she had to do was lift up her heart to her Lord, and ask Him to comfort her and everyone she cared for in time of trouble. She asked for guidance, and for strength to carry out whatever course of action He wished her to take.

Some words that Hamilton had often used came into her mind. Part of a morning prayer. Well, this wasn't the morning, but it had the right sentiments. Something about being ready to go out into the world to right wrong, to overcome evil, to suffer wounds and endure pain if need be . . .

The rest of it had vanished from her mind. She repeated the few words she remembered over and over to herself. To right wrong. To overcome evil. To put up with Maggie's dreadful hee-haw of a laugh. Oh dear, that made her giggle. Would God be bothered to listen to such a trivial prayer as that?

She sat there a long time. A blackbird came and sang in the

tree above her. A light breeze ruffled the leaves. Some nicotiana nearby scented the air.

Perhaps she'd sleep better tonight.

Friday, late evening
Noel was planning what he'd do to Maggie. Where should he take her, for a start? Back to her place? No, her aunt lived there, and she might interrupt just when things were getting interesting. He didn't want interruptions.

Should he bring her back to the flat? Mm. No. Mummy might object if she had to do too much clearing up afterwards, and he was planning to make a mess, wasn't he?

He snapped his fingers. He'd book a room at the hotel, put it on the plastic. Why not make it the honeymoon suite? Yes, why not? He'd be off before the staff were up in the morning, and they could clear up the mess afterwards. He'd be long gone.

He'd lure Maggie upstairs with a message from her aunt, perhaps give her a drink with something in it. He'd topped up his stock of useful pills while clubbing this last week.

Of course, he might have to choke off that silly little slapper of a receptionist. However many times had she tried to phone him today?

He must remember to put a pair of thin latex gloves into his dinner jacket. No need to leave fingerprints. And Maggie wasn't going to talk afterwards, was she?

Fourteen

Saturday, morning
B reakfast was tiresome. Maggie was over bright and noisy. Oliver wasn't looking at Maggie, either because – like Bea – he liked peace and quiet in the mornings, or because he couldn't stand the sight of her with her hair chopped off. Bea decided she felt too frail to cope with either of them, sipped

her coffee, ate some fruit and announced in a cheerful tone that she expected them to be ready to leave for the dress agency in fifteen minutes.

She took them there, told the manageress exactly what she wanted for both of them, and drove on to Green's Hotel. She wasn't convinced that she was doing the right thing, but didn't think she could live with herself if the hotel made a big loss on the evening. She had another crisis of confidence when she spotted a receptionist slotting a card announcing the charity function into the board in the foyer.

She went down the corridor and into the function room, which was being prepared for the event by a team of four or five people, all of whom would expect to be paid for their time and trouble.

'May I help you?'

It was the manageress who'd shown Bea round on Thursday. She was wearing the same sharp black suit, with a different blouse. She was just as well turned out as before, but there was a suggestion of strain about the eyes and mouth. Was the staff shortage really so bad?

Bea said, 'Mrs Abbot. You remember I called the other day? I wonder if we might have a quiet word?'

The manageress hesitated. 'Perhaps we could fix up a time for you to call early next week? I'm afraid I'm rather tied up—'

'It's about the function tonight, and it's important.' Apparently she'd put sufficient urgency in her voice to convince. The manageress led Bea to a quiet office off the foyer. 'Some coffee?'

'That would be good,' said Bea, forgetting that she was supposed to be cutting down on caffeine. On the other hand, she really needed it this morning.

The manageress' hand hovered over the internal phone, but then she withdrew it, and vanished to some inner region to fetch the coffee herself.

So, thought Bea, they're so busy the manageress can't get someone else to run an errand to the kitchens for her? What sort of hotel is it that gets so short-staffed in the holiday season?

'Sorry about that.' Coffee appeared. Nicely laid out on a tray. With shortbread. The kitchens appeared to be working normally, then. 'Milk, sugar?'

'Black. I think we're both going to need it.'

A professional smile. 'Oh, I hope it won't come to that.' She poured black coffee out for herself as well.

'Don't count on it.' Bea sipped her coffee. Black and strong. She shuddered, but the caffeine did help. She laid one of the agency cards on the desk. 'When I called on you the other day, it was on something of a fishing expedition.'

Another bright smile. 'I see you are, what . . . a detective agency? You weren't serious about making a booking, then?'

'No, we're not a detective agency and yes, I might well be looking for a room in which to hold a party in a while. What I really came about, what I really wanted, was some background information on the people whose charity function you are having here tonight.'

The smile disappeared. 'What might your interest be?'

'Unpaid bills from previous functions.'

The manageress' mouth tightened. 'I really don't think that—'

'Was their cheque for the deposit honoured?'

The woman put her coffee down on the tray, untouched. 'Yes, of course.' But her tone was guarded and her eyes flickered to a drawer in her desk.

'At the second attempt, perhaps?' said Bea. 'Were they full of apologies that their first cheque bounced, and promised to give you another? Has this second cheque been presented yet?'

'It only came in the other day. I was going to bank it on Monday. True, there had been a problem with their first cheque, but that was all explained away. Do you have any reason to believe this one will bounce, too?'

'It's happened before. Have you by any chance checked their references? No? Well, perhaps I'd better explain why I'm here. I've just returned from some months abroad, during which time the Abbot Agency has been run down . . .'

When Bea reached the point at which Coral had been gulled into taking on a second event, the manageress reached for her cup and swallowed her coffee in two gulps. When she'd finished, Bea sat back and waited. Now all would depend on the manageress' reaction. She might choose to reject Bea's story. Or she might decide to cancel the function, cutting her losses.

Or she might want revenge.

'What a story!' The manageress tried on a smile, which didn't adhere to her face. 'This is the week for tall stories. First the police come about a missing member of staff and then, well, where's your proof? You come in off the street with a fanciful tale about wanting a booking which you have no intention of making and then—'

'Check the references,' said Bea. 'You'll find they're false.'

'I'm sure they're perfectly all right. Mrs Briggs is most . . . I can't believe this is happening.'

'Believe it. How much are you set to lose tonight, if they flit without payment?'

'They wouldn't do that. Why, we'd slap a solicitor's letter on them, sue them.'

'Check their address and telephone number. Both are false. The address given is that of a small corner shop. The telephone number on the fliers is out of commission.'

The manageress delved into her desk for a file, and drew out a letterhead for the false charity. She reached for the phone, and dialled a number. Listened to the voice at the other end of the phone, replaced the handset.

'The Bolivian Embassy?' asked Bea.

The woman attacked the phone again. Bea excused herself to visit the toilets. She didn't see any reason to sit and watch the manageress' humiliation.

Returning, Bea noticed that the receptionist behind the desk in the foyer was fiddling with her hair and blowing her nose, shuffling papers aimlessly. Distrait. Staff shortage? What was it the manageress had said about the police and a missing member of staff? The commissionaire was an elderly man with a hostile expression, busy with a couple of large American tourists. Well, it was no business of hers.

When she got back to the manageress' office, she found the woman retouching her make-up. The coffee pot was drained dry. 'Sorry about that.' She held out her hand to Bea. 'The name's McNeice.'

'Bea Abbot. Would you care to see the bills from the other places?'

A nod. 'I've alerted the managing director and he'll be in shortly, when we'll have to decide what to do. Frankly, he's a bit of a ditherer and it'll be me who makes the decision.'

She scrutinized the papers Bea passed to her. 'They're upping the numbers each time, aren't they? Tonight we're catering for two hundred and fifty.'

'Among whom is at least one Member of Parliament who is bringing a party. I myself am bringing a party of four, which will include my ex-husband, the portrait painter. Everyone will be wearing evening dress, sporting jewellery, driving up in limousines. They'll have paid high prices for the tickets and they'll donate money freely under the impression that it will go to charity. They'll go away happy, but you, the caterer and the cabaret will be out of pocket. So will the charity.'

Ms McNeice was accustomed to making decisions. 'Right. Two ways we can deal with this; cancel and cut our losses or go ahead. I don't want to cancel because it will upset all the people who've paid to attend. It's a cut-throat market, all of us hotels trying to attract corporate hospitality, and this is exactly the sort of function we want – no, that we need. I agree with you; the guests are not the ones who will suffer. If we go ahead, they'll have a good time and remember us when they want the same again.

'The hotel will be out of pocket for the hire of the room, the wine we're serving and the wages of the people we've employed to set up. Under the circumstances I'm going to suggest that the hotel stands the loss. We were going to supply a rather good wine, but we can downgrade to plonk and that will save a few pennies.'

'Maybe you can stand the loss,' said Bea, 'but what about the caterer? A new, young firm, who are going to bust a gut to produce food to die for, thinking it's their golden opportunity to break into the market. What about them?'

Ms McNeice dismissed the uncomfortable thought. 'They'll have some insurance.'

'Would you care to check?'

Ms McNeice licked her upper lip. 'You must understand my position.'

'I do,' said Bea. 'I can also see a second caterer being driven into bankruptcy. Plus all the other people these con men have hurt along the way. Plus the charities whom I think we may say will never see a penny of the money that's been raised for them.'

Ms McNeice fiddled with her earrings. They were faceted black earrings this time. She took them off. 'I won't cancel. Anyway, it wouldn't help anyone if I did.'

'Agreed. You mentioned the police earlier. They haven't been round asking about these people, have they?'

The woman blinked. 'No, nothing like that. A member of staff went missing, that's all.'

Bea nodded. 'Normally I'd say we should bring in the police, but two of the victims reject that idea.'

'Yes, yes.' Ms McNeice was abstracted. 'It's made us very short-handed. I shall have to get on to an agency for . . .' She picked up Bea's card. 'You don't supply . . .? No, you said the agency was being wound down, didn't you?'

'In normal times we would be able to help you out but . . . wait a minute. Would the services of a fully-trained silver service waitress help? I might just be able to help you there.' Would this be a way of getting Coral into the hotel that evening?

'Heavens, yes. Anyone who can serve wine without spilling it all over the place.'

'I'll see to it,' said Bea, making a note. 'There's one other thing. This is exactly the sort of function where people like to have their photos taken and these people have been supplying their own photographer who likes to pose the guests with a pretty Asian girl. He sells Polaroids on the spot and pockets the cash, which means he can avoid snapping the organizers. So far I haven't been able to track down a single photograph of them.'

'We asked if they wanted the photographer we normally use for these events, but they said they'd bring their own.'

'Understandable. Can you arrange somehow for their photos to be taken this evening without them knowing? Perhaps with one of these new phone-cameras?'

'Yes, I can do that. But . . .' She threw herself back in her chair. 'Let's get this straight. If we go ahead, we lose. If we cancel, we lose. Any bright ideas about how we can come out of this in one piece?'

'We know what they look like, and if we can take photographs of them, that will help. We've found their accommodation address – which is local – but we don't know where they're actually living. We don't even know if the names they've given are genuine. The best plan I can come up with is that we take them off into another room at the end of the evening and confront them with what they've done, and with the photographs we've taken of them. Then we ask for recompense. Can you let me have copies of the cheques they've given you so far?'

'I'll give you copies now.' She switched on a printer-cum-photocopier, and set it to work. 'You think they'll divvy up, just like that?'

'No, I don't. I think we might have to threaten to go to the police if they don't pay us – and you – what they owe.'

'I really don't want to bring in the police because it'll get into the papers and that frightens the customers away, but if they hold their nerve, they could just walk out of here and disappear.' She handed over photocopies of a couple of cheques.

'Have you got a better idea?'

The woman pulled a face. 'Not a legal one. I know a couple of guys who play rugby . . .' Her gaze shifted from Bea.

'Tommy Banks, the manager of the Garden Room, would like to have a go at them, too. But would that sort of pressure work? I mean, we could get them to sign a bunch of cheques tonight, and they could cancel them first thing Monday morning.'

Ms McNeice continued to gaze at the ceiling. 'It's only a fantasy, of course. I'd rather like to hold them incommunicado in one of our cellars till the cheques have been cleared.' She gave herself a little shake. 'But of course we can't. It would be illegal and they could have us up for false imprisonment.'

Bea caught her eye, and they both laughed. 'It's a tempting thought, but no, we can't do that. Leave it with me, will you? I have a computer geek who might be able to think up something. Meanwhile . . .'

'I convince my managing director that we've got to go ahead, get a photographer lined up, and arrange for a suitable room to be available for a quiet after-hours chat with our friends. How many do you think there will be?'

'We think there are four people operating the scam: Mrs Somers-Briggs – who seems to be the brains behind the outfit – that's one. Then there's the man who does the auction and acts as MC. He also plays the piano rather well. His name is Jerry, or Richard, something like it. Then there's a handsome lad who may or may not be Mrs Somers-Briggs' son. I'm not sure whether he's the DJ or the photographer, but either way, he's supposed to be a wow with the ladies.

'Apart from those four there's an Asian girl, name unknown.

We're not sure if she's part of the team or not; she's certainly helping them by telling a sob story and milking the punters. We're pretty certain that the cabaret people are victims rather than predators.'

'I'll get on to it.' Ms McNeice replaced her earrings and stood up as one of her phones rang.

Bea stowed the photocopies of the cheques in her handbag, while Ms McNeice answered the phone. 'Yes, well . . . tell her we're relying on her . . . yes, I know she's upset, but . . . no, the police have all gone now . . . tell her from me that if she doesn't turn up this evening, she's lost her job . . . yes. Must go.

'Sorry about that,' said Ms McNeice, showing Bea to the door. 'Another problem. A receptionist not wanting to work tonight. She's upset by what's been happening here but I really can't afford to have another of my staff go missing.'

'Staff, always a problem,' said Bea, sympathizing.

'He came with such good references, too. Eight years in a five-star hotel in Cheltenham. You'd think he'd know better. But there, the freedom of the great big city, I suppose it went to his head.'

'Mm,' said Bea, not knowing or caring what that was all about. They halted in the foyer, shaking hands, one professional woman having earned the respect of the other. 'See you this evening, then. I'll get my waitress to contact you direct, and if there's any problem you know where to find me.'

Bea went out into the busy street. The hotel had been on the gloomy side, but here the sun was shining. She checked her watch, wondering how Maggie and Oliver had been getting on. Which reminded her that she needed a word with young Oliver. Maybe he was just the right person to operate a scam on the scammers.

Oliver had been fielding messages from all sides since his return from the dress agency. He said Maggie was somewhere around and gave Bea a questioning look, expecting her to ask for details. Bea refused to take the hint. One thing at a time.

She said, 'Oliver, how much do you think these people have raked in so far? Not just from not paying their bills, but also from the auctions and the promises they've got people to give for the charities.'

'No idea. From what Coral was saying, it could be anything from half to a round million. Maybe more.'

Bea whistled. 'Tell me about Internet banking.'

Oliver shrugged. 'I'm no expert.'

'Would it be possible for you to spirit money out of Mrs Somers-Briggs' bank accounts, to pay for what everyone has lost?'

'You're joking.'

'Explain. Hamilton never liked Internet banking, said it wasn't safe.'

'Oh, it's safe enough, nowadays. Let's think what we'd have to know. First of all, we'd have to find out where her accounts are held. She may have used a different bank for each of her scams; let us say one at Lloyds, one at HSBC, one at NatWest, and so on. As far as I can see, she's set up two bank accounts for each of the false charities she's been running.'

'We know this because . . .?'

'She issues dud cheques which bounce, but she's been raking in the money from ticket sales and auction bids and donations so that money must be going somewhere else.'

Bea encouraged him. 'Think like a poacher, Oliver. Tell me how it's done.'

'If I were doing it, for each of the functions there'd be Account No. 1 – which takes cheques in – and Account No. 2, from which she pays out, but which doesn't contain enough money to cover the cheques which are drawn on it.'

Bea dived for her file, and rifled through it. Then she pulled the photocopies of the cheques from the hotel out of her handbag. Oliver leaned over to check as she compared them.

'Yes, you're right. On the flier that Coral gave us, they specify Account No. 1 for paying cheques in, but the dud cheques all came from Account No. 2. What it is to have a criminal mind!'

Oliver blushed with pleasure. 'I imagine that when she got all the money in from the first function at the Garden Room, she transferred it to another account which is probably in her name alone, maybe in a different bank altogether. Then she would close both the original accounts.

'When she came to organize the second function – the one at the Country Club – she set up two more accounts using almost the same name – but not quite – as for the first charity.

Can you see if she's used another bank? Maybe Lloyds for the first, and NatWest for the second? Something like that?'

'Bank of Scotland for the first, Lloyds for the second and . . . where's the cheques from the hotel? . . . HSB for them.'

'That's three banks, with two accounts for each.'

'Right. So where's her slush fund? In NatWest? How do we get at it?'

'I don't see how we can.'

'Come on, Oliver. You're my only hope. If we can bluff her into paying back the money she owes this evening, could she transfer the money to us there and then by the Internet?'

'In theory she could, yes.' Oliver was thinking hard. 'I'd have to take my laptop with me, because she probably wouldn't take hers to the hotel. If she agreed to pay us, she'd have to input her bank account number and sort code, give a password on demand, and then quote from first one and then a second security numbers. These security numbers can be anything up to fifteen digits long and a mixed bag of numbers and letters.'

Bea digested that. 'There's no way you can find out what those would be?'

He shook his head. 'It's a pretty secure system.'

'If we frightened her enough, she could do it?'

'Yes, she could, but there's another problem. It depends which bank she's got her slush fund in. Some of the banks give you up to six working days' grace on Internet banking, which would enable her to cancel the transaction the following day.'

Bea gave a low whistle. 'Six working days! Over a week?'

'Not all of them take so much time. Some take only three days. It varies.'

'Even so. She could set it up to pay us tonight, and then cancel on Monday morning. My idea's a non-starter, then. Bring your laptop tonight, though. Just in case. You couldn't . . .? No, I don't suppose you could.'

He grinned. 'Milk her account by buying stuff on ebay and then selling it on? No, not unless I'd got her bank details. We don't even know which bank she's got her slush fund in, do we? Or even if she's put the money in an off-shore account.'

'Go on, depress me, Oliver. What else can't we do?'

'We can't let them get away with it.'

'That's the cry of the underdog, the world over. Tell me how to stop them, and I'll – I'll help you to get to university.'

For a moment there was an eager look on his face, and then it faded. 'Chance would be a fine thing, and I don't expect it. Oh, there's the phone again. Look, there's some people been phoning all morning. Do you think you could return one or two calls?' He put the sheaf of telephone messages on her desk and left the room.

The sun had gone in, and the sky had greyed over.

Bea pushed the telephone messages aside. She supposed she ought to eat something but really wasn't hungry.

Saturday, noon
Noel was stretching his imagination with the aid of some porn he'd downloaded on to his mother's laptop. He heard his mother letting herself into the flat, and switched off. He was stretched out on the settee with the newspaper by the time she'd slipped off her shoes and asked how his day had been.

There was something about the body on the Heath in the paper. No leads, just a general plea for anyone who knew anything, to come forward. Fat chance.

His mobile rang. It was the receptionist, again. He wondered if he had time to do something about her before they lit out for pastures new. Regretfully, he decided that he could only take on one at a time and tonight was the night for Maggie.

Fifteen

Saturday, noon

Maggie wasn't in the kitchen, or in the garden. She was nowhere to be seen. But Bea could hear noises coming from the top floor, so she climbed the stairs to find the girl polishing the bathroom taps.

Bea suppressed an urge to shout at the girl. Weren't there more urgent tasks to be performed? 'Dear Maggie, whatever is the matter now?'

'Nothing,' said Maggie, short and sharp, head well down,

swilling clean water round the bath. 'You really must pay more attention to cleaning taps. They can't have been touched for ages. I'll be off in a minute but I couldn't leave them like this.'

'But you've got another six days here, haven't you?'

'You could be renting my room out and I'm no good at this agency lark, so it's best I go. I'll keep in touch with Oliver.'

'What's brought this on?'

Maggie poured a bottle of brown liquid down the loo. 'Now don't you bother with all those expensive limescale removers. Vinegar works better and is cheaper. Just don't flush it for a while, let it get to work.'

'I thought you were happy here.'

'Well, of course. In a way. It's more interesting than most jobs but I'm not exactly pulling my weight, am I? Not like Oliver. My mother's got a dinner party on tonight, so I might as well make myself useful at home.'

Bea thought she understood. 'You've been on the phone to your mother, and she's said . . .?'

Maggie wiped over the mirror. 'She says my husband – my ex-husband – is going to be there at this do tonight, with *her,* his girlfriend. They're an item again. So even though you've gone to all that trouble to get me a dress, I couldn't possibly . . . and now I've cut my hair, I look like something the cat brought in. You do see, don't you?'

What Bea saw was an angry, deeply unhappy girl, whose mother was not saying the right things to help her. Well, there was something she could do for Maggie, and that was to pass on her own hair appointment. Bea knew how much better she'd be able to cope if she were properly groomed, not to mention appearing in public at a big function, where every other woman would have spent most of the day in one salon or other.

Bea hesitated. Why should she keep trying to help someone who clearly didn't want to be helped, and who irritated the life out of her most of the time?

At the back of her head, she heard Hamilton say, 'If you let the girl go like this, she'll never fulfil her potential. You look fine as you are, girl. Give Maggie the chance to look good, too.'

Bea said, 'Maggie, my dear. You are worth your weight in gold, or platinum, or whatever is the latest currency. Euros, I suppose. We've only known one another for a short time, but

I can't imagine how I'd ever have managed this last week without you. If you want to leave at the end of next week, then that's your privilege. But don't sell yourself short.' Almost, she meant it.

Maggie polished the seat of the toilet.

Bea said, 'You're a lovely girl, inside and out, and all you need is a good haircut and a tweak or two in your wardrobe to bring out the best in you. It will be my privilege to act as Fairy Godmother. Cinderella shall go to the ball tonight, with a brand new hairdo and a becoming dress, and trust me; she'll wow the punters, and make her faithless ex-husband wish he'd not been so hasty.' She checked her watch. 'Get yourself tidied up and I'll take you round to the hairdressers and see you settled, right? And no more nonsense about leaving today. Understood?'

'As if anything like that could make a difference to what I am.'

'Believe me, it will,' said Bea, holding open the door. 'Let's see what we've got for lunch, and then we'll get going on the transformation scene. Remember, I'm relying on you for tonight, and so is Oliver.'

The girl hung back. 'I know my limits. It's really better if I go back home and make myself useful.'

Bea steered Maggie to the stairs. 'I don't suppose your mother will pay you for skivvying for her, while I'm paying you a proper wage, remember. Oh, and please do give Oliver a kind word. I know he's worried about letting us all down tonight, because he's never worn a dinner jacket before. Do you know how to do a bow tie? I can never get it right.'

Burbling gently away, Bea managed to get Maggie down to the kitchen, and busy supplying them with a scratch lunch. Oliver appeared, looking anxious. Bea continued to chat away about the garden, and the weather and how much Hamilton had been looking forward to seeing Australia, where the weather was of course quite different. She hadn't a clue, afterwards, what she'd said, but whatever it was, it got them through a difficult half-hour.

Twice Maggie opened her mouth to say something, but Bea gently overrode her, refusing to acknowledge that anything was wrong. Oliver followed Bea's lead and actually contributed some chatter of his own. Good for Oliver.

None of them were particularly hungry and there wasn't much clearing up to do afterwards, so Bea took Maggie by her elbow and walked her round the corner into the High Street. There they waited at the pedestrian crossing for the lights to change. Halfway across Maggie stood still and said, 'Look, this is crazy!'

Bea said, 'Humour me, humour me!' and got the girl moving again. Bea was welcomed into the salon with open arms. Oh, Mrs Abbot, how lovely to see you, how are you bearing up, they'd heard the bad news, so sorry, so very sorry, but it was lovely to see her again, but who had she allowed to cut her hair like that? Come this way, we'll soon put you to rights again.

Bea was very tempted to sink into a chair and let her favourite stylist take over, but – with a promise to come in again the following week – she explained that her protégée needed the appointment more than she did. There was some in-drawing of breath as the magnitude of the task set by Maggie's punk style sunk into the stylist's mind, but she nobly shouldered the burden, and bore Maggie off to be dealt with.

'You'll have a manicure now you're here, Mrs Abbot? I'm sure I can fit you in if you can just wait a while.'

Yes, Bea did need a manicure, but she was too restless to sit and wait. 'Make sure Maggie gets one instead,' she said, proffering her gold card by way of payment.

The noise of the traffic enveloped Bea as she left the salon. She hesitated, standing on the kerb. She'd forgotten how loud London traffic could be. She thought of the peace and quiet of the far away hospital in which Hamilton had died. She'd sat by his bedside holding his hand till he left his body behind.

He'd asked for a Christian burial. He hadn't wanted her to have the bother of bringing his ashes back home with her. He'd said it didn't matter where he was laid to rest. In a way, she wished he hadn't been so unselfish. It would have been a comfort, wouldn't it, to have brought his ashes back with her, perhaps to be buried in the garden? But no, he wouldn't have wanted that, either.

'No plaques, no flowers, no mourning. Think of me some-times, as if I've just popped out of the house for a while, but will be back to hear all the gossip later. I'm going on another journey, that's all. To tell the truth, I've got rather tired of all the stresses and strains of this world, and this body of mine is pretty well worn out. It'll be good to be able to rest for a while, and then perhaps there'll be some other task for me to do, but it'll be under a new boss, and He's promised I'll enjoy it.'

Bea blinked. It wasn't safe to cry when crossing a busy road so she turned into Café Nero, and ordered a latte. She tried to relax. One moment she wished she'd stayed in the salon and had a manicure, and the next she was glad she hadn't. She needed space around her, nobody talking at her. Since she'd got back – no, since Hamilton had died – she'd hardly ever had the luxury of being alone and able to relax.

Here in this busy café she could be quiet for a while, taking time out of her busy schedule with no one wanting her to solve problems, no phones ringing, no old friends demanding this and that. No Oliver or Maggie. No family.

It was bliss, she thought. She sipped her latte. She told herself it was good to take time out now and then. Hamilton had always made a rule to take Sundays off, plus at least one other day – sometimes it was only a half day – for them to go out together to an exhibition, to see friends, or just to pootle around the shops and have a coffee and a cake together. They'd often end up in this very place. Gossiping. Making plans. Snatching time to allow the world to settle around them.

She closed her ears to the hubbub around her.

'Well, if it isn't Bea Abbot, back from the dead! Whoops, I didn't mean that exactly, did I? You look good, considering . . .'

Someone she recognized? A face from the past. A blast of good-natured gossip from the past. A divorcee with grown-up children, whose name Bea couldn't for the life of her recall. Not that it mattered. The woman plumped down opposite Bea, disposing of various purchases around her, and chattered away. Key words floated to the surface, complaints about her chiropodist, her husband's new secretary, the new treatment she was on for this, and the investigative procedure for that and . . . and . . . Bea couldn't cope. She stood up without warning. She saw the other woman's mouth gape, and realized she'd been rude.

'Sorry,' she said. 'Got an urgent . . . have to . . . let's catch up next week some time?'

She got herself out of the coffee shop somehow or other,

bumping into people who were entering as she was leaving. Where could she go to be quiet by herself? She crossed the busy High Street at the traffic lights. What about St Mary Abbot's church on the corner of the street? The gates were open and she made her way along the crooked cloisters that led to the church, only to be met by a wave of sound as the bells rang out above her and a noisy wedding party gathered in the porch for pictures. There was no way she could push past them into the peace and quiet of the church, so she fled into the flag-stoned alleyway beyond.

The noise of the traffic was muted here, though the bells still rang in her ears. She remembered other weddings. Max and Nicole's splendid marriage had been in the country church which her family attended, but Bea's mind went back to the quieter, perhaps more meaningful blessing for herself and Hamilton after their civil ceremony.

The joyful clamour of the bells drained her energy. She stood in the oasis of St Mary Abbot's garden, but the benches there were all full of people chattering, playing with children, reading, taking a nap.

She clung to the railings for support. Whatever was the matter with her, giving way like this? She bowed her head, wondering with one part of her mind whether passers-by might take her for a bag lady, living on the streets. Or drunk. Or ill.

If she were to pass out now, did she have any identification on her, to enable people to trace her nearest and dearest? It made her giggle a bit to think of them ringing up Max at the House of Commons to report that his mother had been found wandering around the back streets of Kensington, half out of her mind. Bea knew what Nicole would do; that was easy. Nicole would sweep her mother-in-law into an old people's home, tidying her mercilessly away as someone not capable of looking after herself.

Bea struggled to regain her composure. It would be extremely inconsiderate of her to inflict such a problem on her nearest and dearest, and so she mustn't do it.

Max did love her, she knew that. But his first allegiance must now be to his wife, and Bea had to recognize that there was no great depth to her relationship with Nicole. If Oliver or Maggie or Piers were to see her now, they'd react quite differently. Or Coral. They'd be really concerned, really helpful.

Or would they? Was friendship, perhaps, more meaningful than a blood tie? No, no. That couldn't be true.

'Are you all right?' An elderly man with a walking stick. The walking stick had an ivory head in the shape of a dog.

She asked herself how she'd got like this. The answer lay at the back of her head. Grief. She tried to lift her heavy head to make eye contact with this man who was so concerned about her. 'I'm all right. Just tired.'

'They say you shouldn't drink when you're on medication.'

'Er, no.' The bells ceased their clamour. She pulled herself upright. 'Thanks. I'm all right, really.'

Perhaps he was lonely for company? She had no energy left to let someone else into her life. If she managed to get home without breaking down, she'd be doing well. She wouldn't look any further than that. She smiled in the general direction of the elderly man, looked around, reorienting herself. And set off back home.

There was a strange car parked outside the house. Correction; it was a car she recognized. It was Hamilton's car, which Max had taken for his own use when Bea and Hamilton had flown off on their round-the-world trip. Bea let herself into the house, and said, 'Hello?' expecting Max to answer.

Instead, Oliver appeared in the doorway to the kitchen, holding a phone to his ear, and gesticulating towards the first floor. He held a sheaf of messages in his free hand. He mouthed something which Bea didn't quite catch. She dumped her handbag and went up the stairs to her bedroom, from which she could hear bumping noises.

It wasn't Max in there, but Nicole. Nicole had just come from the salon, her hair was immaculate but she was sweating, trying to shift some of the belongings she'd stored in Bea's closet. Her little dog was sitting on Bea's dressing table, chewing one of her bedroom slippers. Ugh.

'Can I help?' asked Bea, trying not to care at this intrusion, trying to dismiss the wish to fall on the bed and weep, trying to be the Iron Lady.

Nicole gave a great start. 'Oh, I didn't realize you were back. I'm trying to find my Jimmy Choos, which I could have sworn I'd taken with me, but they're not at the flat and I must have them because they match my new dress.' She dashed her hand across her eyes, holding up her hands to show that she'd ruined a recent manicure. Her lips were quivering. 'Now look what's happened.'

Half the packages from the closet were strewn around Bea's bedroom. Some were on her bed. Bea sat on a clear portion of the bed, and closed her eyes momentarily. 'I'm very tired, Nicole. I was just planning to have a nap before dressing to go out.'

'I'll die if I have to wear my old ones.'

You won't die, thought Bea. But you'll sulk all evening. It was all too much. The phone was ringing downstairs. Oliver was working all hours, she really shouldn't ask him to do so much for her.

Bea felt a bump on the bed, and Nicole was seated beside her, noisily weeping. Over a pair of shoes! Bea felt like putting one foot into Nicole's slender back and shoving her off on to the floor. It would be a very satisfying thing to do. She controlled herself with an effort. Instead, she patted Nicole's shoulder. 'You poor thing. What are you going to do?'

Nicole sniffed. 'Wear the old ones, I suppose. But everyone will know they're last year's, the heels are quite obviously not this season's. If only . . .' She sniffed again.

If only, thought Bea, I hadn't come back from the dead. Well, not exactly the dead, but near enough. Poor Nicole, your horizons are so limited. I do understand that to you the wrong pair of shoes is a matter of life and death. I understand, but I do not condone. 'So sorry, dear,' said Bea. 'But maybe it's an excuse to buy another pair? The shops are still open, aren't they?'

Nicole lifted her head. A much smaller sniff this time. 'I suppose. Yes, but Max will kill me if I buy another expensive pair of shoes just because I can't find the others.'

'Perhaps the Second Time Round shop . . .?'

'I couldn't possible wear second-hand shoes!' Nicole was scandalized, but the thought took root. 'Well, I could look, I suppose.' She got off the bed, and inspected her image in the mirror. 'What a fright! And just look at my nail varnish! I wonder if I could get them to give me some first aid?' Nicole picked up her handbag, and rescued her dog. 'Sorry about the mess. I'll get Max to give you a hand tomorrow, shift some of the stuff.'

So Nicole was going to leave the room in disarray? Bea sat up. 'I won't ask you to put it all back in the closet because I'm going to need to get in there myself, but please stack it all tidily away from my bed, right?'

'Oh.' Nicole was disconcerted, but put down her dog and did as she was bid.

'Thank you,' said Bea, seeing Nicole plus dog down the stairs and out of the front door.

Bea had been conscious of the phone continuing to ring all this time. She went in search of Oliver, who was sitting at the kitchen table with his head in his hands, surrounded by pieces of paper. Bea reminded herself that though the boy had been acting like an adult most of the time, he had still only just left school.

'Sorry, Oliver,' said Bea, sliding on to a stool next to him. 'I dumped everything in your lap, didn't I? Most unfair. How have you been coping?'

He firmed his shoulders. 'I'm, like, treading water. I keep telling people that I'll have to ask Mrs Abbot and ring them back. Some of them shout at me.'

The phone rang again. Neither of them made a move to answer it.

Bea said, 'I don't know the answers, either, and I'm supposed to be grown up. I think you've done terribly well, Oliver. I can't think what I'd have done without you.' She remembered she'd said much the same thing to Maggie. 'We're both well out of our comfort zones in this, aren't we?'

His eyes glittered. 'It's exciting, but I keep thinking, what if we fail? I mean, they've only got to keep their nerve, and we're stuffed.'

She'd been thinking the same way, but it didn't do to let him know that. 'Fingers crossed.' She glanced at the clock. Time marches on, etcetera.

Pulling her scattered wits together with an effort, she said, 'Couple of things. Did you get Coral sorted out with a job at the hotel?'

'She rang back to say it was all fixed and she starts at six. Oh, and there was a garbled message from that odd friend of hers, the wine man, to say he thinks he's struck pay dirt but he can't be sure. Whatever that may mean. He enjoys being mysterious, doesn't he?'

Bea stroked her temples. 'Well, I can't worry about that now. Do we have transport laid on for this evening or take a taxi?'

'Piers rang. He'll collect us. That man rang from the Garden Room, Tommy something, wanting to know where we were going tonight, and I told him.'

Oh. Was he going to turn up and alert the baddies that someone was on to their scam? That would be disastrous.

Oliver looked anxious. 'Was that the wrong thing to do?'

'Heaven only knows,' said Bea, feeling tired. 'One thing, Maggie's being transformed from ugly duckling into swan even as we speak. Let's you and I go over everything just once more, make sure we've got all the paperwork on your computer, work out exactly what we're going to say. Then we'd better get ourselves ready for the fray.'

Saturday, afternoon
Noel went over his plans again, point by point, to make sure he hadn't missed anything.

For the first part of the evening he'd play his part as usual, of course, charm the pants off les girls, smarm and smile, take pretty pickies and rake in the cash. Then he'd take the little Asian girl round the tables, drum up some more business. Cash only, no cheques. Mummy would be proud of him.

The complicated bit came just at the end, when he had to separate Maggie from her aunt. Perhaps he could get the DJ or Richie to give her a note to meet her aunt upstairs?

The honeymoon suite was already booked in the name of someone he'd known at university. He might have to keep an eye out for the little receptionist. If necessary he'd promise to take her out the following night, knowing that by then he'd be long gone. She'd believe him. Women always believed him. It was one of his strong points.

Sixteen

Saturday, early evening

Bea massaged her temples with the tips of her fingers. She was getting a pressure headache. Painkillers would dull her senses, so she'd try to manage without. She applied her make-up and pulled a face at herself in the mirror. Nothing bar a face transplant was going to turn her into a raving beauty at her age.

She had a bad feeling about tonight. What they were trying to do was impossible, they were badly prepared, didn't know enough about the con men, had no back-up plan, nothing.

She put on the first evening dress that came to hand, which happened to be in gun-metal grey satin with a long-sleeved black lace jacket over it. Plain black satin court shoes went with it. The jacket was beaded in jet and the whole rig-out had cost a fortune. She'd bought it for a function that she'd been going to attend with Hamilton, but he'd been so unwell that they'd not gone. This would be its first outing. Was that a bad or a good omen?

If Hamilton had been around, he'd have sent up an arrow prayer or two before going out to confront the enemy. In the old days she'd have smiled tolerantly, thinking that if it helped him to prepare then that was just fine by her, but he needn't expect her to go down on her knees and join him. Not that he'd been one for going down on his knees in later years, what with his arthritis and all.

But now she sat on the chaise longue at the end of the bed, calmed herself, closed her eyes, and asked for guidance. *Please, Lord, show me the way to defeat these bad people and restore what they have stolen. Help me to right wrongs and defeat evil. I'm not asking anything for myself . . . well, no. Not really. Well, perhaps I am asking for something for myself, too. Only, I don't know the right words to use.* Hamilton used to say words weren't needed, that you just need to remind Him that you're in trouble. So that's what I'm doing. *Amen and all that.* She could only hope He was listening.

She opened her eyes, clipped on her pearl earrings, swiped the hairbrush across her forehead to make her fringe lie at an angle, and told herself that she was as ready as she would ever be.

Evening bag; she chose the largest one so that she could pop her small camera in it; if all else failed, she could at least take photographs of these people to hand to the police. Oh, and also her specs.

She went down the stairs to the sitting room. No Maggie, no Oliver. Sighing, she climbed the stairs again. Oliver was descending the stairs from the top floor. He'd smarmed his hair down and looked more grown up than she'd imagined he could.

His evening dress fitted him well enough, but his bow tie hung loose.

'I don't know how to do it. I asked them to show me in the shop, but I can't remember how it goes.'

She was soothing. 'You go on downstairs. I'll fetch Maggie. Maybe she knows how.'

She tapped on Maggie's door, and went in. A tall, willowy creature with a close-cut cap of mahogany-coloured hair stood, looking at herself in the mirror. The new haircut showed off the fine shape of Maggie's head, she'd emphasized the lines of her mouth with a gentle colour, and the same pale colour shone on her fingernails. She was wearing a slinky black dress, bias cut and very plain, with a bow on one shoulder. Maggie was transformed from punk to supermodel.

'I feel most peculiar.' This new Maggie didn't take her eyes off her image in the mirror. 'I don't look like me, do I?'

'This is the real "you", I think.' Bea glanced down at Maggie's shoes, which were her own and not particularly sophisticated, but would just about do. Bea glanced at her watch. 'Have you a jacket to wear over that?'

Maggie picked up a Day-Glo pink sweater, and Bea almost fainted with horror.

'You don't think it goes with the dress?' asked Maggie, catching Bea's disapproval for once.

'Er, no. I'll lend you a stole. It's such a warm night, you won't need anything heavier.'

Maggie turned away from the mirror with reluctance. 'Do you think he'll recognize me?' Presumably she was referring to her ex-husband. 'What will I say if he comes up to me?'

'Look through him. He's history.'

Maggie shook her head. 'I may look different on the outside but I'm still the same person inside.'

'Aren't we all?'

Down in the hall, Piers had arrived and was standing behind Oliver, arranging his bow tie for him. 'All hail, fair ladies,' said Piers, giving the tie a final tweak. He was in evening dress himself, and looked impressive.

Oliver gaped. 'Maggie, you look fantastic!'

'Doesn't she just,' said Bea, glad that she'd given up her own time slot at the salon for such a good result.

'The chariot awaits,' said Piers. 'Stretch limo. Champers in the back if you wish. Oliver, don't you dare touch that tie again. Maggie, I'd like to paint you some day soon. Do you have a wrap? Bea, you look cold. Are you all right?'

'Fine,' lied Bea. 'Has everybody got everything? Keys, money, handkerchiefs, mobile phones, the number of the local police station, indigestion tablets?'

Oliver picked up his laptop. 'I'm ready.' He was hoarse with nerves.

'I don't need a wrap,' said Maggie, wafting herself to the front door.

The child didn't even have an evening bag with her, thought Bea, crossly. Oh well, I suppose Cinderella didn't, either. Or a watch. Will a limo summoned up by Piers turn into a pumpkin at midnight? It might, because he might well have forgotten to order it to return for them. She followed Maggie down the steps and into the stretch limousine.

Nobody drank champagne on the way to the hotel. Piers was abstracted, frowning, playing five-finger exercises on his thighs. Oliver wetted his lips. He clutched his laptop as if it would take wings and fly away if he let go of it. Maggie kept looking at her reflection in the window to reassure herself that she looked different. Bea wanted someone to rub the tension away from the back of her neck. Dear Hamilton had always done that for her.

They arrived. For two pins Bea would have asked the chauffeur to keep on driving around London. If she did that, they could all go and dine somewhere on the river. There was absolutely no need to put themselves through what promised to be an extremely difficult evening.

Piers alighted, and handed Maggie out. Maggie looked up at the façade of the hotel, standing straight and tall, her expression remote. Oliver tumbled out, catching his foot as he did so, and almost dropped his laptop. Maggie didn't notice. It was Piers who steadied the lad, and then helped Bea out.

'I don't think it's going to rain,' said Piers.

He led the way into the hotel, and the others followed. Inside, a stream of people in evening dress were making for the cloakroom while others were returning from it. There was a queue of well-dressed people winding their way along the dark corridor to the function room. Bea caught sight of the manageress, fielding an enquiry from some newly-arrived

tourists. The manageress was backed up by a different receptionist, who didn't look old enough to be out this late.

'Mother!' Max bore down on them with a hunted expression on his face. Behind him came Nicole, teetering on new
high-heeled shoes. 'Mother, Nicole's just told me that—'

'There you are, dear!' Double kisses on both cheeks. Velma,
an old, old friend in a blonde wig and a haute couture outfit.
'Didn't you get my messages? I've been trying to get hold of
you ever since I heard you were back. I would have come to
the welcome home party, but there was all that business with
solicitors.'

The queue was gradually easing them along towards the
function room. Max tried to get at Bea, but Velma clung to her
side. 'Never mind him, dear. I've such a lot to tell you.'

'Mother, I must—'

Velma tucked Bea's arm within hers. 'I forget, did you ever
meet Sandy? No? Oh, you'll love him. Everyone says—'

Nicole was bobbing up and down, an agonized look on her
face. Was it her shoes that were causing her to grimace, or
some new tragedy? Maggie stopped dead, just in front of Bea.
Her eyes were on someone ahead of her. Piers noticed, put his
arm around her shoulders, and urged her on. With Velma firmly
on her right, Max wriggled his way to his mother's left.

'It was really strange the way we met, and there was I thinking
he wasn't ever going to get serious, but then he—'

'Mother, you don't really mean to cause a scene—'

'—proposed to me, right out of the blue. He said I needed
someone to take care of me, and if none of my relatives would,
then he was going to do so. He's got this job working for a
charity which pays peanuts but I've plenty of money so that
doesn't matter, and he's such a sweetie pie.'

'—tonight, because it will ruin me! I've got a member of
the Cabinet—'

'Of course there was a pre-nuptial. I couldn't risk—'

'—coming with his wife, and the chairman of my
constituency association and his wife and daughter so—'

Bea turned her head from one to the other. The hubbub in
the corridor was frightful, so many people crammed tightly
together. Was she going to pass out? It was rather airless in
here. Was she running a temperature? Concentrate, Bea! This
is no time to be playing the fainting widow card.

They burst into the light at the end of the corridor. Piers reached a long arm back and steered Bea, Max and Nicole into a ragged line with Oliver and Maggie, as a camera flash went off in front of them. The photographer gave them a Polaroid photograph which turned out to be not bad at all. Piers paid him for it, and the man said he'd be going round the tables later on if they wanted any more.

Velma said she wanted one with her new husband, who appeared on cue at her elbow. Sandy proved to have the fresh looks of a rugby player who hadn't yet run to seed. He was probably twenty years younger than Velma, but clearly fond of her. His name was Weston, which rang a bell with Bea. Hadn't she been getting lots of messages to ring a Mrs Weston? Messages she'd ignored?

Bea wished the newlyweds well. Velma's first husband had been a hypochondriac who had died unexpectedly early from a heart attack. She'd nursed him devotedly through all his imaginary illnesses, and could do with a bit of pampering for a change. Perhaps it would work.

Once in the function room, Bea saw that a bar had been set up in an L shape near the door. Piers bought drinks for them all. Oliver attempted to look as if he were accustomed to going to this sort of function. Maggie had a frozen smile on her face and tried not to look at a nearby group more than once a minute.

Bea spotted Coral behind one of the bar tables, smoothly dispensing more drinks per minute than either of the two barmen working beside her. Coral might be vertically challenged, but her skills were indubitable. Even as Bea looked towards her old friend, Coral did an eye-roll to the right.

Bea's eyes turned in the direction Coral indicated, into the main part of the room, which was laid out with large round tables around a tiny area of dance floor. There were balloons everywhere. There was a stage at the back on which a man in a dinner jacket was setting up turntables under some powerful lights. Helping him was a rotund little man in evening dress, and further over a tall, willowy blonde of uncertain age was talking to a petite Asian girl in the shalwar kameez of Pakistan.

'Yes!' said Bea, recognizing the descriptions she'd heard of the gang. 'We've found her. That's Mrs Somers-Briggs.'

Piers raised his glass to hers in a toast. 'Well done, Bea.'

Maggie turned to Bea with an abrupt movement and took her arm, 'Isn't this lovely, just like a dream, I can't believe I'm really here.'

This effusiveness was so uncharacteristic of the girl that Bea looked round for the cause. A youngish man with sharp features in a group nearby was staring at Maggie with an expression which struggled between doubt and recognition. Was this the ex-husband?

'It is lovely, dear,' said Bea, urging Maggie and Oliver on into the main part of the room. 'Let's find our table, shall we? Are there place names, do you think?

'There's a chart over here,' said Piers. 'It allocates different parties to numbered tables. We're on table nine. Max and his party are also on our table. Shall we drift that way?'

There was some heavy breathing at Bea's shoulder, and Max was back again. 'Mother, I have to look after my guests, but Nicole says that . . . you won't cause a scandal in public, will you? I'm out of my mind with worry.'

'We're not planning to confront them until the end of the evening, so if you leave promptly there'll be no problem. You look after your guests, and I'll attend to mine.'

Max departed and Bea transferred her attention back to the stage, where the rotund man was fixing a mike over an upright piano. His movements were deft and economical. He tested the mike and sent a high five sign to the woman. The DJ was a handsome fellow in his mid thirties, with eyes already roving the room to assess the talent. Who was it who'd said he was too old to be the boss's son? Whoever it was, they were right, even though the lady was probably older than she looked.

Mrs Somers-Briggs had a sharp word with the DJ, upon which he stopped eyeing the talent and went back to his turntables. She moved on to inspect a table full of prizes which had been laid out in front of the stage, and rearranged one or two items to display them to better advantage. She wore a filmy black evening dress with diamond drop earrings and a matching diamond bracelet.

'Bit of a puzzle,' observed Piers. 'Is that woman old enough to have sired the DJ, or are we astray on that one?'

'Late forties, if she's a day,' said Bea. 'I would say he's too old for it. She's definitely the brains of the gang though, isn't she? Maggie,' she turned to the girl, 'don't keep peeping at your ex. Ignore him. Give me your opinion on the DJ. How old is he, and do you fancy him?'

Maggie turned her back on the neighbouring group with an effort. 'The DJ's all right, I suppose. Not as good-looking as . . . the thing is, you won't mind if I stick close to you this evening, will you? I mean, with Noel here as well.'

'Your husband's name is Noel, too?'

'Oh, no. Of course not. I mean, the man who . . . you know? The other night? The photographer.'

Bea hadn't noticed the photographer particularly. She looked back at the entrance to the function room but so many people had crowded in behind them, that the only evidence of his presence was the occasional flash as he took photos of later arrivals.

Her headache was developing into a real rager. Was the photographer part of the gang? Was the man who'd hurt Maggie really the photographer, and was he the boss woman's son? Bea couldn't think straight. Were there three people in the gang or four? Or more?

Mrs Somers-Briggs was moving around the room now, greeting people, towing the Asian girl along, introducing people to her. The rotund man was double-checking mikes, having a word with the DJ, eyes everywhere. Just as Coral had said.

Nicole surfaced to greet Bea with a kiss. 'We've been put right next to the amplifiers. I'm sure to get a headache.'

Bea indicated her evening bag. 'I brought some painkillers with me.' Her eyes wandered to the boss woman, who had met up with the rotund man and was conferring with him by the stage. Bea wriggled her camera out of her purse and handed it to Oliver. 'Can you get a snap of them, do you think?'

He handed his laptop to Maggie to hold and slipped away in the crowd as the boss woman got up on to the stage and flicked the mike into life.

'Ladies and gentlemen – and all you wonderful people who have come here to help those less fortunate than ourselves – would you kindly take your seats? The tables have all been set up with the names of your hosts for the evening, and they will arrange that you don't sit next to your worst enemy.'

There was a titter of laughter and a general movement towards the tables. Piers led his party to their table, where Max was already pulling out chairs and attending to his guests.

Mrs Somers-Briggs allowed a few minutes for people to settle, before continuing her spiel. 'We are delighted that so many of you have responded to the call to help those less fortunate than us. The tsunami that wrecked so many lives has dropped out of the headlines, but that doesn't mean that the scars have been healed, that all the villages have been rebuilt, that people are no longer dying for lack of food and clean water. Or that people have ceased to mourn the dead. The big aid agencies have moved on to deal with other issues, but I want us to do something for the forgotten ones, which is why I have organized this event. We are so comfortable in our lives here in Britain, we have so few tornadoes and monsoons and devastating floods, that it is hard for us to realize how fragile people's hold on life is in other countries. It is greatly to your credit that you are prepared to do something about it.

'You may ask what we can do to help, living so far away from the seat of the great disaster? Well, every pound that you pledge, every bid at the auction, allows us to provide safe drinking water, secure shelter, and basic foods for at least some of those who have suffered so much. Some people can harden their hearts and turn away from the terrible sights with which we've all become so familiar after the floods, but you are not of their number. You have stood up to be counted among those who care, and who not only care but are prepared to put your money where your mouth is. At least you will be able to sleep more easily tonight, knowing you have done what you can. Remember, every pound you donate makes a difference.

'Now on each plate you will find a small gift, courtesy of our generous sponsors, whose name you will see emblazoned on the back. We'd love it if you could show your appreciation of this little gift by dropping a fiver or so into the begging bowl placed on each table. I see the caterers are dying to get the food on the table, so I won't hold you up any longer. *Bon appetit*, as they say in France.'

Bea exchanged glances with Piers, seated on her right. 'That was well done, wasn't it?'

'Softened us up nicely. A pity she doesn't put her talents to use in a worthier cause.'

Max was taking orders for wine and passing them to a waiter. Max was flushed and expansive. Nicole was listening to one of Max's guests with an expression of interest on her face. Bea wondered, in an idle moment, whether Nicole had ever wanted to enter politics herself. Somewhere under all that superficial glamour, there was a brain of sorts.

Piers ordered wine for his party, but saw that they had a glass of water each as well. A swarm of black-clad teenagers appeared to dish out plates of food. One girl or boy to each table. Bea tried to think how much this would cost in wages. She hoped they'd get their money. Horrid to think of these pleasant boys and girls working their butts off and then not getting paid. The starters were prettily laid out, smoked salmon roulade with cream cheese on rounds of crusty bread, a small side salad.

'I've had worse,' said Piers, 'but the wine's not up to much.'

'Mm,' said Bea, remembering that the hotel had down-graded the wine for the function in case they made a loss.

The waiters removed the first course. The second course was duck's breast with red cabbage and mashed potatoes. A little heavy going. Bea told herself to eat it all up before she took any painkillers. Piers was talking easily to a woman in Max's party, about an eccentric nobleman he'd been painting, who kept a menagerie on his estate.

The sweet was a bit icky, but there was a pleasant enough raspberry sorbet to compensate. Then the tables were cleared and coffee brought round with – Bea was glad to see – some chocolate mints. If there was one thing Bea had a weakness for, it was chocolate mints with crunchy bits. She took two, and reached for her painkillers.

The lights overhead dimmed, and the lights on the stage came up. The boss woman took over the mike again.

'Well, ladies and gentlemen, I hope you are all feeling well fed and at peace with the world. The catering tonight has been done by a new company, Passion for Food. Would you all put your hands together for them, and for the delightful young people who have looked after us so well.'

Applause, not overly enthusiastic, but good enough. The students looked pleased, and refilled coffee cups with a smile. Bea hoped that the applause was not going to be the only thing they earned that night.

'I imagine you expect long speeches from the worthy charities who help to alleviate the woes of the world,' said Mrs Somers-Briggs, 'so you'll be glad to hear there are going to be no speeches tonight. Instead, I'm going to tell you what happened to my friend Ana, who was there on the day the sea destroyed her old life.'

She gestured to the Asian girl to come up on to the stage and stand beside her. 'English is not her first language,' said Mrs Somers-Briggs, 'although she is studying it. Because she still cannot speak of these things without breaking down, she has asked me to tell you what happened to her.'

She took a sip from a glass of water. 'Ana lived in a fishing village, which was home to twenty or so families. Her father and the other able-bodied men went out in their boats every day, the children played on the beach and between the houses, and the mothers – ah, the mothers – looked after everybody, as they do all over the world, don't they?'

There was a murmur of amusement as, indeed, they did.

'One day, to everyone's amazement, the sea receded. Fish which had been swimming in the sea a few moments ago, flopped around on the sand. The children, laughing, ran about to pick them up. One of the old people remembered what happened when the sea disappeared. She screamed that everyone should run inland. Ana was working in their garden with her mother, who was pregnant. They ran down to the beach to find the younger children.'

Mrs Somers-Briggs' voice faded, and she took another sip of water. 'Ana found the toddler. Her brothers and sisters were little dots, far out on the newly naked sand. Her mother ran, calling to them to come back, come back. The oldest boy started walking back, too slowly, too late. The others didn't hear her.

'Then they saw the tidal wave coming, faster than a horse could gallop. Ana turned and ran, weighed down by the toddler. She reached the first house on the beach, the largest, strongest house in the village. She was breathless, could run no more. She tried to get into the house but was thrust away by those inside. Burdened by her little sister, she managed to climb a little way up the nearest palm and tied herself to it before the wave overwhelmed her. The water closed over her head.

'After what seemed like hours during which she was pummelled and torn at by the wave, she found her head above water. She lived, but her little sister died. All that was left of the big house were some baulks of timber. Everyone in it had died. Ana was taken inland to where the survivors sat, staring at nothing, or wandered around asking for news of friends and relatives. Not one of the fishing boats ever returned to the village.'

Mrs Somers-Briggs paused to touch tears from her cheeks. She pulled Ana closer to the mike. 'Can you take it from there, Ana?'

Tears marked trails down Ana's cheeks, too, but she spoke up in a small but clear voice. 'The sea go back to its place. We find the bodies of friends, of family, but not my father. It is seven days when people come from outside, with food and fresh water. These people have mobile phones. They ask, have we other family? My father's cousin comes to Britain many years ago. He sends us money once. The people with the phones talk to my cousin in Southall, and he helps me come to Britain. Now I learn English. Then I learn to be a nurse, and after I go back to help my people.'

Noel was standing at the back of the room, waiting till he could take some more photos. The key to the honeymoon suite was in his pocket, and he'd already doctored the bottles of soft drinks from the minibar.

Watching Ana perform for the public, seeing how she lowered her eyes and pretended to be modest, gave him an idea. Ana would do anything for money, so he'd use her to get Maggie away from her family.

He'd already spotted where the girl sat with her aunt. He thought her new look rather appealing. Yes! It excited him, thinking about what he was going to do to her later that evening.

Seventeen

Saturday, mid-evening

During the cabaret people began to move around, swapping seats, paying visits to the toilets or visiting at other tables. Max called for more wine for his party, and Piers ordered another bottle, even though he'd only drunk one glass. Bea had hardly touched hers. The painkillers she'd taken seemed not to have had much effect on her headache, but they had distanced her from what was going on around her.

Looking around, she spotted several people she knew and waved to them. They seemed restrained in their return greetings, which puzzled her. She couldn't see Velma and her new husband; they must be on the other side of the room.

Piers went to 'stretch his legs', which entailed paying a short visit to Coral at the bar and a circuit of the function room, chatting to people he knew. Piers knew a lot of people from all walks of life. Oliver had drunk a bare half of his first glass of wine, which was just as well. If anybody needed a clear head tonight, it was him.

Maggie was given a note by one of the young waitresses. She read it, went crimson, and tore it into pieces. A little later she went to the ladies', and on her return was stopped between tables by her ex-husband, who put his hand on her arm and indicated she join his party.

Bea had a good look at the people on that table and identified the Other Woman without any difficulty; a brittle blonde, anorexic, with a greedy look in her eyes. The problem for Maggie's husband was that his lover's eyes were currently turned not on him, but on a minor television celebrity who was sitting next to her. Was Maggie's ex-husband trying to make his lover jealous by paying attention to Maggie, or did he really feel he'd made a mistake and want to get her back?

Maggie listened to what her ex had to say, took in what his lover was doing, turned on her high heels and stalked back to her seat beside Oliver. Her cheeks flamed red, but otherwise she seemed in command of herself.

'Well done, Maggie,' said Bea, though she didn't think Maggie was listening.

The cabaret turn was a rap singer; Jamaican in origin? Dreadlocks and all. He had the volume turned up high, so the room and everyone in it reacted to the recorded beat of his drum. Oh dear. Then the pianist took his place, thumping and trilling away. Apparently people enjoyed his performance, but it didn't go down well with someone who had a headache.

The auction began. The pianist and Mrs Somers-Briggs worked this together; they were so polished a double act that

Bea had to applaud. She asked Oliver to make notes during the auction, so that they could estimate how much money was being raised. Oliver, given something to do, stopped gazing into space in bored fashion, and started jotting down figures in his notebook. What had he done with his laptop? Was it on the floor beside him?

The photographer was working the room with the Asian girl. Everyone wanted to be photographed with her, and he was doing a good trade. Another note was delivered to Maggie. She read it, stood up, looked over to her ex-husband on the next table, tore the note into shreds and let them drop before resuming her seat. This time she didn't blush, but turned pale. She reached for the wine bottle in front of her, only to find it was empty. Piers had not returned, and Bea wasn't going to get any more wine for the young people. Unfortunately a middle-aged man on Maggie's left – one of Max's party – noticed that her glass was empty and poured her some wine from his own bottle.

'Is that man over there bothering you, little lady?' he asked, all geniality.

'My ex,' said Maggie, gracelessly. 'Are you married?'

That was too abrupt, thought Bea. But the man apparently didn't think so, because he launched into a spiel which turned into, My Wife Doesn't Understand Me.

Piers put a warm hand on Bea's shoulder, and resumed his seat at her side. 'The auction's going well. I've spoken to a few people I know, and they all say this is a really worthwhile charity to support. You're looking a little peaky. Are you all right?'

'As right as I'll ever be, I suppose. I've just realized why I've been getting some odd looks from people. In their eyes I'm a scarlet woman, shuffling off one husband only to take up again immediately with you. They think it's a bit naff, and come to think of it, so do I. Whatever am I doing here, Piers? I'd far rather be tucked up in bed with a glass of hot milk.'

'You're here to stop an unscrupulous gang tricking generous hearts out of a fortune. I'm here because Hamilton asked me to look after you, which is not to say that I wouldn't have come, anyway. I disapprove of Robin Hoods who steal from the rich but don't pass the money on to the deserving poor.'

On the platform, it was time for the DJ to start up. He turned up the volume. Bea winced, feeling pale. A well-known MP came over to talk to Piers, and had to bend close to his ear to be heard. Piers stood up and they went off to the bar together. Possibly the noise level was a trifle lower there. The dance floor was small but was soon crowded with people dancing on the spot, gesticulating wildly, enjoying themselves. Bea bent over to Oliver and suggested he ask Maggie to dance.

Oliver recoiled. 'I don't dance.'

'There's always a first time,' said Bea. 'I don't want Maggie's husband to think she hasn't anyone to dance with.'

Oliver gulped, but leaned over to Maggie to issue an invitation. Maggie's eyebrows went up and she hesitated, but finally nodded. Of course she dwarfed Oliver when she stood up in her high heels, but that didn't matter. The great thing was that she wasn't seen to be a wallflower.

Mrs Somers-Briggs circulated, sweeping up all the fivers that had been donated for the favours earlier that evening and stowing them in a capacious black velvet bag. She was gracious to everyone. Bea wondered which of the Royal Family the woman had based her act on. When she arrived at their table, Bea excused herself to visit the ladies'. No way did she want to have a confrontation before the proceedings were over.

On her return, Bea found the noise from the disco even more overpowering. The DJ couldn't possibly have upped the volume again, could he?

Oliver leant over and said something into her left ear. She said, 'What?' He repeated it. Something about going to the gents'. Was he leaving Maggie to sit all by herself? No, Maggie wasn't in her chair. Maggie was on the dance floor with the middle-aged man from Max's party who'd been chatting her up earlier. Well, that was all right. A trendy young man cut in on Maggie, and her middle-aged partner returned to their table, perspiring. Good.

This left Bea isolated in her chair at the table, with just one of Max's party opposite her, smiling gently into the middle distance. Everyone else seemed to be on the dance floor.

The DJ announced that they'd worn him out and he was taking five, but the pianist tinkled the ivories and quite a few people stayed to dance to the golden oldies he was playing. Including Maggie and her new partner.

The photographer was working his way around the tables on the outside of the room. Bea wriggled round in her chair to see if she could get a good look at him, but he was mostly standing with his back to her, jollying people along into having their photographs taken with the little Pakistani girl who, to give her her due, was doing her best to sing for her supper, smiling at all the women, demure with all the men.

Would the evening never end? Their table filled up again. Oliver returned, looking pale. Had the food not agreed with him? Or was it excitement? He hadn't had more than one glass of wine, had he? Maggie was still dancing with her new admirer. They were well matched, he being over average in height.

Piers drifted back, eyes snapping, mouth curving at some story he'd just been told. The photographer finally reached their table, armed with his Polaroid camera for instant results. Piers said he'd love to be photographed with Ana, so Bea and Oliver pushed their chairs closer together and Bea collected another snap to put into her bag.

The DJ returned with a rousing number or two, and then began to wind down. Finally he announced he was going home to his mother, who fretted if he was out after midnight . . . which got quite a laugh as he didn't look the sort to be still living at home. Besides which it was after one in the morning. The boss woman thanked everyone for coming and for helping to give so many people a better future, and wished them all a safe journey home.

People began to leave, looking pleased with themselves and the way the evening had gone. Piers was engaged in close conversation by one of Max's guests.

Some people were still standing on the dance floor, and the photographer was taking his last few shots there.

Max and Nicole were being thanked for making up the party. Max put his arm round Bea. 'Are you all right, Mother? I can put Nicole into a taxi and stay on to help you, if you like?'

'No, dear. Thank you. I've got lots of back-up and it's best you don't get involved, don't you think?'

Piers said, 'I'll take good care of her, Max. You look after your wife and guests.'

Bea thought Max might argue, but he didn't. The room was clearing fast. Bea looked round for Maggie, but she was nowhere to be seen. Before Bea could become anxious, one of the waitresses hurried up to her. 'Are you Mrs Abbot? I have a message from the girl in your party. She's gone on to a club with someone, said not to wait for her.'

Bea was a little annoyed, thinking that Maggie might have had the courtesy to make her apologies in person. But there; youngsters nowadays never thought to say 'thank you' when given a present, didn't bother to reply to written invitations, or even think it was important to do so. It was a sign of the times. Bea reminded herself that Maggie had been going through a bad patch and deserved to find a boyfriend who'd treat her well. If she hadn't thought fit to advise Bea of her plans, well, Bea wasn't her mother, was she? And it didn't matter very much if Maggie opted out of the forthcoming showdown, because she'd no particular role to play in it. Unlike Oliver, who was drinking a glass of water, and shaking his head to clear it. Nerves, definitely. Hopefully Oliver would be all right.

Bea could see the manageress of the hotel hovering near the bar, which had now been cleared of drinks. Bea collected Oliver and Piers and, making the usual farewell noises to all and sundry, she led them off to where Ms McNeice was waiting for them.

'My office,' said Ms McNeice. 'You know the way? I'll bring them there as soon as I can.'

Bea nodded and led the two men down the corridor. The manageress' office was just as she'd seen it the previous day, except that all the paperwork had been cleared away, apart from one file on the desk. The room was shadowy, lit only by a desk lamp.

Coral was there already, huddled into a padded jacket. Also there was Tommy Banks, the bulky manager from the Garden Room. Even as she greeted them, Bea thought that the moment the gang saw them and made the connection, they'd realize they'd been found out, and try to run for it. How was she going to stop them? By brute force? By bringing in the hotel staff to form a human barrier?

Coral said, 'Where's Maggie?'

'Gone on to a club with someone,' said Bea. 'The man she was dancing with, I suppose.'

'Hope you don't mind my butting in,' said Tommy.

Coral was bursting with news. 'Tommy turned up to help

us clear the bar, but I said he had to keep out of sight and he did. But what I wanted to say was, that the DJ is not one of the gang. He's well known around here, the other bar staff say he's been around this area for yonks and they know his name and where he lives and all. He played at a function here only last week, not a charity do, and he's doing another at the Town Hall at the end of the month. So if you do want to talk to him at any time, you can.'

Bea stroked her temples. 'He's not her son, is he?'

'Who? Oh, no. No way. I think her son's Noel, the photographer. One of the receptionists here has been going out with him, thinks he's gorgeous, which I suppose he is if you like that sort of thing. She made an excuse to come into the function to see if he was making up to the Asian girl because of his working with her behind the camera. Anyway, it seems to be just a business arrangement, because there's a minicab booked to take her – the Asian girl – back home at the end of the evening, and she'll be going back solo. Or so the receptionist says.'

Bea was worried. 'You didn't let on to her that we suspect Noel of being crooked, did you?'

'No way! All she wanted was to feast her eyes on him, make sure he wasn't kissing and cuddling the Asian girl. Which he wasn't. From what I could see, he was being very professional, concentrating on the guests. Then Ms McNeice spotted the receptionist where she wasn't supposed to be, and shooed her back to her desk. She went off to text him a love message, hoping to connect up with him when he leaves tonight. So what happens now?'

Bea had been trying to think about this all evening. 'We have the advantage of surprise, and Ms McNeice is on our side. She says she'll bring them here to her office for a confrontation. I expect they'll bluster and argue but in the end we should be able to make them see the wisdom of paying up. What we don't want is them taking one look at us and running for their lives. We want them to get well into the room before they realize anything's wrong, and then I think we must block the door so they can't get out till we've made them see reason.'

Tommy Banks folded beefy arms across his chest. 'Count on me for that. I'll lurk behind the door and when they're well in, I'll close it and stand in front of it. They won't get past me in a hurry.'

'They may be some time,' said Bea. 'They have to clear up, pay the singer, give out dud cheques to one or two people. I think – if you're all agreed – that we should turn off the light and sit down in the dark to wait for them. That way, they won't realize they're walking into a trap until they're well into the room and find they can't get out.'

'Good idea,' said Piers, with his hand on the lamp. 'Everybody take their seats, concentrate on how much money they've raised this evening and how little they intend to pass on. Oliver, any idea how much yet?'

Oliver gave a little cough. 'Fifty thousand from the auction, then there's the favours on the table, the tickets, the promises. Two hundred and fifty thousand? Multiply by three, to include what they took on the other dates.'

'Something to think about,' said Piers. 'Is everyone sitting comfortably? Then I'll switch off the light.'

Noel was pleased with himself. He'd raked in a good amount with the photographs and it amused him to think that it was all honestly earned. Mummy always let him keep what he earned from photography, as well as giving him a cut of the proceeds.

He'd taken the key off Ana and given her a fifty-pound note when it was time for her to go. Money well spent.

Mummy was looking tired. Well, she did bear the brunt of it on these occasions. Richie was helping the DJ take his stuff out to his van. Richie was stupid. Why bother to help the DJ? They'd never see him again. Noel stuffed a wad of notes into his pocket and gave the rest, with his camera, to Richie to take out to the car. Richie grumbled but did it.

Noel put a careless arm around his mother's shoulders. 'Forgive me if I cut and run. Some unfinished business.'

She was writing a cheque for the singer, who didn't realize it was from Account No. 2. 'Not the receptionist, I hope? I saw her leering at you earlier.'

He laughed. 'Not the receptionist. I'll make my own way back. Don't wait up.'

He kissed his mother's cheek and left the function room, loosening his tie. He wouldn't take the lift to the honeymoon suite because he wanted to avoid reception. However, there was an unobtrusive staircase around the corner which would take him up to the first floor unobserved.

Now let the fun commence!

Eighteen

Sunday, two in the morning

A clock ticked somewhere in the darkened room. Bea rubbed her temples. Her headache was not going away. Was it just nervous tension? She massaged the back of her neck. There were several green points of light on the far side of the room. Standby lights for the computer and printer? As her eyesight became adjusted to the lack of central light, Bea made out the seated figures of her friends, and of the darker shadow where Tommy Banks stood beside the closed door.

She fancied, after a while, that she could distinguish between Oliver's rapid breathing, and Piers' slower tempo.

She tried to relax, to slow her own breathing. Perhaps that would help with her headache. She tried counting to five as she drew in a deep breath, and then counting to five again as she let it out. She'd heard somewhere that this exercise helped one to get to sleep. She was too tense for that, but it did help. This might be a good time to pray a little. She uncurled her hands, closed her eyes and tried to think what words to use. She thought she wasn't much good at this lark because words always eluded her and though she knew in her head that He didn't need her to go into detail when she was in trouble, she suspected He might like her to make an effort. All she could manage was, *Please. Please. Please.*

What was the time? She opened her eyes to glance at where her watch would be, but it didn't have a luminous dial. She heard a ruffle of cloth as one of the men turned their wrists to check the time. Piers.

The corridor outside was heavily carpeted, as was the office itself, so it was something of a shock – even though they'd been expecting it – when the door opened, and Ms McNeice said, 'Go on in, and I'll turn the light on.'

Bea closed her eyes, blinking, as an overhead light came on.

She heard the door close. She'd been expecting to see three people from the gang, but there were only two; the woman known as Mrs Somers-Briggs, and her partner. No gorgeous young man.

Mrs Somers-Briggs looked at Bea and Piers, and didn't know them from Adam. She looked at Oliver, and frowned. What was this?

Coral made a small movement with her hands, and Mrs Somers-Briggs focused on her. It was clear that, out of context, the boss woman didn't recognize Coral. And then, she did. Bea saw her eyes widen slightly, and then the woman's face froze. Her eyes glittered in a porcelain mask. Bea saw her decide to play the 'bewildered' card. 'What . . .? I'm afraid I don't understand . . .'

The man behind her was looking around him. His eyes seemed to recede into his head as he narrowed the lids. He stood stock still, mentally computing the facts. Then he turned his head and saw Tommy Banks standing with folded arms in front of the door.

Ms McNeice eeled around the woman and seated herself behind her desk. 'Let me introduce you. Mrs Somers-Briggs; you know Coral, of Coral Catering, of course. And Mr Banks, the manager from the Garden Room. These others are friends of theirs, anxious to see that all debts are paid before you leave.'

The woman firmed her jaw. 'Ms McNeice, you asked me to accompany you to your office to pay the balance owing to you. Naturally I am more than happy to do so. I don't know what you've heard from these . . . these others. I have come across them before, and I will admit that quite frankly no, we didn't pay them everything they demanded. The services they rendered were not up to the standard we expect, and naturally we discounted their very overpriced bills. I'm amazed that they have the nerve to complain to you about their sordid little scams. Also, if they'd any real grounds for complaint, they'd have gone to the police, right?'

Coral's face flared red, but Ms McNeice put up her hand to

forestall an outburst. Bea couldn't help but admire Mrs Somers-Briggs' nerve, and for the first time she wondered whether Coral's bill really had been inflated. She remembered the man at the Priory Country Club; yes, his bill probably had been inflated. But no, Coral wouldn't do that. And neither would Tommy Banks.

'The police?' said Ms McNeice, 'Yes, we'll bring them in if we have to.'

The woman wavered for only a second, and then returned to the attack. 'If we owe anything – which I dispute, by the way – then the remedy is simple. These people should apply to the small claims court for recompense.'

'We would have done,' said Coral, through clenched teeth, 'if we could have tracked you down. You gave us a false address and a discontinued phone number, remember?'

'You are mistaken. True, I lost my mobile phone recently, but that's no reason to say I've given you false information.'

Oliver lifted a finger. 'On the adverts, the phone number was for the Bolivian Embassy, right?'

The woman stared at him. 'Who might you be?'

Oliver stared back. 'A friend of Coral's.'

'As are we all,' said Piers, speaking for the first time. 'I don't suppose you realized you'd left a trail behind you, but you did. We know all about the accommodation address, and the way you've cheated everyone you come across.'

The woman reared her head on her long neck, making her diamond earrings flash in the light. 'Of course we used an accommodation address. We were moving house, and needed a base for our mail. I've already explained about the mobile phone.'

'Losing one mobile phone,' said Bea, softly, 'is a nuisance. Losing two is a tragedy for all those concerned.'

'Who might you be?'

'Bea Abbot of the Abbot Agency. Coral is an old friend and I want to see her righted.'

'A detective agency?' The woman was scornful. 'I suppose you're charging the earth by way of retainers and hourly rates? I pity Coral, for I don't suppose she'll see a quarter of what she's owed in the end.'

Coral looked confused. Mrs Somers-Briggs was good, wasn't she!

Bea said, 'No, Mrs Somers-Briggs. We are doing this for love, and for our reputation's sake. Coral gets one hundred per cent of what we collect from you.'

'Minus a finder's fee,' put in Oliver, being sensible.

'If that is all . . .?' The woman shrugged. 'Very well. I'm prepared to pay the balance of her bill, if that's what you want. It's under protest, mind, because as I said before, she wasn't worth it.' She was still carrying her black velvet bag. From this she drew a chequebook, which she laid on the desk. 'How much do we owe you?'

'No cheques,' said Coral. 'Twice bitten, twice shy. Cash only, please.'

Mrs Somers-Briggs was amazed. 'You can't be serious!'

'Never more so,' said Bea. 'You've raked in enough cash this evening to pay off Coral. So pay her. Then we'll talk about the other people you owe money to.'

'Don't be ridiculous!' the woman said, staring hard at Bea. 'This is nothing but blackmail.'

'If you think we're blackmailing you,' said Bea, 'then you should call the police and lay information against us.'

'But . . .' Her hands opened and shut. She glanced back at her confederate, who seemed very relaxed, listening to all that was going on with a slight smile. He acted as if they'd done nothing wrong.

'Well,' said Mrs Somers-Briggs, regaining confidence, 'I have nowhere near enough cash on me to pay you. The proceeds from the auction were mostly by way of cheques which are made out to the charity, and I shall have to pay them into my bank account on Monday.'

'There's the money from the favours, and from the photographer. He's your son, isn't he?'

'My son?' For a moment her eyes wavered. 'My son has nothing to do with this. He takes photographs, yes, and is paid for them. That's his money, not mine.'

'You mean that he didn't hand it over to you at the end of the evening? Where is he, by the way? We expected him to join you.'

The woman frowned, and then smoothed the frown out. 'He has a girl in tow, I believe. I suppose he's with her.'

Coral asked, 'The receptionist?'

'How should I know?'

Ms McNeice yawned. 'All this is wasting time. Mrs Somers-Briggs, you have enough cash on you to pay what is due to Coral, I assume. You also owe us here at the hotel for the evening, and I have taken the precaution of getting a bill for the food you ordered tonight. Then there is the small matter of the bills for the functions you ran at the Garden Room and at the Country Club, not to mention the wine bills.'

'Not to mention,' said Piers, 'the amounts you've raised for charity on these last three events. So, how do you propose to settle your accounts?'

Oliver was grinning. 'I know one way. She can make over all those cheques she's taken to us. All she has to do is sign them on the back, and hand them over.'

Piers lifted his hand. 'Which doesn't recompense the charities from whom she's stolen. I'm rather keen to see they get what's due to them.'

'You are mad, quite mad!' said Mrs Somers-Briggs, showing the whites of her eyes. 'What makes you think I can be bullied into—'

'Doing what you promised?' said Bea. 'All those bouncing cheques you handed out, promised to pay for services delivered. So pay up, or we get the police.'

The woman looked at the door. 'Do you intend to hold me here against my will? If the police come, I'll have you charged with kidnapping and blackmail and demanding money with menaces. Oh, and slander, too.'

Bea spread her hands. 'What slander? What menaces? What blackmail? If you are arrested for the three scams that we know about, how many more people are going to crawl out of the woodwork to say that you've scammed them in the past? Won't your photograph be all over the papers? We're doing you a favour by asking you to settle up without making a fuss.'

The woman thought about it. 'You're bluffing. You don't want to go to the police any more than I do. You'd have had them here already if you'd meant to bring them in on it.' She picked up the chequebook and put it back in her bag. 'I'm leaving now, and if your man on the door tries to stop me or offers me violence in any way, I'll sue him for every penny he's got. Come on, Richie, we're out of here.'

Ms McNeice sprang to her feet. 'What about everything you owe?'

'I was going to give you a cheque tonight since you'd been so pressing about payment,' said Mrs Somers-Briggs, 'Now you can send in your bill in the usual way. You know the address.'

Piers was on his feet, too. 'Which address? The newsagent's? That's not good enough. Bea, I think we do have to bring in the police on this. I know Coral would prefer that we didn't, but—'

'Nor the hotel,' said Ms McNeice, 'but we can't—'

'Mrs Briggs, or whatever your name is, you leave over my dead body,' said Tommy Banks, who remained, rock-like, blocking the doorway. 'I'm likely to lose my job over this anyway, so I'm not bothered if we have to call the police.'

'I agree,' said Bea.

Mrs Somers-Briggs produced a mobile phone, and pressed buttons. 'I'm dialling my solicitor. He won't like being pulled out of bed at this hour, but—'

'Who cares?' said Piers, also producing a mobile phone. 'Nine nine nine it is.'

'Hold on a minute,' said Ms McNeice. 'What's that noise?'

They'd all been so wound up they'd not noticed that someone was banging on the office door, and shouting. Mrs Somers-Briggs stopped dialling, as did Piers. 'What . . .! Who . . .?'

'Your son?' asked Bea.

'Noel? No. He's not involved, I tell you.' The woman was worried. For the first time she looked uncertain of herself.

Tommy Banks lifted an eyebrow at Bea, and then stood away from the door. In burst a young girl in receptionist's uniform. She was red in the face, her hair had come down, and she was crying. 'Oh, why didn't you open the door? She may not be dead, you must get a doctor, quickly!'

She bit her fists, falling against the wall, laughing and crying, 'He thinks I'm dead, too!'

Mrs Somers-Briggs turned to ice, but her confederate edged towards the door.

'Oh, no you don't!' His exit was barred by a beefy arm.

Oliver shot to his feet. 'Maggie? Is it Maggie? Where is she? No, she's gone clubbing. It can't be her.'

Bea was on her feet, her mind going into overdrive. 'It can't be Maggie. She left us a message saying she'd gone on to a club, and not to wait for her.'

'You idiots!' screamed the receptionist. 'It was him, wasn't it! All the time it was him! He said he loved me and then he went off with her, didn't he, one of the guests, and he lied to me, he lied . . . and he hit me so hard, and I can't bear it!' She slid down to the floor, her legs all over the place. Her hair fell over her face. She pushed it back, revealing a darkening bruise on her jaw.

'What girl? Who lied to you?' Bea restrained herself from shaking the girl with an effort.

The girl pointed at Mrs Somers-Briggs. 'Her son, the photographer! He took her up there just to spite me, and then he hit me and she's dead!'

'Dead?' whispered Oliver.

'No!' said Piers, sharply.

'What girl?' said Bea, her heart beating faster.

'How should I know! A girl with dark red hair. Oooooh!'

Bea spotted a jug of water and a glass on a side table. She considered throwing the contents over the hysterical girl, but desisted in favour of less drastic action. She poured out a glass and took it over to the girl. What she wanted to do was to run out into the hotel and search for Maggie – if it was Maggie – but the hotel had many rooms, so where should she start?

'Slander!' Mrs Somers-Briggs had hard work to get the word out, and suddenly she looked her age and more. 'Noel wouldn't harm anyone. Not even a girl who'd spurned him. You are mistaken. We're leaving, right now.'

Bea knelt by the receptionist, and put the glass to her lips. 'Drink this.'

Ms McNeice was on an internal phone, trying to raise someone at the front desk, but – Bea glanced at her watch – it was after two in the morning, and maybe the girl was the only one on duty?

The receptionist gulped and wept. Bea said, 'Take another sip. That's right. Now, tell us what happened.'

The girl made an effort to comply. 'I was watching, waiting for him to leave, but he didn't go out with the guests. The doorman said that he was looking in the mirror – you can see right down the corridor to the function room if you look in the mirror in the foyer – and he said he'd seen the photographer going up the stairs in a hurry. Oh, my face!'

Bea took out her handkerchief, dunked it in the water, and pressed it to the girl's jaw. 'Go on.'

'I thought he'd taken the Indian girl up to one of the rooms, but the doorman said she'd gone off in a cab, so Noel couldn't have been with her. I checked the register and there was this one name, something Middle-Eastern and nobody could remember a man who might be Middle-Eastern staying with us tonight, so I didn't know what to do, but I couldn't leave it, could I, so I took the master key and went up to the honeymoon suite and knocked on the door saying it was room service, and oh . . . he opened the door and . . . oh!'

At this point she started to hyperventilate. Bea pushed the girl's head down between her knees and told her to breathe in and out, slowly, slowly. All the time she could feel a pulse beating in her throat, and she wanted to scream for Maggie . . . if it was Maggie and not some other poor girl, who surely couldn't be dead, no, she wouldn't believe it! But suppose she was? That Noel! She wanted to hit someone. Preferably Mrs Somers-Briggs. She made herself keep calm, and tried to help the girl.

'Honeymoon suite!' said Ms McNeice, keeping calm, sorting out keys with hands that shook. 'We'll just take a look, shall we?'

'Nonsense!' Mrs Somers-Briggs' mouth worked some more. 'You can't just break in on your guests at this hour of the morning, on the say-so of some hysterical little chit who's been stood up by her boyfriend and got herself into a state. Noel's gone home, of course. Or he's out clubbing with his new girlfriend. Noel has lots of girls.'

'You, Mrs Briggs, or whatever your name is,' said Ms McNeice, 'sit down there! And your side-kick over there. Sit still and don't move an inch. The men will stay here and watch that you don't move. In fact, I'm going to lock you in, so you can't walk out till we've got to the bottom of this affair.'

'I'm coming with you,' said Oliver.

'I rather think,' Piers began, 'that we ought to call the police right away.'

Ms McNeice gave him a hard look. 'Not till I've found out if there's anything to worry them about. You stay here and you,' she nodded to Tommy Banks, 'while I go up and see what's what.'

Mrs Somers-Briggs sank into a chair, gazing into space. 'The girl's hysterical.'

'Hysterical she may be,' said Mrs McNeice, 'but you must agree this has to be checked out, because if your son has indeed assaulted a girl . . .!'

The receptionist tried to raise her head, and Bea let her do so. 'She's lying on the bed, tied up, blood all over her.' She shuddered, and began to cry again.

Bea felt herself go pale. If it was Maggie up there . . .! With an effort she stood up. She tried to keep her voice steady. 'Coral, would you look after this girl, please? I want, no, I need to see what's happened upstairs.'

Oliver was hopping from one foot to the other. 'If it's Maggie, if he's harmed her, I'll—'

Piers said, 'If he's harmed Maggie, there'll be no pit of hell that he won't suffer, believe me. Bea, I think I'll be more use here than coming with you. Take my mobile phone, so's you can ring for the police if . . . if . . . the worst. That is, can you cope?'

Bea nodded. Tommy Banks stood away from the door, letting Ms McNeice, Oliver and Bea out into the corridor.

The door closed behind them, and the manageress locked it before setting off down the corridor. 'We'll take the back stairs. This way.' She led the way through the foyer and round a corner to a stairwell.

Bea lifted her skirt in front to climb the stairs after the manageress' neat black shoes. Oliver followed, mumbling to himself what he would do if Maggie had been harmed. It sounded as if he were crying.

Bea's own eyes were dry. She castigated herself for having allowed Maggie to come that evening, for letting her dance with anyone she pleased, for not realizing until too late that the photographer and Maggie's earlier assailant were one and the same people. She went further. Maggie had come under her roof and she, Bea, had accepted responsibility for her. If Maggie had been killed . . . it didn't bear thinking about, but she couldn't stop thinking about it. Except, of course, it might not be Maggie, pray heaven it wasn't. *Dear Lord, please . . .*

They reached the door marked 'Honeymoon Here'. Mrs McNeice knocked, softly, and then more loudly. She got out her master key, and turned it in the lock.

The place was in darkness. Oliver was breathing hard, pushing his way in. 'Maggie, are you there?'

There was no reply.

Noel told himself not to run. A man running through the streets at this time of night would look suspicious. People might remember him, especially as he was wearing red-stained evening dress. That slag! Who'd have thought she'd have so much fight in her?

He didn't think he'd killed the other girl, but maybe he had. It was so easy to hit them a little too hard and, pfut! They went limp and died. It really wasn't his fault.

He forced himself to walk normally. He passed a couple arguing about whose flat they should go to. Don't make eye contact. That way they won't register your face. Anyway, they're too absorbed in themselves.

He wished he'd brought his own car; he'd decided against it because it was so recognizable. That was one good thing about Richie, that he always knew where to borrow a car for you. For now, he was reduced to walking. He couldn't take a taxi at this time of night because the driver might remember him. He couldn't risk checking to see if Mummy's car was still there, either. Anyway, she'd be long gone.

Passing a lighted shop window, he gave himself a bad fright. Who was the dishevelled figure mirrored there? He ran his fingers through his hair, straightened his jacket. He'd lost his bow tie somewhere. Oh well, it didn't matter, did it?

He reached the front door of the flats and delved into pockets for his key, only to bring out one that he shouldn't have on him. The key to the honeymoon suite. He swore, shoved it back into his pocket. He sorted out the key to the front door of the flats and let himself in.

Nineteen

Sunday, the early hours of the morning

The honeymoon suite was in darkness. It smelt of something sweet. Wine?

Ms McNeice snapped on the overhead light and Oliver cried out, 'Maggie?'

They entered a well-appointed sitting room. There was a comfortable seating area to the right, with a plasma screen TV on the wall above. Beyond that was a small bar. There were empty bottles and used glasses on the bar, some for wine and some for soft drinks. The room was empty.

Ms McNeice rushed to a door on the left and went in, switching on more lights. This was the bedroom, lavishly furnished with a four-poster bed and a lot of drapery. Doors led off to a walk-in wardrobe and a bathroom.

Maggie was lying on the bed with her arms stretched out above her head, her wrists tied to the bed posts at either side. Something white had been thrust into her mouth. Her eyes were closed. Her dress had been ripped apart to the waist, and pushed up above her hips. Her legs were bare, but she was still wearing her high heeled strappy sandals, which had done some damage to the bed covers in her struggle to free herself.

Bea clapped her hands to her mouth. Was Maggie dead? Pray God, no! Yet there was a horrible red stain running down from her mouth and over her throat and shoulder.

'Maggie!' Oliver thrust past Bea to run to her side. He stumbled and nearly fell over an empty wine bottle, which rolled away under the bed.

Bea told herself to keep calm. It did no good panicking. Maggie's eyelids fluttered. She wasn't dead! Praise the Lord!

The girl had been tied up with her own tights, one leg to each arm. The more she'd struggled, the more the nylon had tightened around her wrists. It wouldn't do any good trying to tackle the knots. Bea dived into her evening bag for a pair of nail scissors.

Oliver tugged fruitlessly at one of Maggie's arms. 'Who was it? Was it Noel? I'll kill him!'

At that moment Maggie opened her eyes fully and moaned. Oliver was getting nowhere with the knots. Bea eased the gag out of Maggie's mouth. The girl spat and moved her lips, tried to speak and failed.

Ms McNeice disappeared into the bathroom and returned with a glass of water while Bea started to saw through the nylon on Maggie's right wrist. The material was so taut that it was hard to cut but Bea concentrated, clipping her way through the material till one of Maggie's wrists was free.

Maggie tried to work saliva into her mouth. Ms McNeice held a glass of water to the girl's lips. Bea went round to the other side of the bed and started work on the other tie.

Ms McNeice looked at the damp square of fabric which had been in Maggie's mouth. 'One of our face towels.'

Bea sawed through the second nylon tie and helped Maggie to sit up with an arm under her shoulders. Maggie held her hands up before her. They were bloodless. In her struggles, she'd pulled the knots tighter, and the nylons had made grooves in her wrists.

Ms McNeice encouraged Maggie to sip water. 'Another sip, that's right.'

Bea told Oliver to massage one of Maggie's hands while she took on the other. Oliver was shaking so much he didn't make too good a job of it, and returning circulation made Maggie mew with pain.

'Drink some more,' urged Ms McNeice. Maggie did as she was bid, tears of pain and frustration standing out on her cheeks.

Close to, Bea smelled wine even more strongly. Was that really blood on the girl, or was it wine?

'Did he . . . did he do it to you?' asked Oliver, his own eyes bright with tears.

Maggie tried to shake her head, but the effort obviously hurt. She mumbled, ''M'all right.'

'You're far from all right,' said Ms McNeice. 'All that blood. I'll get an ambulance.'

Maggie managed to sit upright by herself. ''S'wine. Not

blood. Girl. Hit her.' She pointed a wavering hand towards the door. 'She OK?'

'What girl?' said Ms McNeice.

Bea got it. 'Your receptionist? She must have come in just as . . . before he could . . . Maggie, did he . . .?'

'Not . . . time. Said he would, but . . .' She tried moving her legs, and with Bea's help, managed to sit on the side of the bed and cried out, 'Aaaagh, my hands!' Bea massaged one wrist while Ms McNeice took over from Oliver on the other.

'Can you tell us what happened?'

Maggie nodded, grimacing as feeling came back into her hands. 'The Asian girl, Ana, dancing next me, collapsed. I helped her stand up. She said, go to loo, would I go with. Then she said not the loo, but go up to her room. She said hotel had booked a room for her overnight.'

'Now that was a lie,' said Ms McNeice. 'Did she have a key?'

Maggie nodded. 'She was stumbling around, all over the place, but I got her up here safely. She wanted a drink, some juice, bottle open already on the table. In the other room.' Maggie pointed to the outer room. 'She said would I like one and I said yes, and then . . . I suppose it was drugged? I woke up on the bed, with my arms tied above me. Ana had gone, and that . . . that bastard was trying to force more wine down my throat. I threw up and got him, I hope, oh I do hope! And he'd taken off my tights and put on my shoes again, which was really weird, but apparently he has a thing about shoes. So I kicked and kicked, trying to get him, though I don't think I did! Oh, I do wish I had done! I'm fed up with being used as a toy and I'm going to make him pay for it if it takes me for ever, and ah . . . my hands!'

'He didn't rape you again?' said Bea, wanting to be sure.

Maggie shook her head. 'He thrust that thing in my mouth to stop me screaming, and he had a pocket knife and cut my dress down and pushed up my skirt and he was stroking my thighs and telling me what he was going to do to me, and then that other girl came in and saw us and he went for her! He just launched himself at her, and hit her and she fell down against the wall, and I couldn't see properly because of lying down, and then the light went out and I heard the door close. I wanted to call out to the girl, but of course I couldn't. I was so afraid she was dead . . . and then . . . and then I must have passed out, I suppose, because I don't remember anything more till I heard Oliver calling my name.' Maggie wept noisy, difficult tears.

Bea held her close. 'The receptionist's all right. She thought he was up here with Ana and that's why she burst in on you, but she's not dead. She came down to tell us what had happened. She thought *you* were dead, you see.'

'Me? I'm all right. Never better. At least, I will be when I've made him pay for what he's done to me. Just look at my dress, and it's not even mine! How dare he! I'll kill him!'

'Let's get you cleaned up,' said Ms McNeice.

'I have a better idea,' said Bea. 'If Maggie's up for it. Let's take some photos of her with the wine-cum-blood all over her, and her dress torn. Oliver, here's my camera. Record everything, including the nylon ropes. Then we take Maggie downstairs just as she is, or with a wrap over her – here, take my jacket – and we show Mrs Somers-Briggs just what her son has been doing behind her back. She seems devoted to Noel, and I think she'll pay up if it means we don't bring the police into it. What do you think, Maggie?'

'Yes, yes, yes! Ow, my hands!'

Oliver took the camera and started working the room.

'Is that wise?' asked Ms McNeice. 'I mean, he can't go round attacking young girls and get away with it.'

'I'm weighing up what he's done here to Maggie and to your receptionist, against the unpaid bills and possible bankruptcies the gang has caused. Maggie will survive, won't you, dear? Your receptionist will survive. Yes, he ought to go to jail for what he's done and yes, it's probably unethical to make a deal with them, but if we get him arrested there's no reason to suppose he'll make things easy for Maggie. He's taken her out on a date before this, remember, and he could say she consented. Oh, I know she didn't, but that's what these scumbags claim, when they get into court. They can say Maggie knew what she was doing because she'd been married before, and is no innocent. Then there'd be the long wait for a trial, and no guarantee that a jury would find him guilty because he looks so . . . so little boyish.'

'I'm game, definitely,' said Maggie, forcing herself to stand. She wobbled, and Oliver rushed to put his arm around her. Tears were still running down her face, but she made herself take a few steps. 'Count me in. Let's hit them where it hurts, in their pockets.'

'Are you sure?' asked Ms McNeice.

Maggie accepted Bea's jacket, and thrust her arms into it. 'Ouch. Oh, my wrists! Let's take them to the cleaners – and talking of cleaners, you'd better make him pay for this dress while he's at it, too.'

'We-ell,' said Ms McNeice, looking at the ruined bedding, 'you've got a point there. The hotel must add something for compensation.'

'Let's go,' said Bea.

Ms McNeice unlocked the door of her office, called out that they were coming in, and was everything all right.

'Yes,' said a couple of voices at once. Ms McNeice led the way in. The atmosphere in the office was tense with worry, and with so many people in it the temperature had risen. The receptionist was holding a pad to her jaw. Coral had taken off her jacket, and the men had all loosened their ties.

Mrs Somers-Briggs looked haggard, though perhaps that was the effect of the harsh office lighting.

'Give Maggie a chair,' said Bea, steering the girl in. 'Take off your wrap, Maggie, and show everyone what young Noel's been up to this time.'

Maggie's face, throat and breast were still parti-coloured from wine stains, and she held the torn front of her dress together with one hand. Bruises had darkened on both wrists, adding to the ones Noel had inflicted before.

'Oh, you're not dead, then?' cried the receptionist, her mouth puffy from the blow that had felled her.

'Where's Noel?' muttered Mrs Somers-Briggs, looking at the empty doorway.

'He was interrupted and fled,' said Ms McNeice. 'He probably went out by the fire exit. Now, Mrs Somers-Briggs, we can call the police and have your son arrested or we can cut a deal.'

'I want to see him in jail.' The receptionist was feeling vicious. 'He deserves it after all he's said and done to me.'

Mrs Somers-Briggs sent her eyes to left and right, seeking a way out. She shifted on her feet to interrogate her partner without words. He shrugged. 'Best settle up. He's forfeited his share, anyway.'

She chewed on her lip. 'Very well. You can have what cash I have and I can sign over the cheques to you as well.' She pulled a wad of them out of her bag, borrowed a pen from the manageress, and began to sign her name on the back.

'That's not enough,' said Oliver, producing his laptop from behind the desk. 'I have a list here of everything you owe and a provisional total. I hope we've got everybody's accounts here but in case we haven't, I'm going to suggest we add ten per cent for contingencies, which we'll either use to pay bills as yet undiscovered, or send on to the charities which you've falsely represented. All you have to do is instruct your bank to pay this amount to us, and we'll see that everyone is reimbursed.'

'Take these and be content.' She continued to sign the back of the cheques, passing them one by one over to Oliver.

'You've got Internet banking sussed. We know you've been depositing money in different banks, one per function. Then you've withdrawn it from those accounts and put it . . . where?' He booted up his computer, and settled down at the desk to take her instructions.

'You can't expect me to give you that information,' she said, signing away.

Oliver nodded. 'Oh, I do. Take a good hard look at what's been done to Maggie and to the hotel receptionist, and think of how many years Noel will get for that if you don't clear these debts.'

Mrs Somers-Briggs' breathing became harsh. 'No way.'

Her partner said, 'I'm not going down for what Noel's done.' And to Oliver, 'I think it's NatWest.'

Oliver typed it in. 'Now your account number and name, and then the first of your security numbers.'

Mrs Somers-Briggs' colour had risen. 'You're being ridiculous! If you know anything at all you'll know we've been using several different banks, all of which have passwords. I'm no financial genius. I don't keep numbers and figures in my head, you know.'

'I'll give you the benefit of the doubt on that,' said Oliver. 'If you can't remember them off-hand, I suppose you have a written record which you keep with you at all times.'

'Nonsense!' But her eyelids had flickered, and her hand made a movement towards the capacious black velvet bag which she'd laid on the desk.

Oliver laid his hand on the bag and she turned her head away. He said, 'You have a diary or something like that in here?'

Her voice sounded dry. 'Of course not.'

Her partner said, 'Do it, girl. There's a time to cut your losses, and this is it.'

She made no movement to comply, so Oliver opened the bag and emptied the contents on to the desk. Out tumbled a thick wad of notes and three bank-issue bags of coins, cosmetics, throat pastilles, aspirin, tissues, house keys and a mobile phone. Oliver isolated a miniature silver-backed notebook and pencil, returning the rest to the bag.

Flicking through the notebook, he held up one particular page for her to see. 'This page is headed NW – for NatWest? Are these the passwords we need?'

She shrugged, hesitated, then nodded.

Bea said, 'I'd like you to say it loud, please. Are you giving us permission to take the money from your account?'

'Oh, very well. Take what you want.'

Oliver clattered away on his laptop, stopped. Looked pleased. 'So far, so good. Now they're asking for a password. Is this the right one?' Again he held up the notebook so that she could see. She pinched in her lips, looked away from him, but said, 'I suppose so.'

He nodded to himself and typed in the relevant numbers. 'Now they want . . . yes . . . yes, it's all here.' He tapped away. 'Now I'm going to ask for the current balance,' said Oliver. He whistled, and looked up at Bea. 'Care to see how much she's got in here?'

Bea looked at the total and felt stunned. Why, this was enough to buy a couple of mansions in the most expensive part of London, and she wasn't thinking Northolt or Hanwell, but Knightsbridge. She shivered, clutched her upper arms. Without her jacket, she felt cold. 'Take the lot, Oliver. We'll pay everyone what they're owed and pass the rest on to charity, which is where it was supposed to go in the first place.'

Mrs Somers-Briggs said, 'You expect me to believe that you're going to pass it all on? What nonsense. You're no better than we are, stealing from me, and keeping it all for yourself.'

'Surprising as it may seem to you,' said Bea, 'some people play straight.'

Oliver held up one finger. 'We'll take a small percentage,

equal to what a normal fund-raiser takes, and not a penny more.'

'Oh, three choruses of *Hearts and Flowers*!'

Oliver's fingers hovered over the keys. 'I've put in our own name, bank, account number and sort code. Fine. Do I press send?' Everyone nodded. He pressed it. 'Now what guarantee do we have that this transaction won't be annulled as soon as Mrs Somers-Briggs gets back to her own computer?'

Mrs Somers-Briggs smiled, not nicely. 'You have my word, of course.'

'Your word's not worth a penny,' said Bea. 'On the other hand, we hold the evidence against Noel. We also have photographs of you and your partners, plus photographs of what you did to Maggie. If you try to cancel the order, then our file goes straight to the police.'

Again Mrs Somers-Briggs' eyes went to her partner, and again he nodded, saying, 'Let it go. I told you Noel was more trouble than he was worth.'

'Very well. I'll let the transaction go through if Noel goes free.'

Piers lifted a hand. 'I'm not sure we can trust you, and I certainly don't trust young Noel. What if he finds some other girl to rape tonight, or tomorrow night? What if he tries to intimidate Maggie into refusing to give evidence against him? We wouldn't be bound to silence in that case.'

'He wouldn't do that!' She was sharp.

'I think he's running out of control. We're not offering you a blanket Get Out of Jail Free card. If he's had up for anything else that he's done or will do in the future, then the deal's off.'

Lines deepened on her face. 'You're being very hard.'

'Probably not hard enough,' said Piers. 'I imagine these are not the first scams you've run, and that you've left a trail of damaged and bankrupt people around the country.'

'Ridiculous!' But the rebuttal was perfunctory.

'Ms McNeice,' said Piers, 'am I right in thinking there is some kind of association of hoteliers? Would you care to put photographs of these two people on their website with a warning about them?'

'What?' For the first time, the woman looked alarmed. 'You can't do that.'

'Will do,' said Ms McNeice. 'With pleasure.'

The receptionist wobbled to her feet. 'What about what he did to me?'

'And to Maggie,' said Bea, noting that Maggie was sagging in her chair.

Piers stroked a chin that was showing a distinct shadow. 'Yes, Mrs Somers-Briggs, what about these two girls? Those diamonds of yours are the real thing, if I'm any judge of the matter. Suppose you throw them into the kitty and we give them to the girls by way of recompense for all they've suffered.'

The woman clutched her ear lobes, and shivered. Slowly she divested herself of her bracelet and earrings, laying them on the table. 'Can we go now?'

Bea collected nods from around the room. Tommy Banks stood away from the door. Ms McNeice said she'd see their guests off the premises. Mrs Somers-Briggs swept the black velvet bag off the desk to take with her, but Coral said, 'No, you don't. That's my cash in there.'

Mrs Somers-Briggs delved into the bag and withdrew the wad of notes, throwing them into the air and letting them flutter down all over the desk and floor. Perhaps she thought this would distract everyone, for she made a grab at the pile of cheques she'd counter-signed. Piers put his hand over hers, and leaned on it.

She shrugged. He took his hand away, she shouldered the black bag and walked out, followed by her partner.

Coral began to laugh, but as her laughter climbed towards hysteria, she managed to stop herself. Oliver shut down his laptop.

Anticlimax. Bea was too tired to think straight and Coral was blinking to keep herself awake. Ms McNeice seemed as fresh as ever, as did Tommy Banks.

Piers collected the notes into a neat pile. 'Have we an elastic band to put round these?'

Ms McNeice said, 'I suggest we count the cash now, and total the cheques. If you agree, I'll then give you a receipt for them and the diamonds, and put everything in the safe until tomorrow when we can have a meeting to work out who gets what. Do you all agree?'

'I'll help,' said Tommy Banks.

Oliver was staring at something on the desk. He said,

'Eureka!' in a hushed voice. He picked the little silver-backed notebook up. 'She forgot this! Which means—'

Bea began to laugh. 'Which means that if she was speaking the truth, this may be the only record she has of her passwords.'

'She's probably got the original records back home,' said Oliver. 'Or she could go into the bank in person on Monday and cancel the transaction. I think it's fifty-fifty that it goes through, even with what we've got on Noel.'

Suddenly Bea felt too tired to cope. 'I'm taking Maggie home and putting her to bed. Piers, can you find us a taxi? Coral, have you got your van with you?'

Coral said she'd stashed it in the square opposite and was looking forward to putting on the electric blanket in her bed when she got home and perhaps having a hot toddy to help her sleep. 'For you must admit it's been quite an experience, hasn't it?'

Ms McNeice said they'd put up the receptionist for the night – though not in the honeymoon suite – and in twos and threes they dispersed.

'Thank God that's all over,' said Piers, as they got into a cab. 'Though I don't think we'd have got the money out of her if Noel hadn't behaved so badly.' He consulted his watch. 'I'll doss down with you tonight, Bea, if you don't mind. Too late for anything else.'

Bea nodded. She was past speech. She envied young Oliver his seemingly endless supply of energy. If it hadn't been for him, they'd never have known how to get the money. Even Maggie, who'd been so appallingly badly treated, was able to summon up a smile when Oliver asked if she were all right now.

Bea wondered what Hamilton would have done, if he'd been in charge tonight. The thought made her smile. He'd have tried to keep Bea and Coral out of it, probably. He had old-fashioned ideas about men looking after their womenfolk. Mind you, there was a lot to be said for his ideas when you were as tired as Bea was tonight.

She remembered something that he would also have done if he'd been around tonight, and that was saying thank you. She said it now . . . *Thanks, Lord. Oh, thank you. From the bottom of my heart, I thank you.*

Sunday, early hours of the morning, continued
Someone was waiting for Noel on the first-floor landing outside his flat.

'*Remember me?*'

At first Noel couldn't place the little man, taking him for a beggar who had somehow managed to gain entrance to the flats when another resident had gone in or out of the front door. '*Out of my way, old man.*'

'*I am making a citizen's arrest,*' the pompous old prick said, grasping Noel's sleeve.

'*What the . . .!*' Noel shook him off. '*Go home and sleep it off, do you hear?*'

'*I want my money and I'm not leaving till I get it.*'

Noel laughed, short and sharp. '*If you don't get out of my way immediately, it'll be on your head.*'

The little man drew himself up to his inconsiderable height – Noel topped him by six inches – and ran his forefinger left and right over his almost non-existent moustache. '*My name is—*'

'*Wait a minute. I remember you. At the Country Club? Weren't you the waiter in charge of the wine or something?*'

'*I provided all the wines for that evening,*' said Leo, with dignity,' *for which I have not yet been paid. It's taken me some time to track you down, Mr Noel Briggs – or whatever your name is – but now I've found you, I'm not leaving till I get my money.*'

'*My name is not Briggs,*' said Noel, automatically. '*You have the wrong man.*'

Leo produced a bundle of soiled and torn bills. '*Once I'm on the trail, I never let up. I watched outside your accommodation address this afternoon till I saw you leave, and I followed you all the way here. To make sure I'd got the right person, I've spent hours going through all the rubbish downstairs in the various bins till I found the proof I needed. Your mother rents flat number four under the name of Briggs and we are outside flat number four at this very minute.*'

'*Mistaken identity. Come back tomorrow afternoon when my mother's here, and you can talk to her about . . . whatever.*'

Leo flourished the papers. '*By tomorrow afternoon you may well have flitted. I've been sitting here waiting for you to return for hours, and I'm not leaving till this is settled. Look, here's a pile of envelopes addressed to Mrs Somers-Briggs at the accommodation address which we know you've been using, and some spoiled tickets for the affair tonight at the hotel. That ties you and your mother into the false charity. Here are some letters from people you've cheated out of their pay-packets; this one is from a singer, and another here from a car rental company. They give the licence number of that red car you've been driving, Mr Briggs, and say your first cheque has unfortunately not been honoured. Oh, I've got the right person all right.'*

Noel drew his mouth back into a rictus. 'Old man, if you know what's good for you, you'll stop right there. I'm in no mood to listen to your whinging. And there's one thing you've forgotten. You're on private premises which means you're trespassing, and I can throw you out at any time I like.'

'Fisticuffs, eh?' Leo thrust his papers back into his pocket and put his hands up in a boxing stance. 'Well, come on, then. I used to box a bit, you know.'

Noel laughed, but his anger grew. 'As if . . .! I could swat you as easily as I kill a fly.'

Leo danced up and down on his toes. 'Go on, then! It looks as if you've been fighting already this evening. Been beating up a girl? That's about your weight, isn't it?'

Noel reddened. 'I've killed before, and if you know what's good for you . . .'

Leo knew the truth when he heard it. His mouth gaped in shock.

Noel realized he'd said too much.

Leo turned to run, but before he could reach the first stair, Noel caught him a blow on the back of his shoulder. Leo tumbled down the stairs and lay still, arms flung up above his head. Eyes closed.

Noel hung on to the railing, breathing hard, listening. Had anyone else heard?

Silence. Nobody had heard, or perhaps the other people on this floor were out for the evening and hadn't returned yet.

Noel pulled his sleeve across his mouth. He hadn't intended to kill the little man, but if he had . . . well, it wasn't his fault, was it? Noel had warned him, not once but twice.

Now what was he to do? His mother would know, but she wasn't back yet. She ought to be back. She oughtn't to have left him all alone. She was probably out celebrating somewhere with Richie, which was most unfair.

So, Noel would have to manage things by himself. He crept down the stairs and bent over the body in an effort to find a pulse. He was nervous, couldn't find one. Perhaps wasn't doing it right. He shrugged. Surely the man was dead. It was just so easy to kill, wasn't it?

Furious with everyone but himself, cursing the evil fate that dogged him this evening, Noel went through Leo's pockets, removed his mobile phone, some twenty-pound notes from his wallet, and the paperwork he'd so painstakingly disinterred from the bin. He hoisted Leo on to his shoulder and took him down the stairs into the basement, dumping him with the rubbish bins at the back of the garage area. The bins wouldn't be emptied till the following Thursday, by which time Noel would be long gone.

Noel went back up the stairs, got out his keyring and let himself into the flat. Time to pack.

Twenty

Sunday, early hours of the morning

What Noel had no way of knowing was that it had been a point of honour for Leo to keep himself fit. Yes, he looked rickety, but his heart and lungs were sound.

Leo had been stunned by the fall, but not killed. He came back to consciousness slowly. It took him some time to work out where he was, and then to check that his arms and legs were still functioning. He rather thought he'd cracked a rib and he was bruised all over, but good heavens, he'd suffered worse than that in his time, hadn't he?

He staggered up the slope from the garage to the street, only to find a large car bearing down upon him. He was caught in the headlights. There was no escape. It would be just his luck to be trapped on the ramp by the rest of the gang!

In fact, the car was occupied by a middle-aged couple from one of the top flats, returning from a late night out. And they had a mobile phone on them.

Richie was a careful driver, sometimes a little slow for Lena's taste. Tonight there was hardly any traffic on the roads, but he still slowed for intersections and stopped for red lights.

Lena wept a little, and then began to make plans.

'We'd better shift from the flat tomorrow morning. Once we're away, they won't know how to lay hands on us. The air tickets and the new passports are in the desk. On Monday I can use my laptop to tell the bank to cancel the transaction. It could be worse. We've lost the cheques and that cash . . . and my diamonds. I can soon replace them.'

Richie said, 'I told you Noel was bad news. I think he ought to see a doctor.'

'There's nothing wrong with him bar high spirits. He's so attractive to women, it's not surprising that they fall over themselves to . . . and if he does lash out occasionally, well, it's just that he doesn't know his own strength.'

'I don't blame you for sticking up for him, Lena, but this is where I bow out. I'll change my air ticket tomorrow for another destination, and let you know where to send my cut.'

'I don't want to lose you, Richie.' And perhaps she meant it, in a way.

He was silent. He was sorry for her, a little. He didn't think Noel was ever going to be anything but trouble with a capital T.

He turned into the road in which their block of flats lay, and put on the brakes.

'What . . .!'

For a count of five, he stared at a police car parked slightly askew outside the front door of the flats.

She whispered, 'What?'

Richie took his foot off the brakes and drove on past the flats and round the corner. He found a space and parked. 'Ring Noel on his mobile. You've got yours on you, haven't you?'

She delved into her bag with shaking hands. 'The police . . . it can't be anything to do with Noel. Can it?' She pressed numbers, swore with vexation. 'I can't, my fingers are slippery.'

He took out his own mobile, and pressed numbers. They

could hear the phone ringing at the other end. An ambulance,
lights flashing, crossed the road behind them, followed by
another. The phone at the other end went unanswered.

Richie said, 'Can you think of any reason why Noel isn't
answering his mobile phone? Unless he's been prevented from
doing so.'

'He might be with a girl. I don't understand why the police
should want to home in on Noel now. The hotel people wouldn't
have called them in, would they?' She answered her own ques-
tion. 'No, of course not. They don't know where to find him
and anyway, they stand to lose too much. That Abbot woman
is not the sort to double-cross us. No, the presence of the police
is nothing to do with Noel.'

'I don't believe that and neither do you, really. As the man
said, Noel's running out of control. We know he's killed before.
Suppose he's killed again?'

She made a move to get out of the car. 'He wouldn't. He
couldn't. The police, the ambulances, they're nothing to do
with him. Someone's been taken ill, that's all.'

He reached out and held on to her arm. 'Hold it right there.
We don't want to walk into an ambush, do we? You stay here.
Take off your wig and make-up, put on one of the jackets I
keep in the back of the car. I'll see if I can find out what's
happening.' He took off his dinner jacket, fished a dark sweater
out from the back of the car, and pulled it on. Then he set off
down the street, hands in pockets, a man out taking a stroll in
the dark.

Lena did as she was bid, transforming herself from glam-
orous party-goer to elderly frump. Her own hair was pepper
and salt, fading from red. The jacket she huddled into was too
large, but covered her evening dress. She sat on in the car,
fidgeting, her iron control breaking up.

Ten minutes. She kept looking at her watch. Fifteen. She'd
give Richie one more minute and then go looking for him.

Richie slid back into the car. 'The ambulances stopped outside
the flats. A man was being helped into the first one when I
arrived. I couldn't see his face. A small man, elderly. A
policeman went with him. That ambulance was driven off
straight away. Then after a few minutes, Noel was brought
down in handcuffs, between two policemen. It looked as if
they'd been in a fight.'

'Oh, no! Poor Noel! What have they done to him?'

'You'd best ask what he did to the policeman who went in the ambulance with him. Cracked his jaw, I think. There's not just one but three police cars outside now. There's not enough cover around for me to stick around, but I spotted a couple we know slightly, they live in one of the top floor flats, looks as if they've just come back from an evening out. They're talking to another couple of policemen.'

'Which means . . . ?'

'It means Noel's been losing his temper again. First the elderly man, and then a policeman. You might be able to talk the police out of charging Noel for attacking an old man, but not out of assaulting one of their own.'

'Noel's hurt?'

'Walking wounded. Whatever he's done or not done, he's in police custody, and that means the flat's out of bounds.'

As the truth of this sank in, Lena ground her teeth. 'My clothes, my jewellery, my laptop.' At this she stifled a cry. 'My laptop! If I can't get at that . . . no, I have the passwords in my notebook, don't I? I can still cancel the payment, and then we can get a good lawyer to represent Noel, and replace everything we've lost.'

She scrabbled in her evening bag, upending it on her lap. With nervous fingers she sought for that all-important notebook, but it was not there. As the truth sank in, she whimpered. 'I must have dropped it at the hotel!'

'Surely, you can go to the bank on Monday and—'

She was becoming hysterical. 'Idiot! I'd have to prove my identity, show them bills, credit cards, chequebooks, all that sort of thing, and that's all back at the flat. I haven't even got my credit cards on me.'

He fished a wallet out of his pocket. 'I've some.'

'Yes, but they don't identify me, do they? If they've got Noel . . . we don't know for what or if it's safe to . . . those dreadful people at the hotel said that if he did anything else . . . they'll testify against him and I'm sure those women egged him on and . . .'

He scratched a bristly chin. 'There's the small matter of the barman as well. You can't deny that Noel killed him.'

'It wasn't murder, it was manslaughter, it was a mistake.' She was feverish. 'Anyway, there's no way the police can connect *the barman with us. I'm sure it's safe to go back to the flat.'*

'You know it isn't. Sorry, Lena, but I'm overruling you on this. We'll go out to my brother in Greenwich for the rest of the night. I've got a bag of my things out there already, remember? His wife can lend you some clothes, and tomorrow you can find out what's happened to Noel, what they've got him for. Then you can get him a brief, who'll see if he can get Noel out on bail, right? Only then can you judge whether it's safe to go back to the flat or not.'

'But our flights are for tomorrow.'

'Forget it,' he said, starting up the car again. 'Passports, tickets, access to the money, everything's out of reach.'

She whispered to herself, rather than to him, 'What are we going to do?'

'There's Noel's camera in the back, and the money he took for the photographs.'

'If he gets bail, he'll need his camera.'

'If he's assaulted a policeman, he won't get bail.'

Silence. She didn't want to believe him.

He said, 'Whether he gets bail or not, I think I'll go back up north. I can always get gigs in the working men's clubs. Come with me?'

Her brain was starting to work again. 'What would I do up there? I need to stay down here to see what I can do for Noel. I'll get myself some decent clothes from second-hand boutiques or charity shops. I know someone who runs an escort agency and would be glad to have me work for her. That's more in my line.'

He nodded but he was thinking that she was probably getting a bit long in the tooth for that kind of work. Once or twice over the years, he'd thought of offering to marry her, but he knew – deep down – that it would never work.

Sunday, morning
Bea slept late, showered, pulled on some casual clothes, brushed her hair but didn't bother with make-up. She yawned her way down to the kitchen in a bemused state. She could hardly believe what had happened the previous night. Had they really faced down a gang of con men and come out on the winning side? Perhaps she'd dreamed it. But if she hadn't dreamed it, any credit due must go to Oliver.

And oh, poor Maggie. When they'd got back from the hotel, Bea had helped the girl in and out of a hot shower, and then put her to bed with some painkillers and a glass of hot milk. Presumably the girl was still asleep, for there was no sign of her in the kitchen.

Piers followed Bea into the kitchen, also yawning. He'd had to resume his evening dress, and hadn't bothered to shave or brush his hair. He didn't even say Good morning, but stumbled on to a stool at the table while she made a cafetière of coffee, strong and black. She thought of offering to lend him some of Hamilton's clothes, but didn't bother, for they'd never have fitted him.

She rather thought the phone had been ringing on and off while she'd been on her way downstairs, but presumably somebody – Oliver? – had attended to it. Nobody in their senses could expect her to attend to business this morning. Anyway, it was Sunday, wasn't it? Her day off.

She found a tin of frozen croissants in the freezer and stumbled around, preparing them for the oven. Piers looked as leaden-eyed as she felt.

Oliver came running up the stairs from the basement, all excitement. Good Lord, all that energy! How did he do it? 'You'll never guess,' he said, his voice too loud for her ears, his gestures too wide. 'It took some time but I've been working on her little book, and I've got into all the accounts she's still got running. There's not all that much in the other accounts, a couple of hundred here and there, but we'd be justified in taking that for charity too, wouldn't we?'

Piers yawned, pouring coffee into mugs. 'Cut the volume, will you, youngster?'

'Oh. Sorry. But it's so exciting, isn't it? I've been up for hours, you see, and it seemed like, well, *meant* that she forgot her book. Oh, I took a cuppa up to Maggie about an hour ago, but she was still asleep so I didn't disturb her. She's going to be all right, isn't she?'

Bea nodded. Speech was still beyond her. She put the croissants into the oven, and took the first sip from the mug of coffee that Piers pushed in her direction.

Nothing was going to dampen Oliver's enthusiasm. 'What I think is that we ought to set aside a fair amount for bills we haven't got in yet. Leo's isn't in yet, is it? I suppose he'll

surface some time today. He said he'd struck pay dirt yesterday.
I wonder what he found out.'

'Mm,' said Bea, not really caring, thinking that after they'd
eaten, she might go back to bed for a while with a trashy novel
and some Belgian chocolates.

Oliver looked at his watch. 'Oh, and Ms McNeice just phoned
and is coming round straight away.'

Bea groaned, and closed her eyes.

Piers said, 'Couldn't you have put her off? Bea, the croissants
are burning.'

Oliver looked uncertain. 'She said it was urgent.' The front
doorbell rang, and he went to answer it. Bea concentrated
on putting plates, knives, butter and jam on the table, while
Piers reached for the first hot croissant, burned his fingers,
and blew on them. Serve him right if he did get his fingers
burned.

Oliver ushered Ms McNeice into the room. The hotel
manageress was as point-device as ever, flashing black earrings
and all. She was smiling and very wide awake.

Piers reached out a long arm and unhooked a mug for her,
gesturing that she should help herself to coffee, which she did.
Bea shovelled croissants out to everyone.

'Hope I'm not too early for you,' said Ms McNeice, meaning
that she'd been up with the lark, and thought them very lazy
for not having done the same. 'Is that girl of yours all right?'

Bea moistened her mouth with coffee. 'Still asleep.'

'Good, good. Well, I came straight round because I thought
you ought to know that all bets are off. The police have arrested
Noel Briggs – or whatever his name is – for the murder of our
barman.'

Bea and Piers suspended operations on their croissants, eyes
and mouth wide.

'Good news, isn't it?' smiled Ms McNeice. 'It gives us a
cast iron excuse to take that money and distribute it to the poor
and needy. Yes, I wouldn't mind a croissant. Thank you. Much
appreciated.'

Bea found her voice. 'But how . . . what about . . .?'

'I'd better start at the beginning, hadn't I? I stayed at the hotel
overnight. I was worried about our receptionist, whom you may
have noticed was not exactly herself. We have a room set aside
for staff, so that's where she spent the night. She's perfectly all

right this morning, planning an expensive holiday on her share of the proceeds. I sent her off home this morning in a taxi, just before the police arrived. During the night they'd been called to a disturbance at a block of flats not far away, and found an elderly man who said he'd been assaulted and robbed of his mobile phone by someone living in the flats. The police went upstairs to question the man and he went berserk, assaulted one of the policemen. So he was arrested for that as well.'

Wordless, Piers pushed a second croissant in Ms McNeice's direction.

Smiling, she accepted it. 'Yes, you've guessed it! It was the man we know as Noel Briggs, though whether that's his real name or not, I don't know, and neither do the police. Anyway, when they searched his pockets, they found the victim's mobile phone and . . . and, wait for it! . . . the key to our honeymoon suite! That rang bells with the police, so they asked him why he had that key, and he started shouting that it wasn't his fault that it was so easy to kill people, some girls he'd picked up, and our barman, of course. I think our two young things have had a lucky escape, don't you?'

Ms McNeice cast down her eyes, trying to look meek. 'The police wanted to know if I knew Noel and of course I said he was the son of the woman who'd been organizing a function at the hotel last night, that he'd been the photographer, in fact. I didn't say anything about fraud, or a notebook or millions going missing. Or diamonds.'

Bea blinked. 'Won't the police find out?'

'They don't know anything about a late-night meeting in my office. They don't know that we've managed to retrieve the stolen money, and it seems to me that they've no need to know. If they did know, they might impound the money as evidence and although we could put in our claim for it, it might be months and months before the matter came to trial, and the Crown Prosecution Service might keep it and the charities would suffer, wouldn't they?'

Bea exchanged glances with Piers. Was this ethical?

Ms McNeice chased crumbs around her plate. 'The thing is, Noel is down for manslaughter at the very least, plus the assault on the policeman, plus the assault on his victim last night; whoever he was, poor man. Noel's going to go down for a few years, isn't he? So he really doesn't need to have any extra charges brought against him for the assaults on your Maggie and my little receptionist, which saves them a lot of hassle and court appearances.'

'And it means we can recompense them for what they've suffered at his hands,' said Piers, thoughtfully. 'What about Mrs Somers-Briggs and her partner?'

'Nowhere to be found,' said Ms McNeice. 'They didn't return to the flat last night and the police are looking for them as Noel's accomplices. We've got their cash, I'm putting out a warning on the website to other hoteliers to beware of them. On the whole I'm inclined to think that if they disappear, all well and good. I'm content with that, if you are.'

Bea wasn't sure what she thought about that. 'Are we doing the wrong thing, in order to right a wrong?'

Piers took the last croissant. 'Possibly. But if we don't keep more than a small percentage to cover our costs, that's OK in my book.'

'Precisely,' said Ms McNeice, draining her mug of coffee. 'I must be off. My day to take my mother out for a run. She's in sheltered accommodation, you know, and really looks forward to Sundays. Oliver, as soon as you've got the money into your bank, let me know, and we'll arrange a time and place to start repaying everyone, right?'

'Right,' said Oliver, beaming. He at least had no doubts that they were doing the right thing. 'I'll see you out, shall I?'

Bea and Piers were left sitting opposite one another. She said, 'What on earth would Hamilton have said?'

Piers shrugged. 'All's well that ends well?'

She looked out of the window, across the garden, to the church spire beyond. She wasn't at all sure that Hamilton would have gone along with Ms McNeice's solution, but she couldn't for the moment think of a better alternative. No, wait a minute; she did know what he'd say. He'd say it was poetic justice.

Piers stretched, yawning. 'I suppose I should shave. I'd like to get back to the work today, do some more on Hamilton's portrait. Thanks for putting me up, Bea. You've been great.'

She recognized the signs that he was getting restless and making moves to depart. 'I've appreciated your help. Thanks.'

'Any time.' His mind was obviously moving on. He was flexing his fingers, anxious to get back to his paints. He went off with a light step.

Oliver came bouncing back. 'All we have to do now is wait for the money to arrive in our account. I'm taking bets that it goes through. Shall I take a cup of coffee up to Maggie now?'

The money went through without a hitch. After a small percentage had been deducted for the Abbot Agency, and everyone else had been paid their due, a sizeable sum was sent anonymously to each of the international charities who worked in areas struck by natural disasters.

Ana, the Asian accomplice, was never traced. Presumably her relative in Southall took care of her. When the police searched Mrs Somers-Briggs' flat, they found a heavy paperweight, coated with what proved to be blood and hairs from the barman, which had rolled under a table and been forgotten. The fingerprints on it were Noel's. If Mrs Somers-Briggs had been a better housekeeper, she'd have found and disposed of it. As it was, it provided vital evidence in sending Noel down for life.

The fraud squad tried to make sense of Mrs Somers-Briggs' accounts. They suspected they were on to a massive scam, but all the people mentioned in her books seemed to have been paid off and the lady herself had vanished, so that case was eventually shelved.

Leo discharged himself from hospital, battered and bruised but in good spirits. Coral took him in for a couple of days, declaring he really wasn't fit to look after himself, but once Leo had been paid everything that was due him, he returned to his own place, and set about rebuilding his contacts in the trade. Coral's first grandchild was named after him.

Bea took some time to recover her equanimity, finding it hard to concentrate for long. She began to sleep better, and to dispose of Hamilton's clothes. Maggie bobbed up like a cork upon water, crashing around the house, singing at the top of her voice, making plans – a different plan each day – to sell the diamond earrings which had fallen to her lot as part of the spoils. She bought some clothes which fitted her new, less raucous image, and went out on a date with the tall lad who'd danced with her at the hotel.

Oliver took delivery of the expected packet of papers from his father, enabling him to apply for jobs.

Neither Oliver nor Maggie seemed to want to talk about the

future, which worried Bea, who had begun to worry about it
for them.

She couldn't justify keeping them on, could she? She was
fairly well off, but to employ Oliver and Maggie was not
sensible. She simply couldn't afford it. And what would they
do with their time if she did keep them on? They were young,
they had their own lives to lead. Her mind went round and
round in circles and came to no decision.

It crossed her mind a dozen times a day that she could
reopen the agency, but she wasn't sure that she was up to it.
Hadn't the case of the false charity proved that she was not
cut out for such traumas? And if she did reopen the agency,
she'd have to find good staff to help her, and that meant Oliver
and Maggie. Now Oliver was someone she felt she could live
with and work with, but could she really put up with Maggie's
hee-haw laugh and bossy behaviour? Bea wasn't at all sure
she could.

Also, didn't she have enough to do, trying to get herself
sorted out?

Max rang several times to check that Bea was all right. He
was very relieved that nothing had got into the papers about
Noel's arrest . . . nothing, anyway, that could be referred back
to him. Nicole did eventually start removing their belongings
from Bea's closet, and Bea began to reply to the huge pile of
sympathy cards and letters.

The weather took a turn for the worse and Bea developed a
scratchy sore throat. Several of her old friends – including
Velma Weston – rang to ask her out, but Bea put them all off,
saying she didn't feel up to it yet.

For hours at a time she sat at the window, looking down on
the rain-sodden garden, just existing, letting the minutes pass
by. Resting. Recovering. Sometimes she wondered if Hamilton
had been right, and that she ought to sell up and move away.
Inertia kept her where she was; that and a feeling that she was
waiting for something to happen to make up her mind for her.

On Friday morning – Oliver and Maggie's last day – Bea
had an appointment at the beauty salon for a haircut and manicure. She told herself she'd feel better once she was at the
salon, but there's always a crumple in the roseleaf, as her mother
used to say. Her favourite stylist was off sick, and though
another of the girls did a pretty good job, it wasn't quite the

same. Also, the manicurist rushed her work, so that Bea felt more jangled than rested as she walked back home.

There she met with a problem. Her nails were still slightly tacky and her keys were at the bottom of her handbag. There was no way she was going to poke around in her bag and ruin a perfectly good manicure. She decided to go down the outside steps to the office and get Oliver or Maggie to let her in that way.

On the bottom step, however, sat a large, capable-looking woman of Afro-Caribbean descent, middle-aged and ever so slightly scruffy. She had brought a cushion to sit on and was making herself at home, drinking out of a thermos flask and chewing on a roll.

Bea blinked. 'Isn't anyone in the office?'

'You work here, love? I been trying to get in for ever.'

'I used to work here once, but not now.'

'Ah, closing up, I hear. I got to speak to someone, if it takes me all day. I tried everything else. Phoning. Calling round. Even been up Westminster, chasing that Mr Max that ought to be ashamed of himself, asking for work to be done and then not paying me for it.'

'Ah,' said Bea, recognizing that this woman was the same type as Coral, with the same terrier tendency. There was no way you could brush her off for good. The only thing to do was to listen and, probably, pay her off. 'I think I've heard about you. Come on in and tell me all about it.'

She rang the bell and asked Oliver to let them in. He did so, pulling a face when he saw who walked in behind Bea. 'But, Mrs Abbot—'

'That's all right, Oliver. I'll take our caller into my office.'

Once seated there, Bea said, 'Now, I'm Mrs Abbot. My husband used to run this agency but when he became ill, my son took over and began to run the agency down. Some staff left and records were not properly kept. If we owe you money, then I will see that you get it. Would you like to tell me your story?'

The woman sighed with relief. 'About time, too. The name's Morris. Belle Morris. Me and my friend Bobby – she's a girl my age, spite of her name – we used to work together, cleaning an office in the High Street these many years. Now and then she'd get an extra job through Abbot's, special clearing out of places when old ladies and gentlemen go into homes, know what I mean?'

Bea nodded. 'Not nice work. I used to do it for the agency, and I know. Very often the relatives can't face it.'

'That's it. So Bobby's knee let her down, coupla months back. Real painful, it was. She had to give up work and go and stay with her daughter that lives in Milton Keynes. Not that she'll be there for long, seeing as she's a proper Londoner and hates the country. Anyway, she said would I do this job for her, she'd square it with you. I was to keep note of my hours and get paid the going rate. Some old lady lived and died in this flat, and there was no other family left in London. The nevvy had taken one or two bits that he fancied, there wasn't anything else he wanted, I was to clear out the rubbish, get the house clearance people in for the rest, clean the flat up ready for it to go on the market. I said, fine, and she give me the keys, right? Up Lancaster Gate way. Nice flat but pooh, what a stink, know what I mean?'

Bea nodded. The old woman had probably been doubly incontinent. It happened, despite everything the family or social services could do.

'So I throw open the windows and I start bagging stuff up, old clothes, bedclothes, cushions, taking loose covers off the settee, you know? And I come across where she'd been stashing her pension money, been doing it for years, I should think, some really old notes, know what I mean? Wrapped up in those old thick stockings that you can't hardly get now, stuck behind the pipes in the airing cupboard. Near on two thousand quid.' She unearthed a stiff roll of banknotes from her bag and laid it on the desk.

'Ah,' said Bea. 'The nephew hadn't checked?'

'Didn't know enough about old ladies and their little ways, I reckon. Or he was put off by the stink. And then –' she pulled a wad of clean tissues from her pocket '– I found these.' She unfolded the tissues and spread five rings out on the desk for Bea to see. They were old-fashioned, heavy gold rings, two men's, and three women's, set with what looked like reasonably weighty diamonds.

'Wow!' said Bea, putting on her glasses for a better look. 'They look real. Are they?'

The woman shook her head in frustration. 'Might be glass, might not. Set in gold, though, so they're probably worth something. I did wonder about getting them valued, then I thought

I better not, because they might have thought I'd stolen them, which a course I haven't.'

'No, indeed,' said Bea. 'Where did you find them? No, let me guess. Stuffed into the toes of some old shoes?'

'Wellington boots, would you believe! So, there's the key to the flat and a note of my hours. The flat's been cleared and cleaned fit to put on the market, and I'd be obliged if you'd give me a receipt for the money and the rings, and pay me what's due.'

Bea reflected that the woman could easily have helped herself to money and the jewellery, but hadn't. She pressed the intercom for Oliver to come in. 'Oliver, some more detective work. Some time ago, before you arrived, Max gave a clear-out job on a flat in the Lancaster Gate area to a Mrs . . . what did you say Bobby's name was?'

'Lucas. Bobby Lucas.'

'Mrs Lucas didn't know the client's name?'

'She was given the key and an address and that's all. She said she trusted you, and that you'd see me right.'

'Which we will. Oliver, can you see what you can find for us? We know the job wasn't filed under the name of Morris; look instead under Lucas. Bobby Lucas. We need the name of our client, urgently, to let him know the flat has been cleared and is ready to go on to the market. And make out a cheque for Mrs Morris to this amount. Oh, and also please count the money and give her a receipt for it and for these five rings which belong to our client.'

Oliver's face showed he didn't know whether to tell Bea she was being taken for a ride, or to believe Mrs Morris' story. But by the time Bea had offered Mrs Morris a cup of tea – which offer had been graciously declined – Oliver was back with a slip of paper giving the client's name and contact details.

'He lives in Northampton,' said Bea, putting on her glasses again. 'No wonder he needed someone to clear the flat out for him. I'll get in touch with him right away. Oliver, the cheque for Mrs Morris?'

'A pleasure to do business with you,' said Mrs Morris, accepting payment. 'And a great relief to pass the money and the rings over to you, I must say. If ever you need something similar done . . .?'

'Leave me your address, and we'll be in touch,' promised Bea.

She saw Mrs Morris out, and returned to the office to put the valuables away in their safe. Then she sat back in her chair, musing on how nearly she had missed hearing Mrs Morris' story, and what might have happened if she had made time to listen to the woman earlier. She felt a giggle rising inside her.

From giggling she went to a soundless laugh. From laughing in silence, she laughed out loud. How absurd she'd been, thinking she couldn't cope any more. Of course she could!

She looked up to see Maggie and Oliver gazing at her with identical expressions of concern. 'Are you all right?' asked Oliver.

'We're a bit worried about you,' said Maggie, arms akimbo, ready to do battle.

Bea swiped the back of her hand across her eyes. 'I'm fine. It wasn't really that funny, but it just struck me that way.'

Oliver and Maggie exchanged glances. Maggie said, 'We wondered whether . . .' Her voice trailed away.

'The thing is,' said Oliver, 'that we don't like to think of you being left all by yourself in this big house, and we wondered, that is we thought . . . we know you can't afford to keep us on, but . . .' His voice trailed away, too.

Maggie pulled herself up to her considerable height. 'What we thought was, we could pay you a rent for our rooms here so that you'd have some money coming in, and we could easily get ourselves jobs elsewhere. That is, if you like the idea.'

It seemed that somewhere along the line, Bea's subconscious had already made up its mind for her. She was not going to sell the house and move away. She was going to stay where she was and get on with the job in hand.

'That is very kind of you, my poppets,' said Bea, 'and I'd be delighted if you both stayed on for good, though I'll be paying your wages, of course.'

'But . . .' they exchanged glances. 'Can you afford it, and what would we do?'

'We're reopening the agency, of course. There are all sorts of people out there who can't or won't go to the police when they meet with a problem. They need our special skills. So, Maggie; the agency rooms could do with a facelift. Will you get me some quotes for rewiring and redecoration, please? You'll find the contact details in the agency files somewhere. And Oliver; what other outstanding cases do we have on file?'

As Oliver scurried off to fetch the paperwork, Bea seemed to hear an echo of Hamilton's voice saying, 'You can do it, girl.' She straightened her back and squared her elbows. Yes, indeed. She could do it. And would.

The phone rang, and she picked up the receiver. 'Abbot Agency. How may I help you?'